Young Jethro

Roy Clews

YOUNG JETHRO

BOOK CLUB ASSOCIATES · LONDON

This edition published 1976 by
Book Club Associates
by arrangement with
William Heinemann Ltd

Printed in Great Britain by
Richard Clay (The Chaucer Press) Ltd, Bungay, Suffolk

In the early years of the nineteenth century, while Great Britain was at war with the Empire of Napoleon Bonaparte, another war was being waged in the Midlands of England. A war of industry against countryside, new ideas against old ways, man against master. This was a brawling, turbulent age that produced a violent, reckless people—and none more violent and reckless than the needle pointers of Redditch town. Men who held God, King and the needle masters in contempt, since all of these had abandoned them. It was against this background that Jethro Stanton, son of a rebel, lost his youth and came to manhood.

CHAPTER ONE

Worcestershire, May 1810

Redditch was built across sprawling hills, a tight-packed jumble of terraces, courts, alleys, factories and workshops that covered their slopes. In the broad valley of the River Arrow, which wandered round three sides of the town, there lay small clusters of farm buildings, and here and there the tall walls of a water-powered needle mill straddled one or other of the many tributary streams of the river. To the south of the town, the land rose sharply in a long ever-narrowing ridgeway, alternately wooded and built over.

The centre of Redditch was a plateau, a large triangular common surrounded by tumbledown rows of terraced cottages. To one side stood the small squat church of St Stephen; opposite, a dirt road ran north towards the nearby city of Birmingham, cutting across the commonland and plunging steeply down to the valley floor. This was called Fish Hill and there at the foot of it stood the imposing greystone edifice known as the Washford Needle Mills.

In front of the huge double gates, now barred and padlocked, that guarded the archway entrance to the outer courtyard of the mills, a short, burly, middle-aged man stamped up and down, fuming and cursing to himself. He was dressed in a long, grey-flannel nightshirt and had a blanket flung over his shoulders and a tasselled nightcap pulled low on his bullet head. His drink-puffed face was mottled by an angry flush. On sudden impulse, Clem Washford, the Master of Washford Mills, had left his bed before dawn.

Suddenly he stopped stamping and stood still, staring at a tall, thin, black-clad figure who had come from a cottage midway up the hill and was walking slowly towards the Mills.

9

'Ahr! So there you am! I thought as much,' the needle master grunted, and his face purpled as he opened wide his mouth and bellowed, 'Get down 'ere, you long streak o' piss! Get down 'ere, I say!'

The tall thin man's heart thumped in sudden terror.

'Oh Lord, save me!' he gasped, and broke into an ungainly run, his spidery legs and arms flailing through the air. He reached the needle master and halted, trembling from exertion, his breath whooping in his narrow chest.

'What time d'you call this, Dick Taylor?' Clem Washford bawled, and, holding up a large silver pocket watch, he rapped on its face with one thick finger. 'D'you call yourself a bloody overseer? It wants only fourteen minutes to 'alf-past five o' the clock, and the gates um still locked ... The morning's damn near gone, and theer's you comin' down the blasted hill as if you was Lord bloody Muck agooin' to take tea wi' a bloody doxy ... What in 'ell's name d'you think I pay you for? Answer me, blast you!'

The overseer could only shake his head and tremble.

'What's up? 'As the cat got your bloody tongue?' the needle master roared. 'I'll tell you what I pays you to do, Dick Taylor, I pays you to get these gates open at five in the morning, come rain, snow, wind or high water ... That's what you're paid for ... That's one o' your duties!'

He paused to catch his breath and the overseer, mistaking the pause for an invitation to speak, began to babble out excuses. Washford brutally cut him short.

'Shut your gob, man. You squeal like a stuck sow.' He reached out and grabbed the lapels of the overseer's rusty black tailcoat in his meaty hands.

'You listen well, Dick Taylor.' The needle master shook the taller man, causing his long sour-faced head to wobble alarmingly on his skinny neck. 'In future you spend less time ranting and raving with them bloody mealy-mouthed Methodys you're so fond of, and more time in your bed ... Then you'll be able to rise in the morning and carry out the duties I pay you to do. Understand?'

'Oh, indeed sir! Indeed I do!' Taylor bleated piteously.

Washford pushed him away.

'Good! Now get them bloody gates open.'

Without a backward glance, he wrapped the blanket across

10

his chest and marched off to the fine house which stood to one side of the tall mills.

While the needle master had been berating his overseer, a small crowd of ragged men and women had gathered by the gates. They were self-employed softworkers, come to collect the packets of cut steel wire which they took back to their cottage workshops to be handworked into rough needles. Even when trade was good, the softworkers found it a hard struggle to live; the slump caused by the war had brought them to a desperate plight. Without the work from the mills, most of them would starve. As Dick Taylor unlocked the padlocks and slid the heavy beam from its sockets, he was sick at the thought that these poverty-stricken wretches had witnessed his humiliation. Hearing a whispered comment followed by hastily smothered laughter, he swung to confront them.

'And what does you lot o' gutter rats find so funny?' he hissed venomously, his eyes searching for those who had sniggered. 'You'd best remember that it's me who gives the work out at this mill,' he went on, threateningly.

No one was bold enough to meet his stare and, satisfied that he had cowed them, he turned back to open the gates.

There was a sudden surge forward as the crowd jostled and pushed, each struggling to be first in line at the wire-store door under the side of the archway, in case there should not be enough work for all. Taylor leant against the open gate and watched the scuffling; then he grinned spitefully and pointed at the elderly man who had won first place in the queue.

'Oi! You there!'

The old man placed one gnarled hand on his chest.

'Does that mean me, gaffer?' he asked, his voice quavering nervously.

Taylor nodded. 'Yes, you ... if I recollects rightly, I give you two packets of work larst week.'

'That's right, gaffer,' the man agreed humbly.

'Ahr! I know it's right, and I know what sort of a rotten job you made on um as well.' The overseer cocked his thumb and gestured at the roadway. 'Go on ... gerrout theer! Don't you come back 'ere again for work, I can't afford to give out stuff for the likes o' you to waste.'

The old man's face crumpled. 'Don't send us away, gaffer,' he pleaded. 'I tries to make a good job on um, only me eyes

11

aren't what they was and I'se got this bloody cramp come to me 'ands.' He realized that he was destroying his own case and changed his plea. 'I'll cut me rate for the job, gaffer, and I'll take care wi' um, I swear I ull.'

Taylor seemed to be considering what he had heard and the man went on pleading.

'My old 'ooman's bin real bad lately, gaffer. I needs the work so as I con get some vittles for us ... We'em fair clemmed, we am ... We'se had nothin' to ate for two days past.'

The overseer let the old man ramble on until he sensed that some of the crowd's tempers were rising in sympathy, then he appeared to relent.

'Awlright, old 'un, shut your rattle. I'll give you one larst chance. After all, I'm a Christian and it's my sacred duty to 'elp a fellow sufferer through this vale of woe. I'll 'ave to lower your rate a bit, though. Master Washford 'ud goo mad if I let you 'ave full rate, after you'se ruined so much work.' He brushed aside the old man's tearful thanks, and went to stand in the roadway.

The inworkers employed by Washford were coming through the gates, their clogs clattering over the rough cobbles of the entrance, some of the men carrying young children on their shoulders, while many women suckled babies at their breasts as they hurried into the mills.

'Come on now, hurry it up ... You knows what 'appens, if you're late!' Taylor exhorted them.

He clasped his hands behind his back and rocked up and down on his heels, leaning forward at times to cuff a lagging boy or girl child across the head. Clem Washford reappeared, now wearing the brown coat, breeches and top-boots he habitually favoured, with a high-crowned hat perched upon his bald head.

'It's turned 'alf past five on the clock, Taylor, shut them damn gates,' he ordered, and when the other hesitated, he demanded, 'Why d'you dawdle, man? Do as I bid.'

'Sir, there's none o' the pointers come yet.'

'That don't surprise me,' the needle master grunted. 'The buggers all went to see Millington fight Batten the Keeper up at the White Hart meadow yesterday evening. No doubt they was all drunk as pigs ... They'll be along sooner or later.' He glanced up the hill in the direction of the town green. 'Theer! Talk o' the devil and he's bound to appear. Theer's some on um now.'

A group of men came sauntering down the middle of the roadway, laughing and joking together as they neared the mills.

'Look at um!' Clem Washford chuckled grimly. 'Hell bent for the grave and they don't give a damn all for it.'

The approaching men wore white aprons rolled up about their hips and square-edged, flat-topped caps fashioned from heavy brown paper. Their breeches were met at the knee by deep-ribbed woollen stockings, which in turn disappeared into iron-studded wooden clogs. On their upper bodies they had only coarse shirts and leather waistcoats and brightly coloured kerchiefs knotted loosely around their necks. These were some of the notorious needle pointers, men whose average expectancy of life was not much more than thirty years, because of the nature of the work they did, dry grinding the needles and hooks manufactured in the district. The fine dust of metal and stone breathed into the throat and lungs during the grinding caused the terrible 'pointers' rot', which destroyed the lungs and ate at the inner organs until the sufferer literally drowned in his own blood and tissue.

The pay was high for this work and the few men who dared to earn it were a breed apart, bowing to no master, for none could ever find sufficient numbers to point his needles. Hard drinking, heavy gambling and fist-fighting filled their leisure hours, and they were feared by all because, knowing that they were doomed to an early grave, they gave no thought to the consequences of their actions and in a brawl would fight with the savagery of wild beasts. To most needle masters, the pointers were a necessary evil, feared and despised as brutal animals. But there were a few employers, such as the tough self-made Clem Washford, who liked them, admiring their courage and the devil-may-care attitude they showed towards their hard life and inevitable fate.

'Now then, you buggers!' Washford shouted jovially. 'What happened larst night? ... And wheer's that bloody Millington? Did he get the blue mould knocked off him?'

As the pointers came up to the gate, one of the older ones indicated the tallest of the group.

13

'Does you mean to tell me, Clem Washford, that you doon't see it's Steve Millington 'ere?'

The tall man's face was an unrecognizable mass of swollen black-bruised flesh and weeping blood-filled cuts.

Old Clem feigned a start of surprise. 'Well, I'll goo t'Hanover! If it aren't my mills' star pug, Marster Steven Millington in person! My bloody oath, Steven! Was it old Carrie Allen's bull you put up the mauleys with by mistake?'

The tall man's split lips cracked painfully into a travesty of a smile. 'I reckon I must on, marster ...' he mumbled. 'That Batten doon't 'alf pack a wallop. Put me out cold, so he did. I saw the bugger comin' but I was too knackered to move me yed out the way of it.'

Nail Styler, a tough-looking young pointer, broke in excitedly. 'It warn't 'alf a good mill, Marster Clem! I reckon Steve 'ere was onlucky to lose, that I does.'

'Ahr! And I reckon Steve's lucky to be alive arter fighting that bugger for twenty-odd rounds,' another pointer laughed.

The needle master patted the fighter's shoulder in commiseration.

'Ne'er mind it, Steven. That Batten is a rare-bottomed un. One of the best in the country, I shouldn't wonder. I've heard as how the Earl is thinking of matching him against Cribb for the championship.' Mock ferocity came into his voice. 'That's five good gold guineas you'se corst me, you great lummox! Now, get in that bloody pointing shop and earn me some of it back, afore I takes me own mauleys to your thick skull.'

The pointers laughed and ambled on through the gateway, pushing Dick Taylor contemptuously to one side. Secretly terrified of them, he contented himself with dark looks and muttered threats of retaliation.

'Hold hard!' Clem Washford called. ''As you sin Peter Stanton this morning?'

'Ahr gaffer, theer 'e comes now ... behind you.'

Peter Stanton walked in from the roadway and stopped by Washford's side. Of slightly over average height, his dark hair and trim hard body made him appear much younger than his forty years, and since he had not been long at the pointing, his health had not yet begun to suffer. He wore the rough pointers' rig with surprising style and when he spoke, his voice was low and cultured.

14

'Were you asking after me, Master Washford?'

The needle master nodded. 'I was, Peter Stanton, I want a private word with you ... Taylor! Get about your business, man!' he snapped at the hovering overseer. 'Give them damned outworkers their packets and get rid of the buggers, they stink the place out.'

The overseer glared jealously at Stanton and did as he was ordered. Old Clem gave his full attention to the pointer.

'Well, man? Have you decided?'

Stanton nodded his head. 'I have, Master Washford. And my answer is no.'

The older man's face showed surprise and irritation.

'You're a bloody fool, Peter Stanton!' he snapped. 'I offer you a damned good position arter you'se only bin two years in my mill, a position that means you'd perhaps someday be second only to me and mine in this place, and you tell me no? Any other man in my service would jump at it. You're a bloody fool!'

The pointer's eyes hardened and a note of menace crept into his tone. 'Don't call me a fool, Clem Washford. I'm no man's servant to jump when he calls. Better men than you have paid a high price for insulting me.'

The needle master faltered, checked by the unexpected authority in the man's voice.

'I meant you no insult, Peter Stanton,' he grumbled. 'But it offends me when I offer my help to a man so that he may better himself, and then that man refuses me.'

Stanton smiled bitterly and nodded to where Dick Taylor was hectoring the outworkers.

'With respect, Clem Washford, if that is what being helped to better oneself does to a man, then I want none of it ... Now, if you'll excuse me, I'll go to my work.'

He walked on into the courtyard, leaving the needle master staring after him in puzzlement.

The mill was constructed around one large outer courtyard where wagons could be loaded and unloaded, and three smaller inner ones. As Stanton went through the narrow, winding covered passages that connected the yards, he felt the by now familiar anger against the system that forced people to toil all their days in conditions such as those that assailed his senses at every step. Crammed into dark, low-roofed, ill-ventilated

15

workrooms, rows of men, women and children sat at benches, fashioning needles by hand with hammers, punches, files and tongs. In the same rooms, forges used for tempering and baking the needles belched out noxious, choking fumes, and every surface was thick with oily filth, swarf and rust.

He glimpsed sweating men filling rolls of emery-powdered buckram with needles for polishing, and placing them on iron tables for other sweating men to roll backwards and forwards under flat heavy weights for hours without respite, until the muscles of their tired bodies cramped in knots of agony. He paused for a moment at one doorway to watch a small girl using the guttering iron, a saw-edged file, shaped like a butcher's cleaver, to cut grooves into the needle which she held in tongs in her left hand. Her eyes were red and watery and she blinked continuously to clear her sight. 'Poor little creature,' Stanton thought, and tried not to imagine what her eyes would look like after fourteen hours or more spent doing the same delicate work ... His lips twisted in sudden scorn. 'And you want me to help you drive these wretches, do you, Washford?' he muttered, soundlessly.

At other benches, boys and women were using hammers and punches to cut out the eyes of the needles. This was done on ends of wire that had been heated and laid along anvils so that they might be flattened precisely. Even at this early hour, the air was thick and foul with the stench of rotten-toothed mouths and stale bodies, while the noise made by the serried ranks of tapping hammers and rasping files, the cane-wielding overseers' curses, the workers' raucous screeches of laughter and howling disputes, and the ceaseless squalling of rag-swaddled babies, made Peter Stanton's brain reel.

He went on deeper into the mills until he reached the pointing shop. Through the open doorway came the clattering trundle and slap of the water-powered pulleys and axles that turned the grindstones at which the men worked. Before Stanton ducked under the low lintel of the doorway, he pulled a rag from his pocket and tied it round his nose and mouth. He entered the cellar workshop, almost tumbling down the flight of rickety wooden steps, and paused to accustom himself to the clouds of fine steel and stone dust that hung in the air, stinging his eyes and rasping maddeningly in his nose and throat.

Sitting on crude wooden stools, the pointers bent hunched over their spinning stones. Deftly they picked the needle-length slivers of steel from the boxes that stood beside them, and holding them in upright rows between their close-pressed palms, rolled them back and forth, pressing them down against the racing grindstones. As they moved them to and fro across the tough stone face, streams of white-hot steel sparks and granite dust jetted out around their heads and shoulders. Peter Stanton went to his place and sat down. His neighbour looked across at him and nodded. Peering through the gloom, Stanton recognized under the greasy mask of grime the impudent laughing face of Nail Styler. Styler pulled the rags from his mouth and bawled,

'Am you agoin' to be a shop overseer then, Peter?'

Stanton shook his head. 'Not I,' he bawled back. 'Clem Washford can find some arse-crawler to beat children awake. I'll not do so.' And if all goes as I intend it shall, then no one else shall do so in years to come, he added silently.

His heart lightened at the thought and he winked at Styler, then settled himself to his shift.

CHAPTER TWO

The ancient half-timbered mansion of the Bartleet family was set in wooded grounds on a high slope overlooking the Arrow valley. At one period, the forefathers of its present occupier, Colonel Charles Bartleet, had possessed vast estates in various parts of the country, but romantic loyalties to a succession of lost causes, the last being the House of Stuart, had eroded the family fortunes. Now the Bartleet possessions were composed of some scattered farms and parcels of land in the Midlands, and a large needle mill in Redditch. What had not been eroded, however, was the respect and esteem accorded to the Bartleet name. To deserve this respect and esteem was one of life's main aims for Charles Bartleet, a widower in his early fifties who worshipped his two surviving daughters, his country and his God in that order, and who counted his responsibilities as landowner, needle master and magistrate as honours bestowed upon him by a blessed Providence.

Every morning Charles Bartleet would rise at dawn, allow himself to be shaved, barbered and dressed by a manservant, then spend an hour or two reading and meditating in his library. After that, he strolled through the grounds of his home, pondering such problems as faced him, until the bell rang to announce that breakfast was waiting. This morning, as on many mornings recently, his thoughts were occupied with his cousin, Emily, a hatchet of a woman who could only be described as a virago. He sat down on a convenient tree stump and took deep breaths of the cool fresh air, mentally listing as he did so the upsetting incidents which his cousin had caused during the preceding months—ever since, in fact, she had arrived uninvited from her home in Cheltenham, and announced that she considered it her duty to help him raise his motherless girls. He smiled wryly. His eldest daughter, Anne, was twenty-two years old and her sister, Abigail, sixteen. Since their mother had been dead for fifteen years, his cousin's sudden display of motherly concern was, to say the least, belated.

'She makes the girls unhappy,' he frowned to himself. 'She's abusive and violent to the servants, and she's most damnably rude to each and every visitor.' He stretched his arms and slapped his hands on his knees. 'Dammit!' he said aloud. 'If she does not mend her ways, then she shall go. I'll send her back to that damned spa. She's for ever prating on about how much happier she was there than she is here, anyway.' He got to his feet and walked briskly back to the house.

Entering by the brass-studded front door, he crossed the hall to go up the majestic sweeping staircase that had been constructed from the timbers of a wrecked Armada galleon. As he mounted the stairs, his sharp ears picked up the faint sounds of someone sobbing. He paused and listened. There came a scream followed by more sobs, and he realized that they were coming from his own library but were muffled by the baize doors he had had fitted to ensure silence within that room. Quickly he retraced his steps and flung open the doors. The sobs welled out, echoing through the hallway. His cousin Emily had her back to him. So intent was she on thrashing the girl lying face down before her that she failed to notice the Colonel until he had crossed the library and snatched the long bamboo walking-cane from her raised hand. She turned on him in fury.

'Leave me be, Charles!'

Bartleet knelt by the prostrate girl whom he saw to be one of the housemaids.

'Stop this noise, girl,' he spoke sharply. 'You will not be struck any more. Now go to the kitchen.'

The maid scrambled to her feet and with both hands covering her face scurried, snuffling loudly, from the room. The Colonel rose and faced his cousin. Her hard face was white, and livid spots of temper marked her cheeks.

'How dare you interfere when I chastise a thieving chit of a——'

'Hold your tongue madam!' His voice was a whiplash,

shocking her into silence. 'How, indeed, dare *you* maltreat one of my servants in such a barbaric manner?' He trembled with the effort of control.

For the first time in her life, the woman felt afraid of him. Never before had she known him be anything but pleasant, even conciliatory, but now the intensity of his anger caused her own to fade into nervousness.

'Will you be good enough to explain your actions, madam?'

She swallowed hard, trying to dispel the lump that had formed in her throat. 'Well ... I caught the little thief ...'

'Do not use that term until it has been proven.' His expression was formidable.

'As you wish,' she mumbled. 'I found her with some books. She was taking them into the servants' quarters. It was quite obvious that she was trying to sneak away unobserved and meant to st——' She bit off the word, 'And meant to spirit them from the house.'

'Did you take the trouble to enquire of her what she was doing with them?' Bartleet questioned.

A touch of the woman's customary arrogance returned, and she tossed her lace-capped head, pursing her lips in contempt.

'There was no need to ask the saucy chit. I am not a fool, cousin Charles! I could see plainly what she intended. Why, her very looks and manner betrayed her guilt beyond any doubt. When I began to chastise her, the lying hussy had the gall to scream into my face that you yourself had told her she might take the books ... I ask of you, cousin, what on earth would a stupid, ignorant serving wench find to entertain her in studies of the Greek philosophers? Tch! A ridiculous story, indeed it is.'

By this time, Charles Bartleet was in full control of himself and when he answered his voice was calm and even.

'I had in fact given my permission to the girl to take the books. They were intended for her elder brother who is the son of one of my tenants. The lad hopes to become a schoolmaster. The books were to help him in his studies. However, that has no bearing on what I wish to say ... You will leave this house, madam, and return to your home. I shall arrange for a post-chaise to come at once. I shall, of course, continue to give you any support you may have need of, but I can no longer tolerate your presence here.'

She began to speak, but he silenced her curtly.

'Nothing you may say or do can alter my decision in this affair, madam. You have destroyed the happiness of my home for too long. Will you please go to your room and remain there until the carriage comes for you.'

She searched his face for some sign that he would relent, but all trace of his habitual kindliness had vanished and his eyes were frosthard. Seeing that nothing would move him, she swept out of the room. Charles Bartleet remained standing as she had left him until he heard the slamming of her bedroom door. Then he made his way down the hall and through the passageways to the servants' headquarters.

In the huge stone-flagged kitchen the servants had abandoned their breakfast and were gathered around the trembling, hiccuping maid. When he came in, they greeted him with wide-eyed stares of alarm and consternation. He smiled at them reassuringly.

'I'm sorry that your breakfast has been disturbed by this unhappy occurrence,' he said, and walked over to the beaten girl. 'There now, my dear,' he told her gently. 'Calm yourself and wipe away those tears.' He gave her his own linen handkerchief. 'Mrs Johns,' he said to the housekeeper, 'I would be most grateful if you would examine the girl and see to it that any bruising she has suffered is treated with salves.'

The housekeeper bobbed a curtsey. 'I will, sir, and gladly.'

'And now I wish you all to listen very carefully to what I have to say,' Bartleet addressed them. 'Mary here,' he patted the maid's shoulder, 'has been most unkindly and unjustly treated. I am truly sorry for it and I wish to apologize to her in front of you all.' He held up his hand to quieten the murmurs that arose. 'I do assure you that I will not tolerate this sort of injustice in my household. Of course, if any of you should behave in such a manner as to merit chastisement, then you shall be chastised. I repeat, that what has happened was undeserved by this innocent girl, and I regret it from the bottom of my heart. Now, finish your breakfast and be about your duties, we will regard the matter closed.' He turned to the housekeeper. 'Send Abram to the town for a post-chaise immediately, if you please, Mrs Johns, and when it arrives, inform Mistress Emily.' She bobbed another curtsey and Charles Bartleet returned to his library.

21

He closed the baize doors behind him and, sighing heavily, rested his back against them, closing his eyes in an endeavour to blot from his mind the vision of his cousin's insane expression as she beat the girl. He opened his eyes and looked with pleasure at the room before him, his favourite of any room he had known during his life. The sunlight dappled through the tall leaded windows, warming and enriching their maroon hangings and mingling its brightness with the gleaming polished oak floors. There were only two pieces of furniture, a set of movable steps and an intricately carved walnut lecturn that a Cavalier ancestor had saved from church-wrecking Cromwellian troopers. Every wall was covered by shelves of leatherbound books, stretching up to the cream plaster and black beam ceiling. Charles Bartleet let his gaze roam over the green, blue, brown and black spines, each with its gold-leafed title and decorative scroll, and inwardly blessed yet again the men who had built up this collection of which he now was proud custodian. He took from the nearest shelf a much-loved Roman history and, opening it on the lectern, he began to read. When the bell rang to summon him to breakfast, he was soothed and refreshed and quite suddenly extremely hungry.

The appetizing fragrance of ham, eggs, kidneys, trout, new-baked bread and fresh cheese and butter wafted from the row of silver dishes on the heavy sideboard, and the refectory table that dominated the long dining-room was bright with sparkling cutlery, chinaware and white napkins, while vases of peonies and roses filled the room with their lavish scent. His lips twitched in an involuntary smile. Yet another ancestor had rescued both sideboard and table from the local Abbey of Bordesley at the time of the Dissolution of the Monasteries, and the stately straight-backed chairs surrounding the table had once graced a bishop's palace. 'I may be a good Protestant, but I certainly owe a great deal to the Church of Rome,' he thought, with satisfaction.

A manservant attended to his needs and he ate heartily. During his meal, Bartleet heard the crunching of iron-rimmed wheels on the driveway gravel and the shouting and bustle that accompanied the departure of his cousin Emily.

'I will not be a hypocrite and go out to wish her God speed,' he decided. 'I've no wish to see her or hear from her again.'

He took a long drink from his glass of cold spring water to toast his liberation from her tyranny.

The post-chaise had barely left the grounds before his eldest daughter Anne entered the dining-room. Charles Bartleet leant back in his chair and regarded her with satisfaction. She was a tall girl who possessed a quiet beauty. Her soft brown hair was partly caught back in classical coils, while the front was swept forward to fall in ringlets around her face and forehead. Her figure was gently rounded and she wore a simple, high-waisted white dress without ornament. Her candid brown eyes were troubled, as she asked him, 'Is it true, what Cousin Emily has told me, father?'

He smiled ruefully. 'What has she told you, my dear?'

'That you have treated her abominably, ordered her from this house without reason and told her never to speak with us again.'

He shook his head and laughed softly, then sobered and looked keenly at his daughter.

'I trust, my dear, that you do not misinterpret my sending Cousin Emily away. I caught her treating Mary with the utmost severity. That is why I sent her from this house, and indeed she spoke the truth in that she will not be welcome here in the future.'

Anne stared at the aquiline features of the grey-haired man sitting anxiously before her and felt, as she always did feel, that no daughter deserved to be as lucky as she was in possessing such a father. She smiled and said quietly, 'I must confess to feeling a great sense of relief that she has gone.'

Charles Bartleet's tension left him. 'Where is Abigail?' he asked.

Anne took her seat before replying.

'She will be down presently, father. She has a surprise for you, she says that now Cousin Emily has left us she can give full rein to her desires.'

'A surprise? Full rein to her desires?' Knowing his youngest daughter, Charles Bartleet was slightly apprehensive. Anne was reassuring.

'Oh, it's nothing too appalling, merely a slight change in her normal toilette.'

Before her father could answer, the double doors crashed open.

'*Voilà! Mesdames et messieurs ... on present, la belle Abi!*'

Abigail Bartleet posed dramatically in the doorway, then, lifting her arms in the air, she glided around the table, trailing clouds of gossamer veils, and threw herself down at her father's side in a posture of supplication.

'I have come at your bidding, oh noble one, and am your slave to command.'

It took some seconds for Charles Bartleet to recover himself sufficiently to speak.

'What in heaven's name, Abigail ...'

Abigail threw herself back in a caricature of dismay and pretended to rend her clothes and hair with grief.

'Oh, ye vile gods that torment me in this way,' she intoned.

'Oh, father! Your face!' Anne exclaimed, and burst into delighted laughter.

Once recovered from his initial surprise, Charles Bartleet could not help but chuckle himself. Abigail jumped up and kissed his cheek.

'Good morning to you, father,' she said demurely, with the devils of mischief dancing in her black eyes.

Bartleet studied his flamboyantly beautiful daughter fondly. 'What have you been doing to yourself, child?' he demanded to know.

She had on a long transparent gown, through which he could see clearly ankle-length pink drawers. These were all she wore underneath except for artificial wax breasts, which pushed out the gauzy bodice of her dress in an alarming fashion. Her flawless oval face was plastered with white paint and rouge, and her jet-black hair was cropped short and dishevelled in the latest London style, known as 'à la Titus'. She showed her perfect teeth in a mockingly cosy smile and tapped his head with an ornate outsized fan.

'Oh Papa, you quiz! You know very well that this mode is all the *ton* now in the smart circles of Redditch and London ... I intend to emblazon the name of Abigail Bartleet in letters of fire across the firmament of fashion.'

'You are not serious? ... Are you?' Charles Bartleet murmured.

She widened her eyes in exaggerated surprise. 'But of course I am, Papa! I shall display myself to all the local Corinthians, *beaux* and *bon ton* this very morning. Do be good and order the carriage for eleven o'clock, one must not miss the Grand Parade.'

'Abi, please, stop it!' Anne begged, tears of laughter rolling down her cheeks.

Her sister turned and glided languorously around the table once more, flashing her eyes at her open-mouthed father over the edge of her outspread fan.

'Papa!' she exclaimed, delightedly. 'How devastatingly dashing you are, with your lower jaw dangling in such an elegant manner. I fear George Brummel must look to his laurels, for you are sure to become quite the rage of London when the Prince sees your jaw waggling so appealingly. You and our cousin, Vinegar Em, would make a deuced handsome couple, I do declare.'

She fluttered her green lashes, then began to giggle uncontrollably as her father's mouth opened and shut soundlessly, at a loss for words. Anne simply buried her face in a handkerchief and wept with delight, while the manservant staggered out into the hallway and leaned against the wall, struggling for mastery of himself.

CHAPTER THREE

Doll Greenaway clashed with her brother Tom immediately she returned from Abner Melen's Mills. She had brought the packets of softwork she had been waiting for since before dawn. A gaunt, ragged, prematurely aged woman, she resembled her brother very closely. He stood facing her in the ramshackle workshop built as a leanto against the rear of his equally ramshackle cottage. The man tore aside the rough canvas sacking that covered the wire and examined it.

'Gawd strewth!' he cursed, and pitched the packet to the ground.

'What's the marrer, our Tom?' the woman questioned anxiously.

'What's the marrer?' he shouted. 'You might well arsk, you gormless cow! It's soddin' German steel 'e's give her, not 'ungarian.'

Her quick temper met his halfway. 'If you was any good at your bleedin' trade, it 'udn't marrer a bugger what steel it were.'

The man's toothless mouth gaped wide as he screamed back. 'If I'se told you once, I'se told you a thousand times that 'ungarian steel is the best. This bloody stuff splinters under the punch. Why didn't you do what I told you to and get the packets from Washford's. Old Clem wun't use German at all, 'e knows it's no bloody good.'

Doll Greenaway felt the gnawing in her empty stomach and remembered that she had gone breakfastless to queue for the work. Without another word, she picked up the remaining packet of wire from the bench and hurled it at the man's head. 'Fetch it yerself in future, instead of lying stinking in your pit. You drunken, lazing pig.'

She stormed from the workshop and along the steep alleyways towards her own cottage which stood in one of the terraces near to the common.

'Sod 'im,' she told herself. 'Brother or no brother, I'll not work no longer for the sod. I'll goo and work at the lye in the mills, so I will.'

A few steps more and she calmed a little. If she went to work at the mills, she would be exchanging the comparatively free life of a self-employed outworker for the rigid work-discipline and time-keeping of the inworker. She also thought about the job. It entailed washing the grease and dross from the polished needles in harsh mixtures of lye soap and boiling water, and Doll had seen too many women weeping from the pain of lye-cracked, skinned, raw hands and arms to relish the prospect.

'Bugger it!' she decided. 'I'll goo back to our Tom in an hour or so and take 'im a drop o' gin to sweeten him ... Fat Will 'ull let me have it on the slate, miserable barstard that he is.'

She came out of the tangle of alleyways and on to the top of Fish Hill. As she turned towards her own cottage, she caught a flash of colour and movement down the hill. She looked and saw that it was a party of soldiers, recruiters by their appearance, struggling up the deeply rutted roadway.

' 'Ere, come and see the pretty sodgers.'

Her raucous screeching brought frowsy, unwashed heads to the broken doors and windows of the houses round about. Facing her, the old Crown Inn was still shuttered and barred. Doll beckoned her neighbour's child.

'Susan! Run across the road and tell Fat Will to open up. Tell 'im there's sodgers come.'

The little girl, clad only in a torn, dirty sack-dress, ran to the inn and hammered on the shutters with her tiny hands. 'Uncle Will, Uncle Will, Aunt Doll says you'm to open up for the sodgers.'

The recruiting party had by this time reached the common. A young Ensign led, riding a black horse. Behind him, on foot, were two sergeants wearing the gay rosettes and streaming ribbons of recruiters upon their black leather shakoes. Following them came a diminutive drummer boy, two privates and a huge corporal, while trailing behind all of them were half a dozen new recruits, whose only uniformity, apart from their self-conscious expressions, was a scarlet ribbon pinned to the front of their tattered clothing.

The Ensign signalled with his hand and the drummer began to beat out a riffle. People poured out from the rows of cottages and formed a crowd some paces away from the Ensign. The young officer's lips curled in distaste, the morning air was still and clear, and the smell of the crowd reached him strongly. For the most part they were women, old men and children, with few younger men. The Ensign rummaged in his saddlebag, and pulled from it a rolled-up scroll, which he smoothed out over his knee. He began to read from it, shouting the words.

'To all loyal subjects of His Most Gracious Majesty, King George the Third. If there are any young gallants among you who have too little money or too much wife ... If you suffer from hard masters or cruel landlords ... Then enlist with the glorious 36th Regiment of Foot, the Saucy Greens, the boldest death-defying blades in the Army, and live the life of a Gentleman ... Good food and plenty of drink for your bellies, fine clothes to set the lasses' hearts abeating, pockets full of gold, and glory enough for ten lifetimes are the rewards awaiting men with fire in their guts and adventure in their hearts. If any man wishes to hear more of the dark-eyed beauties waiting to welcome him with open arms in Spain and Portugal, then let him repair to the sign of ...' He paused and looked about him. As he did so, the door of the Crown crashed open and a short, fat white-haired man ran out.

'Please to come inside, your honour. I've the finest of wines and ales here in the old Crown.' The landlord bowed low and smiled ingratiatingly, showing blackened broken teeth.

The Ensign shrugged and turned once more to the crowd.

'... then let him repair to the sign of the Crown Inn,' he continued, 'where my men will feast him like the fighting cocks they are ... God Save the King!' He rolled up the scroll and thrust it back into the saddlebag, while the drumbeat shattered the air once again.

'You'll get no men from here to fight and be butchered for those mincing buggers in London.'

The voice rang out over the rattle of the drum. The Ensign looked up from his saddlebag.

'Cease drumming,' he snapped.

28

The drumroll died away and all was silent. The officer stared menacingly at the crowd and was met with sullen glares.

'Who said that?' he demanded.

'I did.' Doll Greenaway stepped out from the mass of people and walked up to his horse's head. 'And I'll say it again, sodger-boy ... You'll get no men from here. Better you should bring us bread, not take our sons away to be butchered in Spain.'

The Ensign scowled down at the haggard face. 'I come here in the King's service, woman,' he told her. 'We need more men for the Army of the Peninsula, to fight the damned Frenchie. If you want bread, then go to a baker, and cease interfering in the affairs of your betters.'

He kneed his horse to turn away, but the woman grabbed the bridle.

'You red-jacketed little barstard!' she hissed. 'It was another such pretty boy as you that 'ticed my Billy away, and four more lads with him from this town. And where are they now?' She thrust her face upwards at him and spat the words out. 'Four of um were left dead and rotting at Corunna, and my son Billy is sat in the house back there with his eyes blown out and his mind gone ... And not a penny piece to feed him comes from that mad muck-eating bugger in London that you calls King!'

The Ensign's face flamed with rage. 'You speak treason, damn you!' he shouted. 'Sergeant!'

The sergeants ran forward, drawing their short swords as they came. Doll Greenaway screamed her hatred and jumped at the officer, her nails clawing long bloody streaks down his smooth cheeks. The sergeants reached her and one of them, using his swordhilt as a club, hit the screeching woman as hard as he was able on the side of her jaw. Her eyes rolled up showing the whites and she fell heavily. The horse, terrified by the sudden uproar, reared high, lashing out with its iron-shod hooves and trampling the inert head and body beneath him.

The Ensign calmed the beast and shouted angrily, 'Come forward, you bumpkins, and attend to the woman.'

From the crowd, which had seemed held as though mesmerized while the scuffle took place, several women ran towards Doll Greenaway's body. One of them lifted the battered, blood-streaked head and cradled it in her arms. 'Oh Doll, Doll, why does you allus lose your temper so?' she crooned the words.

The Ensign threw a gold coin on to the ground beside them. 'Take this and get a surgeon to treat her,' he said. 'If more money is needed, you'll find me in the inn there.' With that he rode to where the fat landlord of the Crown was bowing and smirking to receive him.

Gently the women lifted Doll Greenaway and carried her to her cottage. Inside the dark, dirty interior they laid her on the rag-covered planks that served as her bed. A boy was sent to find Doctor Murdoch and, when they had made the injured woman as comfortable as they were able, her friends squatted on the stone floor to wait.

By the burnt-out ashes of the fire a man, clad in the tattered greasy remnants of a scarlet jacket and once grey trousers, crouched on a broken stool. His wreckage of a face, dominated by empty, raw-looking eye sockets, gave no sign that he was conscious of the people crowding the room.

'Billy?' one of the women spoke to him, touching his shoulder. 'Have you eaten yet this morning?'

The tortured head lifted, and cocked on one side in an attitude of listening.

'Have you eaten yet, Billy?' the woman repeated.

'No, sergeant, no.' His speech was jerky. 'I'se only just come from the main guard, sergeant ... I'se bin on the main guard wi' Knacker Collins ... There's bin no sight o' the froggy dragoons, sergeant, none at all ... Does we march today? Does we, sergeant?'

Some of the watchers began to titter their amusement.

'He thinks you'm his old sergeant, Agnes. Must be 'cos your 'ands um so big,' one said.

'Or 'cos her speaks like a man,' another put in, cackling with glee. 'I allus knew that her 'ad summat funny about her.'

The whole room filled with laughter. Agnes rounded on her tormentors.

'A pox on you all!' she screeched. 'Making mock o' the poor loony bugger, and 'is own mother lying there, perhaps dying.'

The laughter died away, leaving only a long uneasy silence,

broken by the snoring breaths of the injured woman. From the doorway, one of the old men noisily cleared his throat.

'Here comes the doctor now,' he told them. 'And the Methody's wi' 'im.'

Agnes Bright went to the door and peered out. 'The bloody doctor's taking 'is time,' she grumbled, and turned back into the room. 'You'd all best goo out,' she ordered. 'I'll bet theer's a few on you that wun't want to see the Methody too close.'

Reluctantly, the people inside cleared the room, not wishing to leave the scene of so interesting an event. By the time the stout, red-faced Doctor Murdoch and his companion reached it, the cottage was empty but for Agnes Bright, Billy Greenaway and the woman on the bed. The doctor went inside while his companion halted at the doorway and grimly surveyed the clustering crowd.

The Methody, or Methodist preacher, was a giant of a man who towered above all present. His shoulders were broad enough to fill the doorway and his heavily lined, middle-aged dourness, allied to the sombre blackness of his clothing, made him a fit representative of the grim, Hell-threatening God that he served. Emmanuel Clayton feared neither man nor Devil, and now, as he glared at the crowd, they sensed his sheer power to command.

'What happened to Doll Greenaway?' His voice was deep and growling. 'Have you been fighting and brawling among yourselves again? Or did she get swinish drunk and fall to hurt herself?' He waited for a reply but none came. Instead, people scuffled their feet and would not meet his accusing glare. From inside the cottage came a low moan, followed by a testy shout from the Doctor.

'Clayton? Would ye be guid enough to step in here for a moment?' The doctor's Scots accent became more pronounced as he repeated his request. The preacher gave the crowd a last angry stare, then went into the low dark room. The doctor was bending over the woman on the bed, trying to hold her writhing body still.

'Come over here, Clayton, and keep this damned besom still, will ye. So I can make an examination.'

Clayton did as he was asked, his dour face softening with pity at the sight of the broken, blood-soaked head on its pillow of rags. Gently he enfolded the wiry arms in his shovel-like

31

hands and held them steady. The doctor finished his examination and straightened, his face grave.

'It's a bad business,' he said, shaking his head. 'Her skull's crushed in, there.' He pointed to a shallow dent in the exposed scalp. 'I'll need to trepan, if she's to live.'

Emmanuel Clayton released the woman's arms and stared at his friend. 'Then we had best move her,' he said quietly. 'You cannot work in this filth.'

The doctor pursed his mouth. 'Well, I canna move her either,' he replied. 'Look at her face, man! She'd not get as far as the door in her condition.'

Doll Greenaway moaned again and her legs drew up to her belly in a muscular spasm. Her face beneath the caked grime was grey, and the thin lips stretched over blackened stumps of teeth were blue and livid.

Clayton nodded. 'You are right, Murdoch,' he said. 'Tell me what you want me to do to help.'

The Scotsman smiled. 'Och! You're a guid fellow. For all the nonsense that ye blether in that chapel of yours ... Agnes Bright?' he called. 'Get these women that were with you to heat some water and find a razor, I'll need to shave the head ... And you, boy.' He pointed to a slim dark-haired youth who was standing by the door. 'What's your name?'

'Jethro Stanton! And it was the officer on the horse who did this to Doll,' the boy answered, his voice angry.

'Well, Jethro Stanton, never mind how it happened,' the doctor ordered. 'Run to ma house and ask ma housekeeper to give you the tincture of opium for me. Have you got that? Say it! Tincture of opium.'

The boy nodded. 'I understand. Tincture of opium.'

'Good!' the doctor told him. 'Here! Take this.' From his pocket he pulled out a coin. 'And on the way back, call at the Crown and buy a flask of rum, and mind you tell that rogue Fat Will that it's for me, and it must be good spirit. None of that water and copper alum rubbish that he sells.'

The boy took the coin and ran from the room. Emmanuel Clayton watched his slender well-made figure running lightly across the common. 'Jethro Stanton?' he mused. 'I don't recall his face.'

'If you please, sir,' Agnes Bright put in, 'his Dad is a needle pointer at the Washford Mills, Peter Stanton.'

'No matter.' The preacher dismissed her and spoke to the doctor.

'He seems a forward young man that one. A deal too much independence for his station in life, I'd think, judging by his manner.'

The doctor was busily laying out his instruments. He glanced up at his friend and said, 'You sound like some of our local gentry and needle masters, Clayton. Grind the noses of the poor into the dirt so they canna look up at the stars.'

The preacher shook his head. 'No, my friend, you misunderstand me. I meant that many a young man's spirit has been crushed because he has displayed too much of it for his betters to stomach.'

Young Jethro Stanton ran easily, following the rutted road towards Evesham. The doctor's home was almost a mile from the common, a long low building that stood on the top of a rising hillside called Mount Pleasant. From its rear windows on clear days could be seen the humped lines of the Malvern Hills, their colours turned to a greyish-purple by distance. As he ran, Jethro thought about the scene he had witnessed. The clubbing down of Doll Greenaway and the casual callousness of the young officer, discharging his responsibilities towards the injured woman by the contemptuous tossing down of a coin. The boy's anger smouldered. He reached the doctor's house and hammered on the door until a plump, white-capped woman opened it.

'You young varmint!' she scolded. 'You'm near on knocking the door flat.'

He was unimpressed by her rage. 'Are you the housekeeper?' he asked.

She ceased her ranting and looked more closely at him.

'Yes I am.'

'Then the doctor asks that you give me the tincture of opium to take to him.'

'How old are you, boy?' she wanted to know.

'I'm gone sixteen, ma'am,' he told her, gravely. 'And now will you give me what I ask for, ma'am. There's a poor woman been sorely hurt.'

The housekeeper was amused by the boy's manner, so old for his years.

'What woman?' she questioned.

33

'Doll Greenaway,' Jethro answered, and told her what had happened.

The woman listened in silence, then clucked her tongue against her teeth and said, 'What a silly, drunken sinful hussy that Doll Greenaway is, to be sure.'

'It was the officer, not Doll, who was the sinful one!' the boy burst out in anger.

The woman made no answer, instead she disappeared into the depths of the house to reappear moments later carrying a small bottle. 'Here!' She thrust it into Jethro's hand. 'Be off wi' you, and mind and be careful that you do not speak so slighting of your betters in the future,' she admonished him.

'My father says that in all God's earth there is not one man who is born better than another,' the boy answered defiantly, and ran back towards the town.

By the time he reached the Crown Inn, Jethro was panting. He paused for a moment to catch his breath, then entered the taproom and asked the landlord for a flask of rum. While waiting, Jethro looked with interest at the far end of the room. There, comfortably sprawled on a wooden-armed chair in front of the fire, was the young Ensign, a glass of wine in his hand, richly laced jacket open, booted feet resting on the guard rail. To one side of him around a long table, the remainder of the recruiting party joked, bragged, sang and emptied their leather drinking jacks of ale as fast as the serving-maid could replenish them.

The big corporal noticed the boy staring and nudged one of the sergeants next to him. The sergeant lifted his beer-flushed face and grinned.

'Sure now ... Isn't that a foine young cockerel,' he said, his chuckling Irish voice not matching the hard, cold eyes with which he measured Jethro. 'Sure now, wouldn't a smart young lad like you'se like to wear His Majesty's coat, and have a bit o' fun foightin' the French?' he called to the boy.

Jethro shook his head.

'Ah well! 'Tis a great pity.' The sergeant sounded truly regretful. 'You'd have made a foine Grenadier in a couple o' years, when the good food the Army gives you had filled you out a bit. Never mind! Commun over here, and take a drink of ale with us, for friendship's sake.'

'I can't,' Jethro said. 'I have to go as soon as I'm served.'

While he was speaking, the landlord bustled in with the flask of rum. The big corporal and the sergeant exchanged a knowing look, and the corporal got to his feet and went to the boy's side. As Jethro reached for the rum, the corporal put his hand on the neck of the flask and stopped the boy.

'You bain't very civil, be you?' he said truculently. ' 'Ere's my friends and me offerin' you a sup o' our ale, and you don't even return the compliment.'

Jethro tried to snatch the rum, but the big man lifted the flask high and held off the boy with one large hand.

'Well! Yo're a mean-souled young devil and no mistake. Not willin' even to offer a mouthful o' rum to gennulmen who'm fightin' for you.'

The soldiers laughed at the expression of bafflement on Jethro's face.

'Listen!' he said, desperately. 'I must take that rum to the doctor ... He needs it to treat that woman you nearly killed.'

'What's that?' The Irish sergeant stood up suddenly. 'What's that you'se are saying, you young hound?' His face darkened and he lurched threateningly towards the youth. Fear dried Jethro's throat and mouth, but he forced himself to stand his ground. The corporal gripped the cork of the flask between his teeth and wrenched it free. He spat it on to the ground and, tilting the flask, he took a long swallow.

'No!' Jethro shouted. 'Give it back.' He pushed aside the restraining hand and jumped to snatch the rum away from the man. His wildly clutching hands knocked the bottle from the corporal's lips, causing the spirit to spill down his chin and neck and over the bright green facings of his scarlet regimentals.

'Rot your bloody eyes!' the big man roared and, using his fist like a club, he pounded at the upturned face of the boy. The blows caught Jethro squarely across the bridge of his nose and he shrieked aloud in agony as he felt the grinding crunch of the cartilage. He slumped to the floor, blinded by blood and tears, moaning in his distress.

'Be Jasus! But you've a heavy hand, Corporal Hodgekins!' the Irish sergeant breathed, admiringly. 'You've knocked all the foight outta this one.'

'So he has, you papist blackguard, just as I shall knock all the fight out of him, if he doesn't stop guzzling that rum like the pig he is, and order another bottle to replace it this instant.'

All eyes swung in the direction of the deep, powerful voice. There in the doorway, filling it with his bulk, was Emmanuel Clayton. He advanced into the room and, bending, he gently lifted the dazed, bleeding boy to his feet.

'There, boy, I'll take care of you now,' he comforted.

Corporal Hodgekins recovered from his surprise at the preacher's intervention. 'I take no orders from a damned Methody,' he growled. 'If you don't bugger off out of here, I'll kick y' damned arse through y' mouth.'

'Be Jasus! And oi'll help him do it,' the sergeant threatened.

Clayton gently ushered Jethro behind him. Then, straightening his back, he faced the two soldiers. 'I see that there is a necessity to use the strong arm of righteousness in the Lord's service,' he said sadly, and sprang forward.

There were two sharp cracks as bone met bone, and the corporal and the sergeant went down as though pole-axed. Straddling their senseless bodies, the preacher spoke softly to the rest of the party, who had jumped to their feet, the other sergeant reaching for his short-sword.

'I would advise you not to attempt further violence, gentlemen. I have no wish to deprive His Most Gracious Majesty of any more of his troops.'

The young Ensign, who had been an amused spectator of the whole of the proceedings, laughed his appreciation. 'Put away that bayonet, blast you!' he roared. 'And sit back on your arses, before the preacher skittles the rest of you.' He got lazily to his feet and bowed mockingly to Clayton. ''Pon my soul, sir! I could wish for a few thousand men such as yourself in the Army of the Peninsula. Dammee! We'd have the French back over the Pyrenees in a matter of days.' He turned to the landlord. 'Don't stand there gaping like a fool, you fat hog. Fetch a bottle of your finest rum for this gentleman.'

The landlord brought the rum and the Ensign bowed once more and handed it to Clayton. 'Please accept this with my compliments, sir; and I beg of you, forgive my men for their appalling ways. But no one learns fine parlour manners dealing with Johnny Crapaud.'

The preacher nodded stiffly. 'We'll say no more of the matter, sir,' he answered and, tucking the bottle under one

36

arm, he put the other round Jethro's shoulders and led him out of the inn and across the common to Doll Greenaway's cottage.

In the cottage the doctor snatched the rum and opium, and began to make up a mixture.

'What happened to the boy?'

'He had a brush with the redcoats over at the inn,' Clayton explained.

'Damned scums that they are!' the doctor burst out. 'But there! What else can you expect, if you torture men with unmerciful flogging and put them under the command of worthless drunken fops?'

'True,' Clayton agreed. 'But someday, when the Lord so wills it, things will change.'

'And pigs will fly when He wills it,' the doctor muttered, irreverently. He pulled Jethro to him and examined the injured nose, which already was swelling badly. 'Here, boy, drink this,' he ordered, and poured the mixture of drug and spirit down Jethro's throat. The boy choked and gagged, but the doctor's hand was firmly clamped across his mouth, forcing him to keep the mixture in his stomach. Gradually a feeling of drowsiness overcame him and the doctor seated him on the floor next to Billy Greenaway. The pain in his nose was reduced to a dull throb. Murdoch placed one hand at the back of Jethro's head and with the other he moulded the damaged nose.

'There!' he said finally. 'That will do it. Your nose is as good as new, boy. But keep your clumsy paws away from it for a few days or you'll have it crooked again.'

Jethro nodded and lay back. The noises of voices and moans seemed to come from a great distance, and the last thing he was conscious of was the voice of the idiot Billy, muttering about Knacker Collins and the French Dragoons, while the doctor kept on repeating, 'Hold her still, Clayton, dammit! Or I'll have the drill in her brain ... Hold her still, man!'

CHAPTER FOUR

Owen Treadgold, General Manager of Bartleet's Needle Mills, was a small, timid man who still favoured the powdered clubbed wigs and wide-skirted coats of his father's day. He was not the usual image of the tough-minded, hard-bitten needle master, but Owen Treadgold was in the forefront of his profession. His inventive genius for improving the quality of his product had earned him the high respect of the entire industry. It had not, however, earned him the respect of his wife.

'Are you listening to me, Treadgold?' Her voice bore into him as he sat trying to eat the bowl of bread and milk which was all his ulcer-ridden stomach could digest.

He sighed heavily. 'I'm listening, Mrs Treadgold.'

'No, you are not!' she contradicted. 'You're sat there like a deaf booby, thinking about some mad hare-brained invention or other, I know you are ... I can tell it.' She paced up and down the room, her grey hair escaping from under her mob-cap, her double chin wobbling in time with her step. 'My family warned me before I married you ... "Agatha!" they said. "Don't be foolish. Don't you marry that madman, he spends all his time inventing flying coaches or some other such rubbish. He's a lunatic!" they told me. But I would not listen ... more fool me! And the Lord above knows how I've suffered. But there, what else could be expected? I was only a pretty country maid, as innocent and pure as a newborn babe.' She swung her huge rump round and lifted her melon-like breasts into a more comfortable position. 'What a silly little simpleton I was ...'

'Never little!' Owen thought, scathingly. 'And as for pure and innocent ... Oh, my God!' He shuddered visibly as he remembered the suffocating eagerness with which his hefty young bride had clutched his small frame to her billows of flesh in the marriage bed. He tried fruitlessly to concentrate his thoughts on the business of the day before him at the mills, but her grating diatribe penetrated relentlessly.

'I could have married a gentleman and had my own carriage and servants, instead of which I have to walk everywhere and the only help I get is that slut who comes to do the washing when it suits her. It's all your fault ... you would not be denied, would you?' she accused, poking his bowed shoulders with pudgy be-ringed fingers and pushing her face to within inches of his own so that her perspiring pimply features blotted out all else. 'You wanted me only because you lusted for my body ... You dirty little lecher!'

Owen closed his eyes and stoically endured, knowing from years of bitter experience that to answer back would only unleash the full gale of her fury.

'Oh God, will you never give me the courage to kill her?' he prayed silently. 'Strike her with a thunderbolt ... Sweep down from the skies in your chariot of wrath and crush this great fat lump of dung beneath your golden wheels. I have suffered this torment for twenty long years, God. Have pity on me and destroy her, I beg you, destroy her.'

A sudden metallic clatter made him open his eyes hopefully, perhaps the miracle for which he had prayed for years had occurred and the heavenly chariot had indeed swept down to crush his hated wife. He felt acute disappointment. She had merely thrown a pan at the wall, missing her target, himself. She went into the kitchen to fetch another missile and, seizing his opportunity, he clapped his tricorn hat on his head, settled his square-rimmed spectacles firmly on his nose and escaped from the house.

At the mills he worked contentedly in his office above the main entrance until, early in the afternoon, the sound of hoof-beats in the street outside told him that his master had arrived. He hurried downstairs and emerged into the cobbled courtyard as Colonel Bartleet was dismounting from his glossy brown mare. Bartleet tethered his horse to a ring set in the wall and greeted his manager pleasantly.

'Good afternoon, Owen, how is your stomach today?'

Treadgold returned his smile. He liked and admired the Colonel.

'It's much easier, sir, my thanks to you.'

'And your lady wife is well, I trust?'

Treadgold's smile dulled. 'Well sir,' he sighed.

The Colonel nodded sympathetically; his manager's marital troubles were well known. 'Do you mind if we wait here for a few moments, Owen?' he continued. 'Abner Melen is coming, and we can all look at the wire and discuss what's to be done.'

The wire in question was a newly arrived consignment from the Derbyshire foundries. It was of German steel, and gave a great deal of trouble in working up. The Bartleet and Melen mills had shared the consignment.

'I dare to venture that I have the solution, sir,' Treadgold said. 'But in the meantime, I wonder if I might tell you about an idea I have for a stamping machine powered by steam which will do away with ...'

The two men walked together, Treadgold waving his arms excitedly as he expounded on his latest invention. They made an odd couple. The tall distinguished Charles Bartleet was clad in an immaculate dove-grey riding coat and breeches, with a plum-shaded waistcoat, high shirt collar and faultless cravat. He wore a black beaver top-hat on his head and shining tasselled Hessian boots on his legs—a startling contrast with the tiny Treadgold in his shabby grease-spotted clothing, wrinkled stockings and large buckled shoes of a bygone era.

Another horseman trotted through the arch and into the yard. Abner Melen, the master of the neighbouring mills, dismounted and shook hands with the two men. In appearance he could have been the brother of Clem Washford and, like him, was also a self-made man, who had inherited a single workshop from his father and built it into a large thriving mill.

'Well, Bartleet? What's to be done about this damn wire?' Melen asked, after the preliminary greetings had been exchanged.

The Colonel shrugged. 'I really cannot venture an opinion, Melen,' he replied. 'But Owen here thinks he has the solution, and I don't doubt but that he has.'

Melen nodded curtly. 'Well, like I allus says, if anybody can beat a problem, then it's Treadgold 'ere.'

The manager blushed and smiled with gratification, and a touch of smugness. 'Yes, gentlemen, I do believe I have found the answer. Follow me, if you please.'

He led them across the yard to a wooden leanto built against the outer wall. Inside were piled stacks of coiled wire from which a man was cutting short lengths with large hand-shears bolted to a bench. The lengths were taken by other men who put them into glowing charcoal pits before laying them red-hot on anvils for straightening and rounding by hammer. Then the wire was reheated and forced through the wire-iron, a fixed steel plate with various sized holes bored through it. A tub of stinking rancid hog-lard stood by the wire-iron and the heated lengths were pushed into it before each drawing. The cloying stench as the wire bubbled into the grease caused even hardened workers to turn their heads and hold their noses, and the first effect on the two masters was to send them choking and gagging into the yard.

'Forgive me, Owen,' Bartleet coughed, holding a handkerchief to his nose and mouth. 'I am becoming quite delicate in my latter years, I fear.'

When they recovered their composure, they returned inside the leanto.

'There's the trouble, sir,' Treadgold told them. 'It's really very simple. We are reheating and drawing the wire too many times. We must cut the number of repetitions and place two men to draw a wire together, to compensate for the extra effort needed.'

'Goddam and blast me!' Melen swore. 'All that soddin' wire gone out to be softworked already, and most on it ull be wasted. I must be in my bloody dotage not to 'ave realized that was the trouble ... Well, any road up! That's easy remedied now.'

'Ahr gaffer, that may be so, but tell me 'ow you'm agoin' to remedy the loss of earnin's for the poor buggers as is workin' wi' the bad stuff you'se give out already?' A burly man dressed as a pointer advanced into the shed.

'And who might you be?' Abner Melen challenged.

'It's my pointing shop foreman, Tom Bright,' Treadgold explained, and spoke to the man. 'What ails it you, Tom? Your earnings have not been affected.'

'My earnings, no, Owen Treadgold. I'se only got Agnes, me

missis, and little Susan to worrit about, but there's others 'as a lot more dependent on 'um, and it's time that working men stuck up for each other.' Bright's brawl-scarred face was contemptuous as he glanced at the other workmen in the shed. 'I guessed that none o' these buggers ud 'ave the guts to tackle the masters, that's why I come over special to see you.'

Charles Bartleet stepped forward. 'Come now, Tom, it's obvious that you have a grievance, let us hear what you have to say.'

'It's not only Tom that 'as, marster,' the workman cutting the wire spoke up. 'It's all on us ...' He faltered nervously, then went on, as he gathered courage. 'We'm on piece-rates, marster, and the rates um rock bottom as it is. We 'as a terrible job to manage, and there's folks in this town damn near starvin'.'

A grumble of assent and encouragement came from the other men.

'It's like this, gaffer,' Tom Bright took up the statement. 'This bad wire means that the earnings ull drop to next to nothin' for everybody, through no fault o' their own.'

'And so ull our damned profit drop to nothin'!' Abner Melen could contain his indignation no longer. 'I 'opes you men knows that you'm breakin' the law o' the land by banding together this way and worritin' your betters wi' your moans and groans. 'As you men ne'er heard about the Combination Acts? Colonel Bartleet 'ere is the Chief Magistrate in this district, and I 'ope 'e'll put a stop to this bloody insolence by getting you all committed to the assizes for unlawful assembly.'

'Shut your bloody rattle, Abner Melen!' Tom Bright shouted back. 'I says bollocks to you and your Combination Act. I'm a free-born Englishman, not a cur dog to be shouted at by a arse-creepin' old windbag like you.'

'Calm yourselves, both of you,' Charles Bartleet ordered. 'I'll have no more of that sort of language from you, Tom Bright, and I want no more talk of unlawful assembly and assizes from you, Melen. These men are my responsibility and have every right to tell me of their problems. We'll settle nothing by shouting and bickering.'

The irate Abner Melen took a deep breath. 'Be damned to it! I'm going, Bartleet, I'll not stay here and bandy words wi' a pack o' ...' He saw the gathering violence in the workmen's faces and decided against abuse. 'Good day to you, sir!' he snapped, and strutted away.

Charles Bartleet was relieved to see his fellow needle master's departure, and had already made his decision about the problem.

'Very well, Bright, and the rest of you men. You will of course have to work up the wire that has already been issued. However, I will see to it that none of you, nor any of my work-people, suffer any loss of earnings because of the bad wire, this will also apply to any outworkers who have fetched packets from the mills. I shall attempt to persuade Master Melen to do the same, I am quite sure he will see the justice in it ... Now, get back to work, all of you ... Come along, Owen, we'll discuss your idea further before I return home.'

When they had gone, Tom Bright grinned at the other men. 'Theer you see, I told you that the Colonel was a fair man. He's a true gentleman, so 'e is. 'E'll see that we're all right.'

'Ahr Tom, that may be so, but he's only one and there aren't many like 'im in this town. Theer's too many bad bastards like Melen an' old Clem Washford to bring us into the muck,' one man observed bitterly. 'Our kid's an out-worker, and 'e's near bloody mad wi' hunger and want, and what wi' the rate-cut and the trade so bad these days, I can 'ardly earn enough to feed my own bairns, ne'er mind 'is as well.'

'Well, I don't know what's to be done about the trade ... But I knows one thing for certain,' Bright assured him. 'The bloody marsters and gentry 'ull drive the likes of us into re-bellion afore it's all over. I know I'll not stand by and do nothin' if my kin um starvin'.'

Much the same train of thought exercised Charles Bart-leet's mind as he rode slowly back to his home. He saw all about him every day the increasing distress of the poor. As far as he was able, he ensured that his own tenants and work-people suffered no deprivation and he knew that there were many among the gentry and masters who did the same. But he could do little. There were always competitors ruthless enough to cut selling prices to a minimum and underpay their workers accordingly, to drive men, women and children to the

43

point of exhaustion and beyond, so as to raise profits. 'I'm between the devil and the deep sea,' he thought sadly. 'If I am to make enough money to enable me to save my people from suffering, then, paradoxical though it may be, I must inflict upon those same people a certain amount of hardship to ensure that I earn that sufficiency of money.'

From a bend in the road he could see the tree-shaded lawns of his home. Even as he looked, he saw his two daughters run across the grass, throwing a ball between them, while the family's pet spaniels barked excitedly at their heels. He felt a rush of love for his children and at the same time the intense pity he always felt for the young children of the mills who would never know what it was to live without care and hardship.

Later that evening, sitting in the elegant comfort of his drawing-room, playing whist with his daughters and Doctor Murdoch, who was a frequent dinner guest, the conversation turned on the misfortune that Doll Greenaway had brought upon herself that morning. Charles Bartleet felt an overwhelming sense of helplessness.

'What, in Heaven's name, can be done for these people that will lift them from their violent brutish ways?' he asked.

The doctor smiled sardonically. 'If I could answer that question Bartleet, I would be God.'

'I sometimes wonder if even He knows the answer,' Anne Bartleet said quietly.

CHAPTER FIVE

The daylight had long faded when Peter Stanton finished his work. He straightened his back and with one finger tested the points of the needles he held in his hands. All around him in the narrow cellar, lit solely by two guttering oil lamps hanging from the roof, the other pointers were also finishing off their final batches. For a few seconds he sat watching them. Their faces were shadowed as they bent over the whirling grindstones, but at intervals the white-hot sparks showered around their heads and illuminated their features with a lurid flickering glare. A line from a poem read long before came unbidden to his mind. 'These were brutes in a Stygian gloom, lit only by the fires of Hell.'

'An apt description! I wonder if the man who wrote it had ever worked in a mill,' Stanton speculated, and placed the needles in a box by his side. He yawned and stretched his arms until the tired muscles creaked, then, getting up from his stool, he left his place.

Outside in the rubbish-filled yard he pulled the rags from his face and drew in great gulps of cold night air, which, even though stinking of rotting ordure, was still pure in comparison with the fug he had worked in. Footsteps echoed in the passageway which led to the front courtyard and a tall slender figure entered the enclosed court. It was Harry Washford, only son of the mill's owner, Clem Washford.

'Hello, Peter, taking a breath of air, such as it is?' His voice was pleasant, in keeping with the narrow face and soft gentle eyes which studied him with interest.

Stanton nodded, his tone when he answered neither gushing nor surly, merely civil. 'That's right, Mr Washford.'

Washford paused in passing, searching his mind for some means of prolonging the conversation. His romantic questing

45

nature was intrigued by Stanton, who had come to the mill two years before from no one knew where. He spoke both to the local gentry and his fellow workers as an equal, and although he never mentioned his past, he yet gave the impression of being a widely travelled, well-educated man.

'How is Jethro?' the young man asked, finally. 'Is it not time that he began working?'

'He's well enough,' Stanton said, then smiled grimly. 'And as to the second question, I'll let no son of mine waste his youth and destroy his health in making other men rich, not while I have the strength to provide for him. There are too many men who have never known other than slavery all their lives as it is.' The mildness of the tone softened the truculence of the words and made them inoffensive.

Harry Washford smiled ruefully and looked about him, at the mean yard with its piles of stinking rubbish and its corners used as middens, and at the hell-holes of noise and filth surrounding it.

'There is justice in what you say,' he replied, and walked away.

By now the clattering of the machinery had stopped and men, women and children came from the workrooms to cluster in the outer yard, waiting for Dick Taylor to unlock the main gates and let them out of the mill. The boys and younger men wrestled and skylarked, while the older ones gathered in small groups to grumble about the delay in opening the gates.

Peter Stanton found himself next to his friend Jamie Fisher, the eldest of three brothers who all worked as needle pointers in the town. Fisher was gaunt and hollow-cheeked, and every few seconds his feeble frame was shaken by a racking cough. After each bout of coughing, he would spit into a piece of rag that he carried clutched in his hand, and examine the sputum.

Stanton waited until the man had recovered from one such bout, then asked, 'How is it today, Jamie?'

Fisher drew in wheezing breaths. 'It's bad, Peter,' he said, gasping out the words. 'I'm fetching the blood up somethin' awful.'

Peter Stanton patted the thin shoulder in silent sympathy.

'Ne'er mind!' Fisher tried to smile, showing blackened, decayed teeth. 'I'll get a drop o' gin on me way home ... That ull 'elp it.'

'Surely it will, Jamie,' his friend reassured him.

A volley of jeering and catcalls greeted the appearance of the sour-faced overseer. Self-importantly he made his way through the throngs of people and, unlocking the huge padlock, he pulled aside the bar that held the great wooden doors shut.

As the workers pushed forward, jostling each other to be first through the gate, Taylor shouted sneeringly, 'It's a pity that you carn't be as eager to come to your work as you am to leave it.'

'Save your preachin' for the chapel, you Methody pisspot!' one man shouted back.

Taylor looked down his nose. 'That's just corst you a shilling fine, my lad. You know the rules about filthy language. It 'ud do you more good to serve the Lord in chapel, than to spend your time like you does, in drinking and fornicating and making abominations in the Lord's sight.' His voice rose to a screech on the last words and the only reply to his outburst was a wave of hooting laughter as the crowd spilled into the roadway.

The road was unlighted and the inworkers were only shapeless blobs in the murk as they made their way uphill into the town. At the common, Stanton left his friend, Jamie, who lived on the opposite side of the town, and walked on alone to his own terraced hovel. He noticed the small group clustered about the door of Doll Greenaway's home, but, assuming it was a neighbours' quarrel, he went past without stopping. His house was in darkness, no fire was kindled in the hearth and no meal laid ready. He went in and called.

'Jethro? Are you here?'

There was no reply. Stanton felt a pang of alarm—Jethro had never been absent from home at this time before. Always the boy had a fire lit and food of some sort prepared. The man left the house and made his way rapidly past the tumbledown rows to the crowd at Doll Greenaway's. Agnes Bright, standing guard at the door, saw him coming.

'Is that you, Peter Stanton?' she called.

'Aye, it is,' he replied. 'Have you seen my Jethro?'

'He's here,' she told him, 'sleeping like a babby.'

'What? Has he been drinking?' he asked angrily.

The woman was indignant. 'No 'e aren't,' she snapped. 'And stop glowerin' like a bloody marster ... The lad's bin hurt.'

'Hurt?' Stanton felt anxiety tightening his throat. He hurried to her, thrusting aside the people in his path.

'What's happened?' he demanded.

The woman stood aside to let him enter, then followed him in, babbling out the story of what had happened that day at the top of her voice. Jethro was still lying where the doctor had left him. His father knelt by his side and gently traced his fingertips over the swollen nose and puffy bruised eyes. A surge of tenderness overcame him and for a long moment he remained still, gazing at his son. Afterwards he went to look at Doll Greenaway. The woman lay quietly, her head swathed heavily in bandages, the caked blood from her wounds still encrusted on her skin and clothes and the rags she lay upon.

'Will she live?' Peter Stanton asked.

'The doctor said her 'ud, but Preacher Clayton said it were in God's 'ands.'

'In the hands of God, is it?' Stanton said bitterly. 'I think that we leave too much in the hands of God. It's time people like us began to do something towards changing the state of the world by using our own hands.'

He looked up and met the blank uncomprehending stare of the woman. He shook his head in exasperation.

'What's the use?' he asked of her. 'You don't even have a glimmering of understanding for what I mean. Can I leave Jethro here?' The woman nodded. 'Thank you, I'll not be long,' he said, and started to leave.

The idiot Billy, still crouching on his fireside stool, cocked his head on one side as Stanton passed him and said, 'Is it time to mount the main guard yet, sergeant? Or am I on the outlying picket? Am I, sergeant? Am I?'

'No, Billy. You're free of duties tonight. You can rest easy,' Stanton said gently, the pity in his eyes matching that in his tone.

Once outside, he made his way across the town until he reached the raw wood hut that served the Methodists as a chapel. Behind the hut was the cottage that Clayton lived in, alone but for his books and scanty possessions. Stanton could see the dim light of a candle shining from the window and the shadow of the preacher's head that was thrown gigantically across the inside walls. He tapped on the window and called, 'Mr Clayton, it's Peter Stanton, can I have a word with you?'

The preacher looked up from the book he was poring over and waved his hand. 'The latch is off the door, man. Come in.'

The room was austere and chilly, the only source of light and heat the solitary candle flame now guttering in the draught across the room.

'Come in, man. Sit down, if you will,' Clayton said, warmly.

'Thank you.' Stanton sat on the only seat in the room, a three-legged stool. 'I wanted to thank you, Mr Clayton, for helping my boy as you did,' he began.

The preacher waved away his hands. 'It was nothing ... I was only too happy to do it. May the Lord forgive me, but I enjoyed teaching those redcoats a lesson.' He paused and looked keenly at his visitor. 'I'm glad that you've called, Stanton. I've been wanting to meet with you and have a talk. It's strange, isn't it ... A small town like this, and yet we've never met.'

Peter Stanton smiled bleakly. 'Not strange really, Clayton. I don't frequent the chapel circles.'

The preacher shook his huge head. 'Just so. Just so,' he said sadly, then went on, 'Mr Stanton, I'm a blunt man and have no patience with frills and niceties. I'd like to know something of you. I have heard that you wield great influence among the pointers and others who work in the needles. It appears that you are held in high respect also, I might add, by your employers. Both Washfords have high opinions of you.'

'Really?' Stanton's voice held contempt, and his face darkened. 'I wish that I could say the same for my employers, but I find it difficult to respect those who make riches from the sufferings of their fellow men.'

'That is a strong statement to make,' the preacher said.

'Is it?' Stanton became vehement. 'I think it is time for strong statements, when men like Jamie Fisher are dying on their feet and him not yet thirty years of age, because the needle masters will not spend money on finding a means of extracting from the air the dust of stone and metal that rots a man's lungs ... When women and children toil until they weep, and die for want of bread, and people live in conditions

49

that the gentry would not keep their horses in, when a woman can have her skull broken by redcoats because she does not want mothers to have their sons sent back to them without sight or sanity ... No, Clayton! I do not make strong statements, I speak only the truth.'

For long moments, the big man sat, head bowed, fingering the pages of the book on the table in front of him. Finally he sighed heavily and passed his fingers through his thick greying hair. When he spoke he sounded curiously humble.

'Forgive me for trying to hector you, as I did. Of course, what you have said is the truth, and perhaps I as a servant of God should shout out against these injustices for the whole world to hear ...' He paused and looked directly at the other man from under his bushy eyebrows. 'But I truly believe, Stanton, that Our Lord has given the world these inequalities and injustices for a reason. What that reason is, I know not. But I believe with all my heart that when the time is ripe then the Lord will come into his own, the evil-doers will be punished, and the righteous will inherit the earth.' His voice became fervent and fanatical.

Stanton rose to his feet. 'I envy you your trust in divine intervention, but I have spent my life in many different occupations and in many different lands, and my faith is only in the belief that man himself must change things ... I, for one, intend to try and gain some justice for my fellows, using whatever means I may, fair or foul, peaceful or violent.'

The preacher also stood up and held out his hand. 'I wish you well of it,' he said. 'But I would add a word of warning. In some ears the words you have spoken could be construed as incitement to rebellion. You must tread very carefully, my friend.'

Peter Stanton shook the proffered hand, then in one swift movement he unbuttoned his shirt and waistcoat and slipped them back from his shoulders.

'This has taught me to tread carefully,' he said, and turned so that the light from the candle fell across his back. Clayton drew his breath in sharply with an exclamation of horror. The other man's back was a livid mass of scars, tormented flesh, left by the lashes of some unknown and unimaginable torture, a flogging, perhaps, long past, but, as Stanton's eyes showed, once endured, never to be forgotten.

CHAPTER SIX

Clem Washford lifted the glass of wine to his lips, drained it in one gulp and reached for the bottle to refill it. This time he sipped the wine, savouring its heady sweetness. At the opposite end of the long polished table, its surface littered with the remnants of an elaborate meal, his son Harry sat, head down, absently toying with the dish of beef in front of him.

'Harry?' The older man spoke sharply. 'What ails you, boy? You're poking at that meat as if it was a lump o' cow dung.'

The young man looked up in surprise. 'I'm sorry, father. I was thinking of something.'

Old Clem grunted disgustedly. 'You does too much thinkin', boy! You're like your mother was, allus daydreaming and moonin' about.'

Harry smiled and said nothing.

'I hear there was some trouble up in the town this mornin',' his father went on. 'That damned Greenaway woman again.'

The young man's face grew animated. 'There was no need for the soldiers to serve her as they did,' he protested.

Clem Washford's heavy features reddened. 'There was every bloody reason!' he shouted irascibly. 'I don't know what the world is acomin' to, when a slum bitch can attack a King's officer engaged on the King's business and a man in your position can say that she was ill-served ... The country's gone to the dogs, what wi' Cobbett and Hunt and the rest o' them Hell-damned Radicals, preaching sedition and calling for bloody revolution. It's got so that every stinking slum-rat thinks that 'e's as good as 'is master. Doll Greenaway should be hung for what she done ... And so should all the rest on um.'

Harry sighed and pushed his plate away. 'Cannot you realize that a new age is dawning?' he said quietly. 'Now that man has mastered nature and is harnessing powers like steam, as they have done at Coalbrookdale with the locomotive coach, a whole new world has been born. The new machines and knowledge mean that we can now satisfy all man's needs in abundance. All must share in the new wealth that we can now create. You talk of slum-rats ... Don't forget that my grandfather lived all his life in one of those hovels up by the common there, and you were born in that same hovel.'

The old man's red flush became almost purple.

'That's enough!' he roared. 'My Dad didn't waste 'is days getting drunk and 'is nights rutting between women's thighs. He took good care o' the money 'e sweated for and used it well. I worked from the time I could stand for fourteen and sixteen hours a shift. While the other lads were enjoying themselves, I was slavin' me guts out in your grandad's workshop, every single bloody day o' the year. We didn't worship Saint Saturday, Sunday and Monday like the rest o' the buggers.' He flung his arm out in the direction of the mills. 'We built that out theer from one hut, me and your grandad; and after he died, then me and your Mam went on building it ... And while I 'as a breath left in me body, then nothin' nor no one shall take it from me.'

His voice stilled and he leaned across the table. 'Listen to me, Harry.' He seemed almost to be pleading. 'Your Mam, God rest her soul, and me wanted time and time again to stop struggling, to enjoy ourselves sometimes, like other people used to do and let the morrow go hang. But we thought on you ... You was the only one God spared to us, we buried six afore they was a year old. We wanted everythin' for you. That's why you was brought up and educated as a gentleman. Because we didn't want you to 'ave to slave and suffer, as we did.'

He straightened his squat, thickset body and the anger boiled from him once more. 'Her died when you was only a babby, worn out by toiling and struggling, but her died knowing that we'd done it ... That the mills was built and prospering, and you 'ud one day be a needle master ...' He paused then shouted. 'And by God! That's exactly what you 'ull be, and no whore's whelp of a Radical will share in what me and mine worked and died to build.'

Harry made no reply, he rose to his feet and, walking round

to where the old man sat, he patted the thick shoulder.

'Very well, father,' he said quietly, 'we'll talk no more of this at present,' and left the room.

Clem Washford listened to the sound of his son's footsteps fade away, his face lost the red flush of anger and the harsh lines etched deep into the leathery skin softened into sorrow. He sighed deeply. 'You're like your Mam, son,' he whispered. 'Too soft, too soft by half. The bloody wolves 'ull pull you down, unless I harden you.' He shook his head and reached for the bottle of wine.

Alone in his bedroom, Harry stood by the window and gazed into the night. To one side loomed the dark mass of the mills, seeming to crouch against the hillside like some threatening primordial beast. The young man grimaced at the thought.

It was a beast, that sucked the strength of men for sustenance and spewed out the drained broken bodies when that strength was consumed. Spreading out from the mills were the dull flickering lights of the hovels where the mills' sustenance was spawned, dragged bloody and screaming from the bloody bodies of screaming women, swaddled in filthy rags and set to battle against death's warriors ... disease ... hunger ... dirt ... ignorance. The mills' sustenance that survived the carnage of this battle grew stunted and mis-shapen, with decayed teeth, twisted bones and dulled minds. As soon as it could perform the simplest of tasks, it was thrown into the maw of the mills, to live out the remainder of its short days satisfying the insatiable appetite of the monster.

The young master of Washford Mills turned away from the window, his mind a seething mass of tormented images, and flung himself still fully clothed on to his bed, there to toss and turn through the long dark hours of the night.

Down below, old Clem sat hunched over the table. Periodically he rang the bell which rested by his arm and bellowed out, 'Sam, you fool, are you dead?'

The manservant would come silently into the room, place a full bottle on the table in front of his master and take the empty one away.

In the cottage on the common, Doctor Murdoch sat on the heap of rags and watched over his patient. Doll Greenaway was unconscious, lying as if dead. Only the faintest sawing of breath through the pinched white nostrils showed that life still remained.

By the glowing ashes of the fire, blind Billy sat muttering and chuckling to himself.

'That's it, Sergeant! That's it! There! I hit 'im ... That Froggy jumped a yard in the air when I 'it 'im, Sergeant ... Do we march? Do we march, Sergeant? ... Gawd! These mountains 'um cold and miserable, aren't they ... All right for the General, I say! It's all right for him, aren't it ... Gawd, I'm hungry! Hungry! Hungry, Sergeant!'

Peter and Jethro Stanton sat side by side in their bleakly clean room. On the rough-hewn wooden table in front of them lay an open book and by candlelight they read together, the older man from time to time exhorting the boy.

'There now, Jethro, do you see what Tom Paine means when he says this? It's very simple. There should be no parasites of aristocracy leeching the blood of working men ... We must do as the French did and sweep them all away ... Gentry, Church and King.'

CHAPTER SEVEN

It was Sunday and the bells of St Stephen's rang out, throwing echoing chimes across the clean blue skies. On the common, the boys and youths wrestled and played tricks on each other, hooted and ran in the gleeful madness of freedom from their workshops and mills. The young girls gathered together in flocks of fresh white aprons, giggling and preening themselves, rivalling each other in their efforts to attract the glances of the young men. The alehouses and beershops that abounded in the town were open and the serious business of getting insensibly drunk was already well in hand. In every street the women sat on steps of houses or leaned from windows and gossiped, suckling grimy babies at grimier breasts and keeping lack-lustre eyes on the antics of the toddlers that swarmed about them, playing in the dust and filth of the narrow courts and alleys.

Summoned by the bells, the devout of the town made their dignified ways to the various places of worship, the gentry and near-gentry going for the most part to St Stephen's, while the shopkeepers and steady artisans tended to gravitate to the chapels.

Jethro Stanton stood at the edge of the common and watched the scene. His father had risen before dawn to walk to the nearby city of Birmingham on some mysterious errand of his own, leaving Jethro to spend the day as he chose.

A heavy weight landed on Jethro's back, sending him sprawling on to the ground. Strong hands gripped him around the neck, forcing his head back and almost choking him. The next instant he was released and he heard a laughing voice.

'How bist, Jethro? I goo t'Hanover! I caught you properly nappin' then, didn't I?'

Jethro rolled on to his back and squinted up against the

sun. A sun-browned, dark-eyed face laughed down at him with strong white teeth. Jethro grinned.

'Jos!'

The boy flung himself down beside Jethro. Of the same age, his muscular body threatened to burst through the sparse rags that covered it.

'I didn't know the Boswells were back in Redditch?' Jethro said.

'Ahr well, we am, bain't us.'

'Where's your Dad and the rest?' Jethro asked.

'We'm settled in Doctor Murdoch's field, bin theer fower days now. Old Simeon says we'em agoin' to stay for a while.'

Jethro crowed his delight at the news. The Boswells were a clan of travelling tinkers whose patriarch, old Simeon, a huge grizzled bear of a man in his sixties, had been a champion prize-fighter in his youth.

'What's you adoin' now?' Jos asked.

'Nothing,' Jethro told him.

'Come on then, let's goo up the woods.'

Side by side, the lads ran across the common and through the town towards the woods that covered the land towards Bromsgrove. Soon they reached the fringe of brush and small trees that formed the outer line of woodland. They pushed into the clinging branches of the young hazels, disregarding the brambles' greedy clawing, and broke through into the clear glades that stretched away between gnarled trunks of ancient oaks and elms.

Whooping their delight, they flung themselves over the pulpy mossbanks; they jumped across the tiny streams, leaping high to catch the lower branches, then bending low to snatch the heads off the thick masses of bluebells that blanketed the ground. On top of one rise the boys halted. Jethro drank in great gulps of the warm, wood-scented air. He felt a wild intoxication with the beauty of this other England, so different from the fetid streets where men lived and breathed in the industrial towns.

Jos touched his arm and pointed. There beneath them, unaware of any alien presence, was a flock of baby rabbits. Jethro turned to his friend and smiled his pleasure. Jos pointed again, not speaking for fear of disturbing the animals. Moving through the long grass, downwind of the rabbits, snaking silently forward with deadly intent, was the supple brown leanness of a stoat. One of the baby rabbits was suddenly still, its ears twitching. The stoat halted, blending into the undergrowth so that only the flickering red streaks of its cold eyes showed that it was animate. The baby rabbit, satisfied, began to play once more and as Jethro watched he saw the stoat hunch forward, bunching its muscles, tensing for the attack. The boy wanted to scream out in warning, to rob the marauder of its prey, but from somewhere deep within him an ancient atavistic lust to see violence and death enacted flooded over him, stilling the cry of warning before it reached his lips.

The brown body hung poised for seemingly endless seconds, then exploded forwards; white fangs gripped and slashed, cutting short the terrified scream of its prey. In a flurry of frantic movement, the doe and the rest of her young disappeared. Only the ripple of grasses marked the retreat of the stoat dragging the body of its victim deep into the bramble thickets.

A sudden rush of tears stung Jethro's eyes, threatening to spill down his cheeks. Jos looked at him in puzzlement, but in the kindness of friendship said nothing, merely turned and raced away down the bank-side, leaving Jethro to recover himself and follow behind.

When Jethro caught up with his friend, Jos was crouching at the side of a beaten track. In his hands he held a rabbit that had been strangled by the wire snare around its neck. Jos looked up and grinned.

'Who does you reckon laid this then, Jethro?'

He ran his fingers along the length of the fine wire until he found the buried stake it was fastened to.

Jethro shook his head. 'Hard to tell,' he replied. 'There are a lot of people near starving in these parts.'

Jos's grin widened. 'Ah well! It's solved our dinner problem anyways.' He turned the limp body and examined it more closely. 'It's a fine young buck, is this one. A few herbs an' some onions ull make it goo down a treat ...'

'Will it now, young gippo?'

The harsh voice coming so unexpectedly made both boys start up in shock. A heavily built man, dressed in the rough cords and gaiters of a gamekeeper, came from the bushes at the side of them. On his head he wore a moleskin cap and the blunderbuss he carried was pointing unwaveringly at Jos's stomach.

'Now don't make a move, either on you,' the man threatened. 'Becos' the one that does ull get his tripes blown to the winds.'

He stopped about two yards from the boys and, putting a finger to his mouth, he gave a piercing whistle. For some moments nothing happened. He whistled again and faint shouts and whistles came in reply. The keeper grinned his satisfaction.

'You'se led us a merry dance, you gippos 'as,' he said pleasantly. 'But I knew we'd catch up 'uv you in the end.'

'Doon't talk bloody daft, man,' Jos began to protest. 'We'se not set this snare ... nor any other in this wood, come to that.'

'Just shut your gob!' the keeper cut him short. 'You con save all them tales for the beaks.'

'But he's speaking the truth,' Jethro cried out. 'We found this rabbit by accident.'

The keeper swung the gun menacingly. 'I shan't say it agen. If you don't shut your rattle. I'll blow your bloody guts out.'

Loud shouts and the cracking of breaking undergrowth sounded loudly and they were suddenly surrounded by men. The keeper touched his cap respectfully.

' 'Ere they am, Mr Batten. I copped um redhanded, so I did.'

Both boys swung to see Batten, the Earl of Plymouth's head keeper. Short, but built like a bull, he was a noted prize-fighter, not just famous locally, but also known further afield.

The head keeper regarded the prisoners, his grim stare made even more forbidding by the shaven head, flat nose and battered face that were the badges of the pugilists' 'Fancy'. He pointed at Jos who was still holding the rabbit.

'Put that down, gippo.' His voice was hoarse. 'And do it gentle,' he added.

The boy bent and laid the limp body carefully on the ground. He straightened and faced the man, trying to hide his fear.

'What's your name, gippo?' Batten asked.

'Jos Boswell,' the boy almost whispered.

Batten chuckled. 'Speak up, gippo, no need to be shy 'cos

you'm in the company o' gennelmen.'

The other keepers howled with laughter until Batten scowled them to silence.

'That's enough! Now boy, what's your name?'

The boy's hot temper banished his fear.

'My name is Jos Boswell,' he said, loudly and clearly.

Batten nodded and repeated the words musingly. 'Ahr! Jos Boswell ... So you'll be one o' the old fighting tinker's brats, will you?'

The boy nodded.

'Ahr! I thought so.' Batten nodded again, then went on, still slowly and musingly. 'They do say as the only thing 'e could ever manage to fight and beat was 'is daughters, when 'e wanted a bit o' what lay between their legs.'

'You bastard!' Jos screamed the words and hurled himself at the man. The keeper parried the boy's wild swing and, with a speed that was remarkable for a man of his bulk, he pivoted and bent at the knees, catching the boy on the side of his hip to send him crashing into the trunk of a tree. Jos slumped to the ground, all breath smashed from his body, his face blackening as he wheezed in agonized effort to draw breath into his lungs.

The keeper shook his head in disgust and turned to Jethro.

'What's your name?' he demanded.

Before Jethro could tell him, Jos struggled to his feet digging his fingertips into the tree's rough bark to drag himself upright. His face twisted in pain, he pushed himself away from the tree and came at the keeper once more.

This time Batten moved to meet him. A straight left jolted him to a halt and a right smashed into his belly. As he started to jack-knife forward, his head swinging down, the terrible right hand of the keeper smashed into his mouth, shredding his lips to red rags against his teeth. Jos's head snapped back, his knees buckled and he would have collapsed, had not the hard square toe of Batten's iron-shod boot caught him between his legs, lifting him bodily off the ground. The boy crumpled and fell inert and twisted; the only sound he made was a continuous high-pitched squeal. Batten prodded him with his toe and spat contemptuously.

'Never met a bloody gippo yet who had any guts for fighting.'

He moved back to Jethro. 'I arsked you what your name was, boy?'

'Jethro Stanton.' The words came from dry lips.

Batten frowned in surprise and stared hard at the boy. After a pause he asked, 'Is your father called Peter Stanton?'

'Yes,' Jethro told him. 'He works at the Washford Mills.'

Batten nodded. 'Ahr! So I know.'

Jethro waited in frightened anticipation for the man to begin insulting his father. He was trying to screw up his courage to react as Jos had done, but deep in the recesses of his being, Jethro knew, with shame, that when the challenge came he would not be able to meet it. He glanced at Jos, still squealing through bloody shredded lips, and felt his stomach lurch.

'Did either o' you set this snare?' Batten asked.

Jethro shook his head. 'No. We found the rabbit by chance. We were only walking through the woods.'

Batten mulled over the answer. 'Am you sure your father is Peter Stanton?' he asked again, surprisingly.

Jethro nodded. 'Yes, of course he's my father.'

'Wheer did 'e work, afore he come to Washford Mills?'

'We travelled a lot,' Jethro replied. 'But before we came here, we were in the north country for a time, in Lancashire.'

The man's grim face softened momentarily. 'All right, young Stanton ... Now take your friend and get off the Earl's land, and doon't let me catch you 'ere again. This is enclosed land now and a hunting preserve, no one is allowed in without the Earl's permission, and the likes o' you and that gippo theer aren't likely to get that.'

'Wait a minute!' the keeper who had caught the boys shouted.

'You aren't gooin' to let these buggers goo free, am you Mr Batten?'

The head keeper stared bleakly at the man. 'Be you in charge 'ere, Reuben Bates?'

The man swallowed hard, but went on doggedly. 'Look 'ere, Mr Batten, theer's a reward paid for poachers, and I copped these two fair to rights. You knows very well that we oughter take um in front of the beaks.'

Batten looked at the other under-keepers. 'Did any o' you lot see these lads settin' snares or lines?' No one answered, they were wary of crossing the man. 'Well, theer you am,

Reuben Bates. It's only your word agen theirs, aren't it?'

Bates reddened. 'You'se never doubted my word afore, Mr Batten. It was good enough to send that bugger for transportation larst month, warn't it?'

Batten grinned at the man, but the grin failed to reach his eyes.

'You listen to me, Reuben. I says that the lads goo free; and I want no more argument from you ... So shut your gob and keep it shut. Or I might just do it for you.'

He swung on his heels and walked away. After a moment, the under-keepers, their faces mirroring their puzzlement at Batten's unaccustomed leniency, followed him.

Reuben Bates spat on the ground. 'Theer's somethin' smells bloody funny 'ere!' He kept his voice low so that only Jethro could hear him. 'I doon't know why 'e should let you get off scotfree boy. 'E's never done it afore for anybody. But I'll tell you this, the next time I sees you in these woods, I'll put a charge o' shot through your bloody guts. No matter even if you be one o' Batten's mates.' With that parting threat, he too went away.

At first, Jethro stood staring after him, then the realization that he was free and unscathed came fully home to him. He felt utter relief, then he heard Jos whimper and he felt a sick shame that he had stood by, too frightened to intervene, while his closest friend had been beaten and kicked. He was near to tears as he knelt by the tinker boy and tried hopelessly to ease the pain he was suffering. It would be much later that he would begin to wonder why Batten had let him go; and when he asked his father, Peter Stanton curtly told him to keep silent about the incident and not mention the keeper's name ever again.

The moon had risen high before Jos had recovered sufficiently to be moved. Jethro took him across his shoulders and began the journey to the tinkers' camp. Before he reached it, he was forced to stop and rest many times, but each time he stopped he saw the pain twisting Jos's features and he would force his aching body onwards.

At last he saw the flickering fire and the huddle of tents and caravans. He lowered Jos gently to the ground.

'Wait here, Jos,' he panted. 'I'll go tell your Dad and Mam, and get help to carry you.'

Jos tried to joke. 'I doon't reckon that I'm agooin' to run off anywheer, Jethro boy!' he gasped.

Jethro patted his friend's shoulder and ran to the camp. When he reached the outer edge of the firelight he could see Old Simeon sitting with his wife and swarm of children around the fire. Savage, half-starved dogs ran barking to drive off the intruder as they scented him.

'Simeon! It's me, Jethro Stanton,' the boy called.

The old man rose to his feet, shading his eyes to peer beyond the firelight.

'Get back 'ere, you useless buggers!' he roared at the dogs. 'Doon't you know a friend when you sees one.' He beckoned to Jethro. 'Come 'ere, boy, sit and talk for a spell, it's good to see you agen.'

Jethro went up to the giant tinker. 'I've left Jos back there, Simeon,' he said. 'He's hurt ... I don't think it's too bad,' he added hastily, 'but it's hard for him to walk.'

The tinker said only, 'Take me to him. The rest on you wait here.'

His sons, who had jumped to their feet at Jethro's words, sat down again.

When they reached Jos the old man placed his finger across his lips. 'Wait till we get to the camp, then you can tell me the story.'

He bent and, lifting Jos, he walked with him cradled like a baby in his massive arms. He placed the boy at the fire's side and began to examine the wounds.

'Tell me now,' he ordered Jethro.

Jethro told him what had occurred, leaving out nothing. The old man showed no emotion until he drew Jos's trousers down and saw the torn and badly swollen genitals where the keeper's boot had landed.

'The dirty animal!' he snarled.

His half-wild pack of sons cursed their hate.

'Get back 'ere, all on you!' Old Simeon roared. 'I'll deal wi' Batten when the time is right. If 'e'd beat our Jos in fair fight, I'd ha' said nothin' ... But to use his boots on a half-grown lad? Well, he'll pay ... I promise that.'

'We con make the bugger pay right now feyther,' one of the sons shouted.

The old man swung his open hand and cuffed the boy's

head, sending him staggering.

'Doon't talk like a bloody loony,' he hissed. 'If you smashes up the Earl's head man, then the beaks ull transport you for sure, that's if they doon't hang you. Enough said! I'll deal wi' bullyboy Batten when the time comes. And if any of you tries to do anythin' afore I say so, then you'll ha' me to answer to. Is that understood?'

Jethro stared in awe at the huge tinker, looking in the ruddy glow of the fire like a warrior from the old legends. His long iron-grey hair was a mane on the leonine head and the rough sheepskin coat he wore seemed to be the mantle of an ancient king.

Satisfied that his commands would be obeyed, the old man gave his attention to Jethro. 'My woman and me, and all our family give our thanks to you, boy,' he said, gravely. 'You will allus find a welcome at our fires.'

Jethro flushed in sudden shame.

'But I failed Jos!' he blurted out.

'How?' Simeon asked.

'I stood by, too afraid to move, while Batten did this to him.'

A hush came over the camp and the whole tribe gathered to stare at the boy standing before them. When it seemed to Jethro that the accusing silence would last for ever, the old man reached forward, and with one great gnarled hand gently stroked the boy's cheek.

'Sooner or later,' the old man said softly, 'terror enters the soul of every man and makes him as helpless as a newborn babby. Today it was your turn, tomorrow it could be mine or any of my fighting sons. Don't feel shamed by it, lad. You didn't leave my son in the woods as you could ha' done, you brought him back to us. I knows in my heart that if this animal Batten was to maul any o' mine as he did today, then you wouldn't stand by and let him do it. I don't reckon that you'll ever fail anyone agen ... Ever!'

He placed his arm round Jethro's shoulders and led him from the camp. 'Goo on now,' he said gently. 'Your feyther 'ull be worrying about wheer you are, and doon't forget what I've said to you. You will allus be welcome at our fires.'

Jethro was too moved to reply, it seemed as though a great weight had been lifted from him by the old man's words.

Almost happily he ran along the dark tracks towards the town.

Early next morning, when Jethro went to see his friend, he found only the warm ashes of the fire and stretches of flattened grass where the tents and caravans had stood. The tinker tribe had gone, and no one knew where.

CHAPTER EIGHT

Redditch, April 1812

'Annie? Do you think he really finds me pretty?' the young girl asked anxiously.

Anne Bartleet's lips twitched in amusement. She put down the book she was reading, removed her reading glasses and gave her complete attention to her sister, Abigail, who was standing in front of the full-length mirror in their bedroom. The elder girl's eyes travelled slowly from the tips of the dainty toes up over the flowing lines of hips and waist to the pert high breasts that thrust out proudly.

'I would think that he finds you very pretty,' she smiled. 'But until you are wed, it would be advisable to put some clothes on when you meet your beau.'

A blush spread across Abigail's oval face and shapely neck, then her dark eyes sparkled and she showed white teeth in a mischievous grin, making her look far younger than her eighteen years. She lifted her hands to her high-piled mass of shining hair, causing the rich nipples of her breasts to rise invitingly, and began to turn slowly, looking at her reflection in the mirror.

'If what some of the other girls say is true,' she giggled, 'then I am sure any man would prefer me to meet him like this.'

Anne tried to frown disapprovingly, but could only laugh. At twenty-four she lacked the flamboyant beauty of the younger girl. Her figure was more gently rounded, her hair and eyes soft brown and her personality more subdued. But to a discerning eye she had as much to offer as her lovely sister. There was in her a quality of strength allied to her gentleness, and her mind was quick and able.

Abigail pirouetted across the room and flung herself on to the old four-poster bed which the girls shared. She lifted one shapely leg into the air and regarded it critically.

'Annie? What do you think of John?' she asked. 'I mean, really think? Deep down?'

Anne shook her head. 'It isn't for me to pass any opinion on Captain John Mence,' she answered quietly.

Abigail pushed herself upright and stared speculatively at her sister.

'You do not like him, do you?' she accused.

Anne closed the book on her lap with a bang. 'No!' she said firmly. 'I do not like or have any respect for the gallant Captain.'

'But why?' Abigail questioned. 'He is always most pleasant and respectful towards you; and besides, I am quite sure that father thinks he would be a fine match for me.'

A note of anger crept into Anne's voice. 'Father thinks whatever you want him to think,' she said sharply. 'He has never been able to deny you anything.'

'You still have not told me why you hate John so,' the younger girl persisted.

Anne smiled ruefully. 'I wish you would not assume that I hate John Mence. I do not hate him ... he is too stupid to hate. I just do not consider him to be a suitable match for you, that is all.'

'But why?' Abigail wailed. 'He is one of the richest men in the county, and is connected with the Earl himself. He is handsome and brave and a fine horseman; and is wonderfully attentive to me. He tells me always how he adores me and how he would die for me, he is very romantic. Why is he unsuitable?'

'Really, Abigail!' the older girl snapped. 'At times you sound like an idiotic child. I will tell you why I despise the gallant Captain, if you wish. He treats his tenants and work-people abominably. He continually brags of his bravery and what he would like to do to the French, but yet is content to play at soldiers as a Captain of Foot Volunteers. While others such as Mark Purcell are fighting in Spain with the army, gallant John Mence parades his troop of fire-eating shop-keepers twice a week on the common and, like the rest of that fearless band, he took good care to buy a substitute when the militia were ordered to send men to the army.

'He comes mooning here, telling you that he adores you and would die for you, and at the same time he fills every poor serving wench he can lay his hands on with parish bastards.' She paused for breath, then went on. 'And as for his wealth and good connections, I will say nothing of how these were come by, but only that such attributes do not make the true gentleman. They serve merely to cover the dirt with tinsel.' She lapsed into abrupt silence, the trembling of her hands showing the depth of her feelings.

For some moments Abigail was still, then, bright spots of colour burning in her cheeks, she blurted out, 'You are jealous, that is all! Because your one and only beau, dull Mark Purcell, is in Spain and my lover is here with me. That is why John did not go to the Peninsula, he has told me many times, because he loves me too much ever to leave me. If it were not for that, then he would go tomorrow to fight the French ... I know he would; and I think you're hateful! A hateful and detestable old maid! In fact I despise you for saying what you have about my John. It is not true, it is all lies! Lies! Lies! Lies!'

Tears began to stream down her cheeks and the rest of her words were muffled by the pillows as she buried her face in them.

Anne sighed and, taking her book, she went from the room. At the foot of the main staircase, she met her father.

'Where is Abigail?' he asked. 'And what were you quarrelling about this time?' The anxiety in his voice was at odds with the strength of his firm jaw and mouth.

Anne felt a wave of love for her anxious father, whose only weakness was his two daughters.

'Nothing of importance,' she said lightly.

His eyes were worried. 'You quarrel far too much with one another. I think that you have become too hard with the child.'

'She is no longer a child, father,' she told him impatiently. 'Abigail is eighteen now, and is a woman. You feel that I am too hard with her but at times it is necessary to be harsh. I have had to try and take the place of a mother for her. It has not been easy, especially since you are always busy.'

Charles Bartleet was quick to placate his eldest girl. 'I know my dear, it is very hard for you. It is only that I love you both so much and wish solely to see you happy together.'

'We were happy until John Mence began paying court to her,' Anne burst out. 'Really, father! I cannot understand why you allow it.'

He regarded her gravely then said quietly, 'My dear, I share your low opinion of John Mence, but what would you have me do? If I were to forbid him to address himself to Abi, then he would appear much more desirable to her. The forbidden is always the most exciting and inviting ... No! This way I hope that her own good sense will eventually help her to recognize him for what he is. Besides, she has had many girlish fancies such as this.'

'But suppose this is not just another of her fancies, and that her good sense fails her?' Anne questioned caustically. 'What then?'

Charles Bartleet smiled. 'I do not think that it will fail our little girl. She has too much of you in her for that ... Now. Are you ready to come into the town? I've had the carriage waiting for over an hour.'

Anne returned his smile. 'You make me feel very gauche at times, father. Of course, you are right. It is the best way to handle this affair ... But I get so angry when I think of Abi being involved with that ... that ...'

Her father laughed and interrupted her indignant splutterings.

'Come now, do not let him spoil your day. Concentrate on your good works instead,' he teased.

Anne ran into the kitchen and came back carrying a basket filled with food the cook had prepared for her, and a worn but clean blanket. Her father took the basket and carried it out to the open carriage waiting in the driveway. A boy stood holding the heads of the two frisky young mares in the shafts. When he saw the Colonel he touched his forelock respectfully.

'They'm a bit lively today, sir,' he called. 'I dursn't lose um to open the door for you.'

The Colonel nodded. 'Don't fret yourself, Abram,' he said pleasantly. 'We are well able to manage.'

Anne arranged the basket and blanket and settled herself comfortably, while her father took the reins and readied the horses. As they were on the point of leaving, Abigail came running from the house.

'Wait for me,' she called. 'Wait for me.' She flung herself into the carriage and smiled brilliantly at her father and sister. 'I feel that in spite of our differences we should still endeavour to present to the world a spectacle of family unity and happiness.'

After a second's surprise, Anne burst out laughing, the Colonel joined in and under the astonished gaze of the boy, Abram, the family began the journey amidst peals of happy laughter.

The distance into the town was soon covered by the eager horses and at the Fox and Goose Inn, opposite St Stephen's Church, Colonel Bartleet halted the carriage while his daughters descended.

'Who are you visiting?' he asked.

'Doll Greenaway,' Anne told him.

He nodded. 'I see ... Well, I do not doubt that the poor woman needs all the help possible. But mind what I say, when you have finished there come directly to Lawyer Guardner's chambers. I'll wait there for you to come if my business is finished.'

While Anne was speaking with the Colonel, Abigail looked about her. Outside the Fox and Goose, a number of men and youths were drinking and playing cards on the wooden benches that were set along the walls of the inn. Most of them wore the white aprons and square-edged flat-topped hats of the needle pointers. One or two of them noticed the girl staring at them with such interest and began to grin and catcall obscene invitations to her to join them on the benches.

The Colonel's face hardened. 'That's enough of that!' he snapped at the men.

'Get along wi' you, gaffer,' one of the pointers jeered. 'Does you want to keep the pretty dears all to yourself? You greedy old sod!'

Bartleet's temper rose. 'Do you know who I am?' he demanded.

The man spat contemptuously, the gob of spittle striking the carriage wheel. 'Yes, old gaffer. I knows who you am; and I doon't gi' a bugger! Not for you nor twenty like you.'

'Why you damned impudent ...!' The Colonel dropped the reins and made as if to jump from the carriage. Anne, her face flaming crimson, put her hand on her father's shoulder and held him back.

'No, father! Please don't!' she whispered urgently. 'It is of no importance. See, Abi and I are going, we'll meet you at Lawyer Guardner's. Please go now, for my sake. Do not fight with that man, promise me that you will not.'

Softened by her entreaties, the Colonel agreed.

'All right, I promise,' he said shortly. 'Now kindly go on your errand.'

Carrying the basket and blanket, the girls went quickly across the green behind the church. The Colonel waited until the bright dresses had disappeared into the huddle of mean alleyways, then turned to the loungers once more. He pointed his horsewhip at the man with whom he had exchanged words.

'You there? What is your name?'

The pointer rose to his feet and lurched up to the carriage. As he came face to face with the Colonel, he belched and said, 'Luke Fisher's me name, old gaffer. Brother to Jamie Fisher, one uv the finest men ever to be destroyed by the load o' thieves 'oo call themselves the needle marsters.'

Bartleet smelt the reeking beer-breath of the man, and drew back in disgust. At this an expression of pure hatred crossed the man's pock-marked face.

'You poxy 'igh-falutin' bugger!' he cursed. 'Our kid's lying in bed coughin' 'is lungs out uv his mouth, becos' o' barstards like you ... You and the other muck-swillin' pigs o' gentry.' His face distorted and he jumped forward, hands crooked and searching for the Colonel's throat. Even as he jumped, other pointers rose and dashed towards him. Now they grabbed and held him, dragging him back as he shouted and struggled.

A lean dark-haired man dressed as a pointer came to the side of the carriage.

'I think it would be wiser if you went on your way, Colonel Bartleet,' he said, politely but firmly. 'If you remain here, others might become enraged as he did.'

'What the devil are you suggesting, man? That I should give way to drunken scum?' Bartlett shouted in anger. 'And who are you, that you should dare speak in this manner to one of your betters?'

The lean man's lips tightened into a thin pale line, and when he answered he seemed to spit the words from between clenched teeth.

'My name is Peter Stanton, and I'll speak as I wish to any man, for I don't acknowledge that I have any "betters", as you term them. That man's brother, Jamie Fisher, who is also my friend, is even now coughing out the last days of his life. He is dying through the fault of people like yourself and the other manufacturers whose only wish is to become rich at all costs, and devil take those others who suffer because of your wicked greed. That is why Luke Fisher is drunk and full of hatred, he has good cause to be ... now go! While you are still able to.'

Bartleet drew deep breaths, fighting to control his rage. Finally he picked up the reins.

'You'll hear more of this day's work, Peter Stanton,' he promised grimly.

Stanton showed his teeth in a savage grin. 'And so will you, Bartleet, and the rest of your cronies.'

He watched the Colonel drive away before turning to the struggling man who was still being held down by the others.

'Calm down, Luke Fisher,' he said. 'Save some of that temper and fight. We'll be needing all we can get of that shortly and a lot more besides.'

CHAPTER NINE

It was almost two years since Doll Greenaway had been injured, and the stringy grey hair once more grew long over the scarred scalp. But the damage to her brain had left her partially paralysed, her left hand was a useless withered claw and it was only with difficulty that she could move her left arm and leg. Unable to carry on working at the needles with her brother Tom, the woman had suffered great privation during the months of her convalescence. It was only the help given by her neighbours, who had little enough for themselves, that had enabled her to fight off the attempts by the parish guardians to commit her and blind Billy to the poorhouse in nearby Webheath village.

Times had become harder for the poor. The needle trade had slumped even further, while the prices of food and goods had risen uncontrolled. Bread, the staple food, now cost two shillings for a half-peck loaf and even when trade was good, a man and his wife could only earn about five shillings a day. For this they slaved for fourteen, fifteen or sometimes sixteen hours to make five thousand needles, and out of this sum they provided their own tools, heat and light. These days practically all the needle workers were near to starving.

Anne and Abigail could see the hardship all around them as they made their way to Doll Greenaway's house. Children, who would previously have been running and screaming in play, now crouched apathetically in the dust. Their elders who had filled the streets with their bustle and work, their laughter and quarrels, now lounged about, too hungry and dispirited even to haggle with each other over who should draw water first from the surface wells which served each group of houses.

Jethro Stanton was also making his way to Doll Greenaway's. At eighteen, he had grown tall and strong. He was still slim-hipped, but his shoulders had broadened and his body become hard and muscular. For more than a year he had been working as a carter for George Heath the local carrier. His father, Peter, had objected strongly to his son working.

'I want you to study, boy,' he repeated over and over again. 'I want you to learn what tyranny people of this country are subject to, so that when the time comes you will be able to confront the gentry with knowledge superior to their own.'

Jethro had countered these arguments with one of his own.

'I must know for myself what it is to work, father. How can I be a leader of working men if I have the soft white hands of a gentleman? Let me go into the mills so that I can know what it is to spend a life there.'

Peter Stanton had been adamant in his refusal.

'No, boy! I would sooner kill you with my own hands than watch you destroy yourself in the pointing sheds. No! If you must work, then do something that is not harmful to your body.'

Finally they had compromised, and Jethro had become a carter. He travelled all over the Midlands and wherever he went, he tried to discover for himself the conditions that men lived in and what they did to earn their bread.

He moved from the coalpits and potteries of Staffordshire to the broad gardens of the Vale of Evesham, from the roaring foundries and furnaces of Birmingham to the rolling farmlands of Oxfordshire and the sheep runs of the Cotswolds. In the mills and factories of Derby and Nottingham, Jethro met and watched at their work miners, potters, foundry and furnace men, farmhands, shepherds, bargees, navvies, factory and millhands. As his body grew and hardened from the loading of wagons and the handling of the huge horses that drew them, so his knowledge grew and his desire hardened to raise his fellow workers from the dirt they had been ground into.

When Jethro turned the corner of the terraced row where the Greenaways lived, he saw the two young women going into the cottage. He stopped and whistled admiringly to himself. 'That black-haired one is a beauty,' he thought. 'But who are they? Unbonneted like factory wenches, yet wearing shoes and clothing fine enough to be gentry, and their hair and skin glowing with health and cleanliness.' He laughed to himself. 'You can find out very easily boy. All you have to do is to carry on into Doll's.'

At the low doorway, he paused and listened to the elder girl saying very firmly in her low cultured voice, 'Now I want none of your nonsense, Doll Greenaway! Even if you have no use for the blanket on your bed, at least it will be something warm for Billy to wrap himself in.'

Jethro registered the fact that the girls were gentry on a charity visit.

Although partially paralysed and worn by hardship, Doll Greenaway had lost none of her old spirit. 'Don't talk to me o' nonsense, young Annie! I smacked your backside when you was a nipper; and if you uses that tone to me, I'll do the same again.'

Jethro laughed aloud at the words and stepped into the room.

'Yes, she will, that's for sure, if she sets her mind to it.' He spoke directly to Anne Bartleet.

For a moment her lips tightened and she seemed about to speak sharply to him, but at her side Abigail began to giggle and in spite of herself Anne smiled.

'I see that you have a good understanding of the lady, sir,' she said, and turned once more to the old woman. 'At least, Doll, take the blanket for Billy,' she entreated.

Doll Greenaway, satisfied, nodded. 'I will, and thank you for it.'

She took the blanket from Anne's outstretched arms and, moving with a peculiar hobble which favoured her bad leg, she went to where Billy was sitting on his old stool by the cold fireplace. She draped the blanket round his shoulders and when she spoke to him her voice had a gentleness that it never held for others.

'Here, Billy, son, feel what the kind ladies brought you. This 'ull keep you warm through the nights.'

The blind man lifted his ravaged face. 'Warm?' he repeated. 'I aren't bin warm since we come up into these bloody mountains, Sergeant ... No ... not warm ... It's cold, Sergeant ... cold!'

'Oh, the poor, poor man!' Abigail was touched. 'He thinks he is still in the army.'

74

Doll covered his mouth with her work-scarred hand.

'Be quiet, son.' She patted his head with the same hand. 'Be easy now, and keep the blanket round you.' She looked directly at Jethro. 'And what does you want 'ere, young Stanton?' she questioned harshly. 'Come to gawp at these pretty maids, 'as you?'

'No, Doll,' he answered. 'I've come to shave and clip Billy as I promised I would.'

Both girls regarded him with interest, wondering who the young man was. Certainly they thought it strange that while he wore the rough fustian of a labouring man, yet his accent was that of a scholar.

'Well, gerron and do it then,' Doll scolded. 'I doon't want a girt lump like you aclutterin' up my kitchen all day.'

Jethro smiled at the girls. 'If you ladies will permit me,' he said easily. 'I'll carry on with my task.'

He opened the cloth bundle he was carrying and, taking out scissors, comb and a large cut-throat razor, he bent to arrange them on the wooden bench that flanked the plain table.

'Take care that you do not cut off his head with that fearful weapon,' Abigail said teasingly.

Jethro looked up at her and felt his heart begin to pound. It was as if, for an instant of time, a veil had been lifted from past incarnations in which he had known and loved this black-haired girl. It seemed to him that she sensed the intensity of his emotion. A delicate flush coloured the creamy skin of her neck and face, and her lips parted slightly, showing a glimpse of white teeth. It was Anne who broke the spell of their shared feeling.

'Come, Abi! We must go and meet father,' she said, and bustled her curiously subdued sister out of the cottage, waving aside Doll Greenaway's words of thanks. 'I will call for the basket another day, Doll; and please stop thanking me, it is not much that we do to help you.'

Jethro went to the door. He watched Abigail walking along at her sister's side. As they turned the corner, she glanced back at him. Jethro lifted his hand in farewell. She also started to wave, then dropped her head in confusion and disappeared from his view.

Doll Greenaway had noticed what had passed between

Jethro and the girl and now she came to stand, hands on hips, in front of him.

'Jethro, boy,' she said, and her voice was kind. 'That's Anne and Abigail Bartleet, the black-haired 'un is Abigail. They'm the daughters o' Colonel Bartleet ... It doon't do for a lad in your station o' life to raise 'is eyes and dream o' gentry women.'

Jethro's eyes held a strange expression and when he answered, it was as though he talked to himself.

'I'll do more than raise my eyes and dream,' he said. 'I'll have that girl for my wife some day.'

Doll Greenaway could make no reply. She shook her head and went back into the cottage. After a moment or two Jethro followed her.

CHAPTER TEN

'What ails the girl?' Anne Bartleet's question was rhetorical and sarcastic. 'I declare that she has been mooning about the house for the last two days as if she were in a dream. I wonder if perhaps she took the vapours when we visited Doll Greenaway?'

Abigail was sitting by the open windows of the drawing-room, gazing out at the sunlit lawns which ended at the wood-flanked dirt road. She showed no reaction to her sister's verbal prodding, but remained motionless, lost in her thoughts. The elder girl wandered aimlessly about the room, running her fingers over the ornate black and gilt inlaid furniture.

'I cannot think what possessed father, can you, Abi?'

'Hmm?' the young girl answered.

Anne sighed in exasperation and said loudly, 'Will you at least have the politeness to pay some attention to me?'

Startled from her reverie, Abigail turned in confusion. 'I'm sorry, Anne. What is it you want?'

Anne threw up both arms and declaimed in mock thankfulness, 'Praise be! You're still in our world.'

'What do you mean? Still in our world?' Abigail looked vague.

'It doesn't matter,' Anne told her. 'I merely said that I cannot think what possessed father to furnish this room as he did.'

She looked deprecatingly about her. Chairs, tables, desk, wall pictures and statuettes were all in the fashionable mock ancient Egyptian style.

'But it is all the rage,' Abigail said.

'That may be so,' Anne replied. 'But I do not like modern furniture. I much preferred our old Jacobean tables and chairs, the craftsmanship was far superior.'

'Perhaps father imagined he was the reincarnation of the Pharoah when he had this room changed.' Abigail laughed. 'Let us be thankful that he did not alter all the rooms, and then finish by having the house rebuilt in the shape of a pyramid.'

The girls' laughter prevented them from hearing their father's entrance.

'What do you find so amusing about pyramids?' His face was stern, but his eyes were kind.

'Good morning, father,' his daughters chorused.

'Good morning to you both ... Why were you not at breakfast, Abigail?'

'I was not hungry, father.'

'I see. You haven't eaten a decent meal for days,' he grumbled. 'Now ... perhaps you'll tell me more about the house being converted into a pyramid?'

Abigail looked demure. 'Anne and I were thinking of acquiring a sphinx, father, and we were wondering where we should place it. I think it would be kinder to the unfortunate beast if we put it there.' She pointed through the open windows. 'Do not you, Annie?'

Her sister giggled and agreed.

Abigail put her head on one side and half-closed her eyes, as though measuring the distance. 'Yes ... that would be an ideal position. We shall have it facing the windows and then it can see inside and imagine itself to be back on the banks of the Nile. It will prevent the poor thing pining away with homesickness.'

Both girls laughed freely. Their father scowled in mock annoyance.

'I like this room,' he stated positively. 'And while you may make sport of it, I regard it not only as the height of fashion, but also as a constant reminder of our glorious victory at the Nile ... Besides, it is the only modern room in the house and it was entirely your doing that led to it being furnished in this manner.'

'Oh father, how could you say such a thing?' Abigail questioned, delighted at her adored father's light-hearted reaction to her teasing. 'Anne and I happened to remark one day on the extreme antiquity of the old furniture and lo and behold! In only hours we had been literally transported back

78

to the beginnings of history. I do declare that I feel like Nefertiti when I sit here ...'

There was a knock on the door and Mrs Johns slipped into the room. She bobbed a curtsey.

'Excuse me, sir, there's a caller to see Miss Abigail, it's Mr Mence.'

'Not again!' said Abigail.

'That is enough, young lady.' Her father became serious. 'John Mence has called here at least five times to my knowledge in the last two days, and you have refused to see him. May I ask why?'

'Because I have no wish to,' his daughter pouted.

'Has he said or done anything to offend you?' Charles Bartleet asked.

Abigail sighed. 'No ... it is just that he bores me, and I find that I no longer wish his attentions.'

'Well, in that case you must tell the man so yourself. I will not permit you to behave with such ill-breeding to anyone, treating them like this, not even John Mence,' her father told her very firmly.

As he was speaking, a large open cart came into view along the dirt road. Abigail noticed it and did not answer her father until the cart came near enough for her to recognize the driver, Jethro Stanton.

'Well, Abigail, I'm waiting for your reply.'

She smiled brilliantly at him.

'I have changed my mind, father ... I feel like riding ... John Mence may accompany me.' She kissed her father's cheek. 'Do be good and entertain the gentleman while I change; and have my mare made ready.'

Charles Bartleet lifted his eyes in supplication. 'Dear Heaven preserve me from young women!' was all he could say.

Abigail Bartleet reined in her horse under the red-fluttering sails of the derelict windmill and waited for John Mence to catch up with her. He was some two hundred yards behind, brutally whipping and spurring his flagging mount over the rough bracken and fern-covered slopes of the Bridley Moor, which lay to the north west of Redditch town. He reached her and reined savagely, causing his horse to rear back on its haunches.

'Dammit Abi!' he shouted. 'You'll have both our necks broken, riding the way you do.'

She laughed at his red-faced, panting bulk, and stroked her own mount's glossy neck. 'Perhaps I am the better rider of we two, for my little mare here is still fresh, and I do assure you, John, I was not for a moment in danger of falling.'

The man's thick throat tightened and he felt a tremor of hungry excitement in his loins as he feasted his eyes on her beauty, set off to perfection by the flowing dark green riding habit, its bodice tight-fitting over thrusting breasts, and the black ostrich-plumed tricorn hat perched upon her raven hair. A frothy jabot half-covered her neck and his lips yearned to nuzzle the soft white skin under the ruffled lace.

Below the moor, stone-laden carts drawn by great lathered horses lurched over the rough track that led almost in a straight line to the ruins of the Abbey of Bordesley.

'I wonder if Jethro Stanton is fetching stone from the Abbey,' Abigail mused.

John Mence kneed his mount until they were side by side.

'Abi, let's dismount and sit here for a while.' He spoke urgently.

She shook her head absently. 'I think not . . .' Her gaze was fixed on the distant Abbey ruins.

Abruptly he leaned across and grasped her, pulling her upper body hard against his. His mouth clamped down on hers and his hands mauled her breasts, kneading and bruising. She tried to push him away but was not strong enough. Her nostrils filled with the acrid smell of his sweat and she could taste the staleness of old wine, tobacco and meat on his probing tongue and wet lips. In desperation she jabbed at his eye with her stiffened thumb.

'God damn and blast you!' He released her and explored his damaged eye. 'What in hell's name possessed you to do that? You have near blinded me!'

Unafraid, she answered spiritedly, 'I will not be handled as if I were one of your sluts, John Mence.'

His handsome florid face, already patterned by the tiny broken veins of a hard drinker, twisted in ugly threat.

'When we are wed, you will be handled, as you put it, every night. So you had best become accustomed to the idea.' He grinned confidently, and straightened his riding cap which had been knocked askew in the struggle. 'Don't worry, Abi my love. You will grow to enjoy it. Every woman does ...'

She tilted her chin and grimaced in disgust. 'I will never enjoy being treated as if I were a gutter trollop ... And what is more, John Mence, there will be no wedding between us. I have no wish to wed you.'

The grin left his face. 'What? Have you been leading me on for sport? I love you, Abi, and I want you. I realize that I may have been hasty today, but it is only that I love you so, and wish to be your husband.'

'Well, I do not love you, and certainly will never want you for a husband,' she told him.

His voice rose in temper. 'I've a notion that there is some other man.'

She smiled enigmatically.

'God rot me! I'll kill him!' Mence raged.

'Kill whom?' she enquired sweetly. 'La! I do declare, John Mence, you grow more childish and ridiculous with each passing day.'

'Childish, am I?' he growled, and grabbed for her again, his desire driving him half-mad.

'Aggh!' He screamed in pain and lifted both hands to his face. 'You bitch!' he moaned. 'You little bitch!'

She lifted her riding crop in readiness. 'I shall do the same again, if you try to touch me,' she warned, and spurred her horse away from the windmill and down in the direction of the Abbey ruins.

Mence traced with his fingertips the red weal that the girl's riding crop had raised across his face.

'I still intend to wed you one day, you hell-cat,' he muttered after her rapidly retreating figure. 'And then, by God! We shall see who is the master.'

He rowelled the flanks of his mount until the blood oozed from its hide, and galloped back towards the town.

Jethro grunted with effort as he lifted the square-dressed grey rock and placed it with the others on the back of the cart. He expelled his breath in noisy relief and wiped the sweat from his forehead with the back of one work-soiled hand, leaving a smear of dirt across the bronzed skin. The sun was high and hot and at the other side of the ruins another pair of carters heaved and strained to complete their loads, which were being used to construct extensions to the Earl of Plymouth's great mansion at Hewell hamlet, some miles from Redditch.

'Good morning, Jethro Stanton.' The soft greeting caused his heart to thud alarmingly and he swung round to stare in glad amazement at the girl who had haunted his thoughts since their brief meeting at Doll Greenaway's.

'Why, good morning to you, Miss Abigail,' he said, when he had caught his breath. She smiled at him and his heart seemed to lift into his mouth. He felt a happy daze of confusion and said. 'I'm loading rocks ...'

Gravely she nodded. 'Yes, I see that you are. Are they heavy?'

Lost in her sparkling black eyes, he replied, 'I don't really know ... well ... that is ...' He cast about in his mind for something to say, but could only give up and grin happily.

She held out her arms. 'Will you help me down?'

As he touched her pliant body and caught the sweet freshness of her, he felt a surge of joyous strength such as he had never felt before. He placed her gently on the ground and all his confusion stilled as his eyes met the flawless oval face lifted trustingly to him. Indeed, Abigail did sense absolute trust as she felt herself lifted easily from the side-saddle and exulted in the strength of his muscled arms. She stood, looking up at his handsome face and gloried in the devotion that shone from his eyes.

'Oh yes, yes,' she told herself with mounting excitement. 'I was right to find this man once more. I was so right.'

'Come, let's walk by the river,' Jethro said, and together they strolled across the thick springy turf where once Cistercian monks had walked, pondering on Life and Death and thinking greedily of the fresh fish suppers of Lent.

Few words passed between them and their hands did not touch. Only sidelong glances were exchanged and shared smiles of pleasure. One other carter nudged his helper and sniggered, 'Oi reckon they'm an 'andsome pair, bain't they?' The carter winked.

His helper stared greedily at the girl. 'Ahr!' he breathed.

The carter caught his meaning and cuffed him banteringly. 'You'm a dirty-minded young devil, you am. You'se got no romance in yer.'

Jethro and Abigail strolled on, until the sun began to fall down the sky and it was time for her to return to her home.

As he lifted her to her saddle, Jethro said, 'I hope that your father will not be vexed with you for walking with me.'

'Why should he be?' she questioned.

'I am a labouring man, and you are of the gentry,' Jethro told her.

She smiled and shook her head, causing the plumes of her hat to sway backwards and forwards.

'I doubt that he will know, and when I consider it to be the right time, then I shall tell him. These are modern times, Jethro, we are no longer living in the days when acquaintance between the gentry and the labouring people was unknown. Today it is possible for any man to rise above the station of his birth and be welcomed by those above him.'

He smiled in return. 'Of course you are right,' he answered. 'This is 1812, not 1412, and the world is changing ... At least, today it has changed for me,' he added.

She reached down and touched his cheek.

'Will you be here tomorrow?' she asked.

'I will, and every day that there is a hope that you may ride by, I shall be here.'

'And what of your work?' she teased, gently.

'My work can go hang!' he laughed. 'Besides, I have the moonlight to work by ... and dream by.'

'Until tomorrow then, and make sure that your dreams are only of me,' she whispered, and rode away.

Abigail Bartleet did ride by the next day, and again the day after that, and the day after that.

CHAPTER ELEVEN

One evening in May 1812, Spencer Perceval, the Prime Minister of Great Britain, was shot dead by the madman Bellingham. That same evening, James Fisher, a needle pointer of Redditch, vomited blood into a broken bucket held under his head by Peter Stanton. His brothers Luke and Matt Fisher cradled his skeletal pain-wracked body in their arms, as he died with the blood still streaming from his gaping mouth.

The death of Perceval sent a wave of fright and horror through the ruling classes of the country. The death of Fisher created not a single ripple of emotion beyond the sorrow of his brothers and a few friends.

After days and nights of sharing a tiny room with the living, the rotting, stinking corpse of James Fisher was bundled into a crudely made scrap-wood box. His hearse was a broken builder's handcart pushed along by his brothers, and a small group of ragged men and women followed him to the pauper's grave that was his entitlement.

A drunken curate hiccoughed and slurred for brief moments over the earthly remains of Fisher and the sole oration was a brief sentence from his brother Luke. 'Jamie's better off wherever he's gone, I reckon. The poor sod!'

After Jamie Fisher's funeral the mourners went back to their hovels and tried not to torment their empty bellies by thoughts of eating.

Doll Greenaway and Agnes Bright had walked with Jamie Fisher's coffin to his grave; now they sat on broken chairs in Doll's cottage and waited for the child Susan Bright to return with the bread they had sent her to get from Humphries the baker. For once, blind Billy was not crouching on his stool; Doll had given a small boy a penny to take Billy on to the common where he could sit in the sunshine.

Agnes Bright cleared her throat and spat into the embers of the tiny cooking fire.

'He was a good man, was Jamie,' she observed, sadly. 'And a fine strong body he had before the rot got him.'

Doll Greenaway nodded agreement. 'Ahr, you'm right there, Agnes. My Lord! I've seen dozens of fine men that the rot's cut down. It doesn't bear thinking on, do it? The poor bugger worked hard all his life and ends up in a pauper's grave.'

'He's not the first,' her friend said. 'Nor he won't be the last. Not by thousands, he won't. This bloody war is going to drive us all into early graves if it keeps on buggering up the trade, like it's doing.'

'Ahr! One way or another, the war's going to finish us all, an't it,' Doll Greenaway said bitterly. 'Mind you, I don't see it hurting the gentry or the bloody masters.' She shook her head emphatically. 'No! Not them! Only us!'

At this moment Susan Bright came running into the cottage, her dusty face streaked with tears. Agnes Bright jumped to her feet at the sight of her daughter's empty hands and shouted threateningly, 'What's you done wi' the bread, our Susan? If you'se lost the money I give you, then I'll break your bloody head, so I will.'

The child's sobs grew louder in her fright, and she choked out unintelligible sentences.

'Wait a minute, Agnes,' the older woman intervened. 'Give the babby a chance to tell us what's happened, before you goes on frightenin' the daylights out of her. Come here, little 'un.'

She pulled the child to her and stroked and petted her to calm her down. The sobs quietened and at last the child was able to tell them what had happened.

'Old Humphries kept the tanner, and he told me to tell you that bread is two shillings a loaf and he'll give you no more of it until you pays him for the last lot you had off him. He said to tell you as how bread was too dear to throw it into the gutter for pigs to guts up for nothing.'

Agnes Bright clenched her massive fists. 'He did, did he? Well, I'll give bloody Humphries what he's got coming to him, so I will.'

Doll Greenaway tried to pacify her friend but her words

only helped to whip Agnes Bright's quick temper into a blind fury. She ran into the street and began to shout at the people there.

'Listen to me, all on you,' she screeched, waving her arms to attract their attention. 'Did you hear what Baker Humphries said to my babby? He said that bread was too good for pigs like us. He said he'd sooner throw it in the gutter. He tore my last tanner from my babby's hands, so he did ... My last tanner! He said I owed it him ... The dirty lying bleeder.' Her fine breasts heaved under her ragged shawl and her voice cracked with rage as she screamed out, 'He forgets what he owes the poor women as opens their legs for him. There's a few wenches in this town as had to do that so that they can put a bit of grub in their babbies' stomachs ... But I'm not going to lay down for him, I'm a decent married woman and respectable too.'

Her vehemence roused her listeners from their apathy and a chorus of growls and applause came from them.

'Does you know what I'm agoin' to do now?' she questioned rhetorically. 'Well, I'll tell you. I'm goin' round to see Randy-balls Humphries and I'm going to throw him headfirst through his own shop winders; and if there's any guts left in you lot, then you'll come and 'elp me do it. That's unless you don't mind being called pigs by the likes of him.'

She stormed off along the street followed by a rapidly growing crowd. Doll Greenaway saw what was happening and turned to Susan.

'Quick, child. Run down to Bartleet's mills and get your Dad. Tell him there's fire and murder going on up here and that your Mam's gone to kill Baker Humphries.'

The child scampered away and Doll Greenaway hobbled after the crowd.

By the time the shop was reached, the crowd numbered more than a hundred; and, because it was market day, there were many hundreds of others in the town who would come running when they heard what was happening.

Baker Humphries, a thin sickly-looking man, as pale as the flour he worked with, came to the door of his double-fronted shop and confronted Agnes Bright.

'Well? What do you want here?' he demanded. 'Have you

86

come to pay what you owe me, now that you've got my message?'

'Yes, you scrawny bastard! I got your message all right,' the woman shouted. 'Where's my tanner?'

'Your tanner?' the baker sneered. 'Where's the rest of what you owe me?'

'All I owe you for is one loaf,' Agnes Bright stated. 'One poxy loaf! You should be too shamed to ask the price you do for bread. It's bleedin' wicked, so it is. There's people near starving in this town with the trade being so bad, and you charge so dear that they can't even buy a stale crust.'

The crowd yelled their agreement. The baker was a brave man. He stood unafraid and yelled back. 'It's no fault of mine that the war has spoilt the trade and brought the costs so high. I make little enough to live on as it is,' he appealed to the crowd. 'You all know me, friends ... wasn't I the last baker in the parish to put his prices up? Haven't I given credit to nearly every one of you at one time or another?'

Agnes sensed the swing of the crowd's sympathy towards the baker.

'Oh yes! That's right! You give credit all right, you scrawny bugger!' Her voice was filled with contempt. 'You gave credit to young Meg Ordsall didn't you, when her man was took for the army; and she's in the workhouse now and the babbies you give her are in there with her. 'Cepting for the one that died of hunger a few months back, after you'd tired of the poor daft wench. Oh yes! We all know about your sort of credit.'

The crowd's feelings veered once more, as the woman's words struck home to them. There was a unified growl of anger.

Humphries was unabashed. 'What's upsetting you, Agnes Bright?' he jeered. 'Is it because I've never offered you the same credit? Well, I'll tell you why not ... You're too much like a big fat cow for my taste.'

The woman's control left her at the jeering taunt.

'You filthy bugger!' she screamed. She swung one massive fist in a roundhouse blow that caught the baker on the head and sent him crashing into the window of his shop. The cheap wooden frames crashed inwards under the impact and the man lay dazed across the heaped loaves on display. Beside herself with anger, Agnes dragged the baker to his feet and, steadying him with her left hand, she hit him with another roundhouse swing. This time he somersaulted across the pavement and crashed into the crowd. They fell back and he slithered to the ground and lay full length in the gutter. His attacker grabbed a loaf in each hand and hurled them into the middle of the crowd.

'Here!' she screamed. 'Fill your bellies for once.'

Like a pack of famished beasts, the crowd surged forward. Men, women and children took off their iron-tipped clogs and used them to smash the windows down. They wrestled and tore at each other for the loaves of bread. Others followed Agnes Bright into the shop itself and began an orgy of destruction, ripping the fitments from their fastenings, turning over the counters and smashing the casements against the walls in their frenzy.

The baker's wife and children ran wailing with fright out of the living quarters at the rear of the shop when a section of the mob rampaged through the splintered dividing door. Some of the cooler heads began a systematic search for money and valuables, while others wrenched open drawers and cupboards, seeking food and drink. One man shouted in triumph and brandished aloft a bottle of gin. He pointed to the corner chest he had forced open. It was full of bottles of spirits. Within seconds, the chest had been emptied and the rum, brandy and gin poured down throats to inflame minds that were already crazed by hunger and hardship.

CHAPTER TWELVE

Owen Treadgold was sitting at his desk at Bartleet's mills, staring out of the window that overlooked the courtyard, lamenting yet again the day that he had married his nagging shrew of a wife.

Littering his desk before him were half-finished plans for steam plant to power the mills instead of horses and water, plans for stamping machines capable of producing a hundred needles at a time, plans for drilling machines, plans for building enclosed windmills, plans for a dozen other ingenious projects; and none of them more than halffinished.

He sighed deeply and stared glumly at the papers. 'If only that nagging bitch would leave me in peace, let me concentrate on my work, I could complete all my inventions ... I could become the foremost inventor in England ... Perhaps the world. Oh God! Why don't you let the house burn down with her inside it? Or let her catch fever and waste away?'

A sudden commotion from the courtyard broke into his thoughts. He rose from his desk and looked out. Half a dozen men and boys were gathered around a small girl who was chattering excitedly to them. Even as Treadgold watched, he saw his foreman pointer, Tom Bright, run out of his workshop and bend to talk with the girl. Treadgold drew back from the window slightly, so that he could watch without being observed, and called his clerk from the alcove next to his office.

'Mace! Come here, will you.'

The clerk entered.

'Go down into the yard and find out what is going on,' Treadgold ordered, then gave his attention once more to the scene below.

By now, almost the entire workforce had gathered around the little girl and even with the windows firmly closed, the manager could hear clearly shouted oaths and arguments. Suddenly Tom Bright grabbed the child and swung her on to his shoulder. He walked from the courtyard and the rest of the workers trailed after him through the covered archway that led into the street. Mace, the clerk, came back to the office, trembling with nervous excitement.

'Master Treadgold, sir! There's murder going on up in the town!'

Treadgold swung to face the man.

'What's that you say, Mace?'

The words came tumbling from the man's lips. 'There's a riot! Tom Bright's girl says that there's fire and murder and that her Mam has gone to kill the baker and a thousand people with her.'

Treadgold was for several seconds open-mouthed with astonishment at the news. Then with a jolt his thoughts began to race.

'Go up to the Colonel's and tell him what's happening,' he ordered. 'Go on, man! Quickly! Tell him not to worry about the mill, I'll stay here and guard it.'

As the other man ran from the room, Treadgold sank into his chair, overcome by the impact of a frightening, yet wonderful idea which had occurred to him as he was speaking. He began to breathe heavily and he struggled to thrust it from his mind, but it persisted and began to grow into a fully-fledged plan of action. His faded blue eyes behind the square-rimmed spectacles glowed with excitement. He swallowed hard and his heart thumped with fearful anticipation. He rose and went from the room. Moving with astonishing rapidity for a man of his years, he checked the various outbuildings and workshops, storerooms and cellars of the mill. Then, satisfied that no one remained on the premises, he jammed his tricorn hat on his head and slipped quickly through the archway.

Up in the town, the drink looted from the baker's house had awakened an uncontrollable lust for more. The mob had looted the shops that were in the same row as the baker's and then broken into a small alehouse that stood on the corner. Barrels of ale and cider were brought up from the cellar and broached on the pavement outside. Men, women and children grabbed whatever they could find to drink from, and those who could find nothing else took off their clogs and used them.

Agnes Bright, still seeking revenge on the baker and unable to satisfy such a craving by breaking furniture, found a keg of oil. She smashed it open and poured it over a heap of shattered fittings, then snatched a burning coal from the baking oven and set the wreckage alight. She waited only to make sure that the fire had caught well, then, laughing like a crazy woman, she joined the crowd struggling to get drink from the barrels.

By this time the rowdier crowds from the market had joined the mob to swell its ranks by hundreds, and already the first wild ones from the factories and mills were arriving.

Salter Allday, the parish constable, was fetched from his garden and quickly gathered a group of his deputies. Carrying the staff that was his badge of office, and leading his truncheon-bearing men, the constable tried to force his way through the mob and arrest the ringleaders.

It was unfortunate for Allday that the first man pointed out to him as a ringleader was a fighting needle pointer, Nail Styler. Until this moment, the crowd had not been excessively savage. The needle pointers who were in the town that day had only joined in the uproar as they would have joined in any rough horseplay. Salter Allday grabbed Styler by the collar and attempted to drag him from the crowd. Nail resisted and some of the deputy constables panicked. They began battering at the man with their heavy truncheons. Nail's shouts brought Steve Millington, another fighting man, running to the rescue at the head of a group of pointers he had led up from the mills.

'Cummon lads!' he bawled. 'They're hammering a pointer there.'

From all over the crowd, white aprons and brown paper hats converged. The constables tried to fight their way out, flailing their truncheons at everyone around, but in seconds they were beaten to the ground by a barrage of fists and clogs.

'Into the pool with um,' Steve Millington bellowed, and the cry was taken up by the whole crowd. The battered, blood-streaked constables were each lifted high by a score of rough hands, and the brawl developed into a triumphal procession, led by the pointers under the command of Millington and Nail Styler.

The town pond was a large pool situated a quarter of a mile from St Stephen's. From somewhere a large drum and several fifes were produced and the crowd streamed through the streets, laughing and catcalling to the pounding of the drum and the shrill of the fifes. When the pool was reached, the pointers lined up at the edge and while Millington bellowed 'Present! Aim! Fire!' the constables were pitched one after the other into the slimy green-scummed water. There they joined the decaying filth and rubbish, the dead dogs, cats, and rats, the rotting vegetables and the assorted outpourings of a hundred chamberpots.

When the last shout of 'Fire!' had been heard, and the last constable had gone flying head over heels, the needle pointers formed up behind the drum and fifes and led the crowd in procession back in search of more drink and excitement.

CHAPTER THIRTEEN

The Bartleet family were entertaining John Mence and three officers of the Nottinghamshire Yeomanry. In the parlourmaid's opinion, the gentlemen were the very essence of martial gallantry. Colonel Bartleet, who as a young officer had fought at Bunker Hill and later served with Banastre Tarleton's Legion during the remainder of the American War, did not share the maid's views as to what constituted martial gallantry. However, as befitted a gentleman, he exerted himself to show the due interested pleasure in his guests' anecdotes about the exploits of the yeomanry.

John Mence was piqued by the rapt attention Abigail was giving to the cavalrymen. Inwardly, he glumly compared his own drab blue and black uniform with the resplendent green and gold of the others', whose silver-spurred hessian boots, dangling sabretaches and curved sabres gave them such a dashing air.

The eldest of the trio, a chubby red-cheeked young merchant, was describing the Luddite troubles which had flared up in Nottingham during the previous year and spread to the neighbouring counties of Derby and Leicester.

'Why, at one stage it looked as if the whole of the North Country would rise in open rebellion,' he told his audience. 'In Nottingham alone there were three thousand regular troops, besides we yeomanry and the militia and special constables.'

Abigail's dark eyes twinkled. 'And were you not afraid, sir?' she asked mischievously. 'Surrounded in your tiny garrison by those hordes of truly dreadful Luddites?'

'Afraid?' he blustered. 'By your leave, ma'am, there's nothing on this earth that can frighten the old Sherwood Rangers.' He clasped his sabre hilt and rattled the blade in the scabbard. 'My only regret is that the Stockingers didn't give us a battle. We'd soon have given them a bellyful of cold steel, I do assure you.' He laughed boastfully. 'I'd like nothing better than to meet this so-called General Ned Ludd, in personal combat. In fact, I issued a public challenge to him to come out and meet me, man to man. To face me on the field of honour like a soldier. Isn't that so, gentlemen?'

His brother officers nodded their confirmation. Abigail gave him the full benefit of her most radiant smile. 'You are uncommon brave, sir. Indeed you are.' She leant forward eagerly, and his eyes moved involuntarily to the artlessly displayed top curves of her breasts. 'Tell me, sir? Did this General Ludd dare to come out and answer you?'

He shook his head emphatically. 'No, ma'am! That he didn't! For the man is an arrant coward, like all his followers. They are brave enough when smashing looms in the dark of night and terrorizing women and children, but they are not so anxious to cross swords with we chaps ... Oh no indeed! They run like frightened rabbits when the Sherwood Rangers come on the scene.'

With a serious expression Abigail said gravely, 'Perhaps, sir, if you had made a tour of the local rabbit warrens, you might have found the notorious Ludd cowering inside one of them.'

The young man's jaw dropped and he stared at her in confusion.

A strange choking sound came from Anne Bartleet as she spluttered into a handkerchief. Her father frowned heavily at Abigail, then he too appeared to be suffering from an unusually violent fit of coughing. Tears started from his eyes and suddenly he gave vent to his amusement in a loud rumble of laughter.

When they controlled themselves once more, they became aware of a strained silence, as Abigail sat demurely, eyes downcast, and the four young men toyed with their accoutrements.

'Do please pardon my daughter and myself, gentlemen,' the Colonel entreated soberly. 'I fear that the sudden affliction that overcame us is one that occurs constantly in this family.'

The officers accepted his apologies stiffly and, with Anne's gentle guidance, the conversation flowed easily once more.

It was then that the panting dishevelled figure of Mace the clerk appeared at the end of the driveway. As the clerk neared the house, he saw the gathering through the windows that opened on to the lawn. He stumbled across the well-kept turf and hammered on the glass panes.

'What the devil!' The Colonel sprang to his feet and opened the windows. 'What is the matter with you, man?' he demanded.

Mace held up his hands imploringly until he had caught his breath enough to gasp out, 'It's the town, sir! There's riots and murder going on up there.'

In a few questions Colonel Bartleet drew from the man all that he could tell.

'All right, Mace,' he said finally. 'You have done well. Now go round to the kitchen and tell cook she is to give you some refreshment. Then wait there.'

The others in the room had clustered behind the Colonel and now he turned to them.

'Do you think it could be an attack by General Ludd's army, father?' Abigail asked sweetly.

The Colonel's voice was stern. 'That is enough, young lady. This isn't the time for jokes. I must go into the town and see what is happening there for myself.'

'Is there anything we can do, sir?' the Yeomanry officer asked.

Bartleet shook his head. 'Not for the moment, thank you. However, I would be most grateful if you would remain here while I'm away and protect my daughters.' He spoke next to John Mence. 'John, I think it would be wise to call out the volunteers. Have them muster at your house. It's near enough to the town for a quick gathering and secluded enough not to attract any attention until we wish to take action; and send some of your men to the other magistrates and masters and tell them that I wish them to meet me at Lawyer Guardner's chambers.'

'Very good, sir.' Slightly pale and with pinched lips, Mence picked up his plumed brass helmet and went to the stable yard, bellowing for his horse.

Satisfied, the Colonel instructed his daughters. 'I want you girls to stay here in the house with these gentlemen and do not let any of the servants wander into the town. I don't think for a moment that you are in any danger, but I want to be easy in my mind about you.' Subdued now, the girls assented and the Colonel kissed them goodbye.

It was more than two hours later when Bartleet joined the gathering at the lawyer's chambers. The rooms were packed with worried men when he arrived. As he entered, they besieged him with questions. He waved them to silence.

'I'll be brief, gentlemen,' he said. 'The situation is very serious. I've reconnoitred the area and frankly I don't like what I've seen. At the moment the rioters are mostly in and around the Crown Inn, they've broached the casks there and they're getting drunk. Humphries' shop is burning and some other premises nearby are also in flames.'

'What are the constables and the volunteer firemen doing?' one man asked.

'They're at John Mence's house, having their wounds attended to,' the Colonel told him.

'What are we going to do about the mills?' an old needle master shouted.

Bartleet disregarded him and went on, 'The volunteers, or at least most of them, have also mustered at Mence's house. I'm not sure if they will be of much use. Naturally enough many of them seem reluctant to use force against men and women whom they have known all their lives.'

'But what about our mills?' the old man persisted.

'The mills are in no danger ... at least not at present,' the Colonel answered. 'This isn't a Luddite rising. The people seem only to want food and drink ... especially drink.'

The masters began to shout and argue amongst themselves, each one putting forward his plan of action. Bartleet attempted to quieten them, but his voice was drowned by the noise.

'Gentlemen! Gentlemen! Cease behaving like a crowd of fishwives.' The bull-like roar overwhelmed all argument. Standing in a corner of the room the Rev. Emmanuel Clayton glowered about him as the crowd fell silent. 'That's better, gentlemen. Now! Instead of arguing, let us listen to Colonel Bartleet's proposals as to the best action to take in dealing with this disturbance.'

Clem Washford held up his hands for attention.

'What makes you so sure, Clayton, that the Colonel knows best what to do? All of us here who are needle masters have dealt with trouble from our workhands before now,' he said aggressively.

'With respect, Mr Washford,' the preacher said, 'this isn't just a drunken brawl. This is far, far more serious than the troubles which usually arise in the mills. Therefore, I feel that the Colonel, who is possibly the only war veteran among us, is the man best fitted to dictate what action should be taken.'

Washford's face reddened and he started to make an angry retort, but his son Harry turned him away from the preacher and calmed him. Clayton nodded at the Colonel.

'Please proceed, sir.'

Bartleet smiled his thanks and began.

'Messengers have already set out to muster the Volunteers in Bromsgrove and to appraise the magistrates in Birmingham of what is happening here. The enrolment of special constables has begun all over the district and Mr Adam Milward, our fellow magistrate, is even at this moment swearing them in. I have also ordered that the Worcestershire Yeomanry be alerted and the regular dragoons at Lichfield. However, I do not consider it likely that we shall need the cavalry. As soon as possible I intend to read the Riot Act and disperse the mob, using the Redditch Volunteers. If the attempt fails, then I wish you, gentlemen, to gather together your loyal workers and servants and to assist the special constables to guard your premises until the Bromsgrove Volunteers and the yeomanry squadrons arrive ... Mr Washford, I would request that you as a fellow magistrate accompany me.'

Clem Washford grunted his acquiescence.

'Thank you,' the Colonel said. 'Now, gentlemen, please remain here until I have attempted to disperse the mob. If I fail, then please proceed as I have requested.'

The two magistrates left together. Once they had gone, the hubbub of argument broke out afresh.

CHAPTER FOURTEEN

'Giddup! Gooo onnn! Gooo onnn!' Jethro Stanton urged on the horses heaving the vast wagon up the hill. By his side on the wagon seat, his father lolled back, eyes closed, dozing. Jethro frowned worriedly as he glanced at the older man. It was at times like this, asleep and unprotected, that his father betrayed the toll that his hard life had taken upon him.

His deeply lined face was grey-tinged and black rims of exhaustion ringed his eyes. Over the last two years Peter Stanton had aged rapidly, the smooth muscles of his arms and shoulders had become stringy tendons and the skin of his strong neck had shrivelled to the wattles of an old man. His hair was flecked with white, and the hands that now lay loose and unclenched in sleep trembled and twitched.

Jethro bit his lip and wondered yet again about the mysterious absences that his father had taken in the last years, leaving without warning early in the morning while the world slept, and returning days or weeks later during the same quiet hours, sometimes with bruised and bleeding hands and head, clothes torn and muddied, sick with hunger and tiredness. Other times he was jubilant with suppressed excitement, head erect, body strong and fresh. But never, in spite of all Jethro's pleading and cajoling, had Peter Stanton said one word about what he was doing. All he would say was, 'Someday, son, I'll tell you ... But that time hasn't arrived yet.' Then he would fall silent and refuse even to acknowledge questions about his absences.

This time he had been away since the night of Jamie Fisher's death and Jethro, returning with a load of needle wire from the Black Country, had overtaken his father walking towards Redditch.

The wagon reached Bromsgrove and as they neared the

centre of the town Jethro could hear the thudding of drums. His father stirred and awoke. For a moment he gazed blankly, then his head cleared and he smiled at his son.

'We're making good time, I see, Bromsgrove already.'

Jethro returned the smile. 'They must be having a fair day. Listen to the drums.'

His father sat bolt upright. 'There!' he pointed. 'It's the militia!'

Far in front of them, at the very end of the long High Street, was a milling mass of uniformed figures, and from the houses and shops more men, hastily donning equipment, hurried to where the drummers were beating the muster.

Jethro laughed. 'Don't tell me that old Boney's finally come across the Channel,' he shouted across to a militiaman who had drawn abreast of the wagon. 'What's happening, master? Have the French landed?'

The man shook his head. 'It's them mad buggers at Redditch,' he answered, 'the needle pointers. They'm burning the place to the ground, from what we'em told. We'em agoin' to march there now and set about them, not that any of us relishes the prospect I might tell you. They'm like a pack of wild wolves, them bloody pointers. Better they should send some cannon and blow um all to Kingdom Come than expect us to control the bloody savages.'

Jethro turned to his father. 'Do you think it's the Luddites, Dad?'

Peter Stanton's face was puzzled. 'It can't be,' he murmured. 'Not in Worcestershire ... not yet ... We're not ready ... this will be the ruin of us. Quick, boy! Whip these beasts up, we must get to Redditch as soon as we can.'

Jethro wanted to ask him what he meant by his strange murmurings, but looking at the hard-set features next to him he decided to wait for a better moment to ask that question.

When they reached the Redditch boundary, Peter Stanton jumped from the wagon.

'I'll see you later, son,' he snapped, and ran into the labyrinth of alleys that led up the hill to the common.

Jethro continued until he came to the mill where he was to deliver the wire. When he swung the wagon into the courtyard the only sign of life was a small group of overseers standing together by the entrance gates. He got down to the cobbles and went to them.

'What's happening here?' he asked.

'Nothing's happening here, carter,' one of them answered.

'It's up in the town where the trouble is, bloody slumrats from the common side creating merry hell.'

'Can I leave my wagon and horses here for a while?' Jethro asked.

'That you may, carter,' the man said, and grinned. 'Mind you, if the Luddites come this way I'm not promising you that we can keep it safe.'

'Is it Luddites then?' Jethro queried.

The man winked at him. 'No one seems to know rightly ... But mind you, there's a lot round these parts who wouldn't be too unhappy if it was Ned Ludd come.' He grinned and winked again. 'Not me, mind you. I'm an overseer and a loyal servant to the needle masters. It's all the other buggers who'll be pleased to see Ned Ludd.'

When he reached the common, Jethro halted and studied the scene before him. By the Crown Inn, a crowd of several hundred men, women and children, brandishing bottles, bricks and assorted clubs, hurled curses and abuse across the open space to where some two hundred yards away stood the silent ranks of the local volunteer corps, a sombre mass of blue tunics and black or grey breeches, ending in black half-boots and topped by dull brass helmets with black horsehair plumes moulded over them. From where he was, Jethro could see the pale drawn faces of John Mence and his two junior officers who sat on motionless horses in front of their men. Directly in front of Mence were Colonel Bartleet and Clem Washford also mounted while to the side of the volunteers were standing a handful of Special Constables, among whom were Harry Washford and Emmanuel Clayton.

Bunched together in the forefront of the mob, Jethro picked out Steve Millington, Luke and Matt Fisher, Nail Styler, Tom and Agnes Bright and Doll Greenaway, clustered round a man whose face was hidden from Jethro's view. They were arguing fiercely. Luke Fisher moved and Jethro saw the man was his father. All round the common, like spectators at a prize fight, swarmed crowds of onlookers. Watchful and attentive, as if waiting for a signal to join in the riot.

Suddenly Colonel Bartleet drove his horse forward, ac-

companied by Clem Washford and Captain Mence. The three
reined in their mounts a short distance from the crowd. Bartleet pulled a piece of paper from his pocket and began to read
aloud from it.

A tremendous howl greeted his words. Jethro realized that
the magistrate was reading the Riot Act. The three men
wheeled their horses and galloped back to the silent ranks of
the volunteers.

In front of the mob, Peter Stanton began to talk again,
gesticulating vehemently.

'And I say disperse, Luke! How many times do I have to
tell you that there's reinforcements of militia coming from
Bromsgrove even now, and next will be the yeomanry.'

Luke Fisher bared his teeth savagely. He swayed, half-mad
with beer and grief.

'Does you reckon that me and me mates here care two pins
for the bloody Bromsgrove volunteers. I tell you, they'm the
same as them bastards across there ... Bloody shopkeepers
and Methody pisspots who can't fight their way out of paper
sacks. AN'T THAT SO?' He turned and shouted to the
crowd, who despite not one in ten of them knowing what he
had said before roared their agreement.

Peter Stanton thrust his jaw out pugnaciously. 'You're a
fool, Luke! Nothing but a fool! Now isn't the time to rise up
against the masters and gentry. Why can't you wait until I
say?'

A tall lean man with a black eye-patch on his scarred face
came lurching from the crowd. In one hand he carried a
wooden crutch.

'You all knows me,' he bellowed. 'Peg Whittington. Old
Wooden Peg.' He pulled up his wide-bottomed trousers and
showed the crowd his brass-studded peg-leg. 'Listen, Stanton,
I like the cut of your jib, and you're a man after me own heart,
but you just listen to me ... And you lot of poxy deck apes,'
he bawled at the crowd and brandished his crutch threateningly. 'I left this eye and this leg at Trafalgar Cape, and all
I've known since then is an empty belly which just goes on
getting emptier. And I says this, that now's the time we fills
our bellies for nothing. And if you think that a bunch of fat-
gutted lubbers dressed up like sodger boys am agoin' to stop
me fillin' my belly today, tomorrow and next week too, then,

101

Peter Stanton, you'm makin' the biggest mistake you'se ever made.'

The crowd cheered its approval of the speech.

Doll Greenaway tugged at Stanton's arm. 'Leave it, Peter, they'll not listen to you ... And why should they? It's our turn now to eat and drink our fill.'

He faced the crowd, desperation on his face and in his voice. 'Listen to me for a minute, will you. I'll tell you why I want you to wait.'

The crowd quietened.

'I've just come back from the North Country,' Stanton told them. 'For the last two years I've been making trips all over the country. In every county and city, in every village and town, men and women just like you, just as poor, just as hungry, just as desperate, have been getting ready.'

'Ready for what?' a pointer shouted.

'Ready to lie down and die,' another bawled, and the crowd burst into jeering laughter.

'No!' Stanton shouted. 'Not to lie down. But for once to stand on their feet ... To get off their knees, lift their faces from the dirt and act like freeborn men. To get rid of the tyrants who rule us and put in their place a government of the people. A government that will give fair and equal justice to all.'

'Who d'you reckon you are, covey?' a drunken harriden wanted to know. 'General Ludd?'

A sudden hush fell on the crowd as the woman screeched the words. Then, from the fringe, a short, bull-like man, wearing a broad-brimmed hat that partly hid his features, pushed his way through to join the group of leaders. He pulled off his hat and there came an audible gasp of astonishment.

It was the head keeper to the Earl, John Batten.

'You may well be surprised,' he sneered. 'But what that drunken slut said is only the truth. That's why you had best listen to Peter here.'

He spoke in a low tone to Stanton. 'It won't do any harm to tell them now, Peter. I spotted Stone and his men this morning. They know we're here, so we've got to move fast.'

A buzz of astonishment and excitement ran through the crowd. Was this really the mysterious revolutionary leader? The man who, so it was whispered, would soon lead his hordes against London itself?

The keeper spoke again. 'Tell them, Peter,' he urged. 'Before they ruin our plans for these parts completely.'

Peter Stanton glanced across at the magistrates and troops who were still motionless, waiting to see if the mob would disperse. Satisfied, he addressed the crowd, his firm voice carrying easily and clearly.

'There are many of us in this country who are known as General Ludd,' he began. 'There are many leaders ... All I ask of you is that you do not bring a mass of troops into this area by attacking the volunteers. There are reasons which you do not know of, reasons that must for the present be kept a secret, for not attracting the Government's "provocation men" to this district. I beg of you to believe in me.' He paused and swept the crowd with an intense regard. 'Go now! All of you! Go back to your homes. Soon I shall return here. When I do, you will have the opportunity to strike out at those who oppress you. I promise you that, and it will be sooner than you imagine. But for now go! Please go!'

The crowd shuffled uncertainly and were on the verge of dispersing when Doll Greenaway screamed piercingly and pointed to the volunteers. 'Look there! They're killing my poor Billy ...'

Struggling and cursing, Blind Billy was being dragged by several men along the front of the militia ranks. John Mence turned his horse to see what was happening and all attention was focused on the scuffle.

'What are you doing with that man?' Mence shouted.

'If you please, sir, it's Blind Billy Greenaway,' a corporal answered. 'He's drunk, sir, and he keeps wandering into the line of fire. We're only trying to get him out of the way so that he won't get hurt if there's trouble.'

'Well, be sharp about it,' Mence ordered. 'And get back into line.'

'Very good, sir,' the corporal saluted. 'Come on, you men, get this loony moving.'

As he finished the sentence, a thrown rock hit him squarely in the throat. His eyes bulged, he choked and dropped to his knees, hands scrabbling at his collar and stock. Even as he dropped a tremendous howl of raging hate filled the air and a barrage of missiles rained down on the militia. The mob of rioters, led by Peg Whittington waving his crutch above his head, swarmed across the common like maddened wolves. Taken by surprise, the volunteers stood as if petrified. Everywhere men were falling injured, reeling from the ranks under the impact of hurled rocks, bottles, pieces of grate iron and a hundred other objects heavy enough to smash and maim. One of the first to be struck down was Charles Bartleet. A bottle caught him on the forehead knocking his round high-crowned hat flying and stunning him, so that he swayed and fell heavily from his horse. Clem Washford's mount, hit by a dozen missiles, reared and bolted with the needle master hanging on grimly, unable to do anything other than try to keep his seat.

In panic, John Mence drew his pistols from their saddle holsters and fired them wildly into the advancing mob. One ball whistled harmlessly over their heads, the other tore into a woman's thigh. She stood for a moment stock still, then sat down abruptly and remained staring stupidly at the blood staining her ragged dress until she was knocked flat and trampled unconscious under the clogs of the crazed rioters, pushing and jostling each other wildly as they tried to come to grips with the man who had fired. Mence hurled his empty pistols at them then yanked his horse's head savagely round and spurred it straight through the lines of volunteers behind him.

Before the junior officers had time to comprehend what had happened, the rioters had reached them and torn them from their horses. For brief moments the militiamen fought to contain and beat back the onslaught of the mob, but with their leaders gone and already unnerved by the whirlwind they had reaped, they proved no match for their attackers. In ones and twos, then in tens and twenties, they ran, throwing down muskets and bayonets, casting off helmets, packs, belts, pouches, anything that impeded their headlong flight. The rioters hooted after them through the alleyways and the swarms of half-starved dogs that infested the town snapped and snarled at their heels.

On the common, only a few isolated groups of volunteers were still or their feet, fighting back to back with musket butts and bayonets against a ring of cudgels, iron-shod clogs and whirling chains.

Jethro had watched the mob burst over the common when Doll Greenaway screamed. He had seen his father and Batten swept aside as they tried to stop the attack and then seen the keeper hustle his father away into the alley. When Colonel Bartleet fell from his horse, Jethro could only think that this was Abigail's father and without conscious volition began to run. He reached the fallen magistrate and knelt, lifting the bleeding head and cradling it in his arms, interposing his body as a shield against the violence crashing over and around them. For what seemed an eternity, he was buffeted and trampled on. Just when he felt himself being battered into senselessness, there came a sudden respite. He twisted his head and looked up, squinting through the mist of sweat and blood that veiled his sight. Standing above him was what appeared to be a black giant, swinging two black clubs which dealt terrible punishment to those rash ones who came within distance. Jethro rubbed his hand across his eyes, blinking fiercely to clear his sight. When he looked again, the giant had become the Reverend Emmanuel Clayton and the clubs the mighty arms and fists with which he hammered his attackers to the ground.

The crowd around them eddied and suddenly thinned as the volunteers gave way and ran. Clayton swung one last tremendous blow, sending a pointer crashing; and all became still. Panting heavily, the preacher straightened his neck stock and smoothed his thick hair. He reset the white linen of his cuffs and settled his black coat into its usual neatness. Only then did he look down at Jethro.

'Well, young Stanton,' he said, quietly. 'I see that once again you've got into difficulties while trying to serve your fellow man.'

Jethro wanted to laugh and cry at the same instant, to hug this huge grim man as a brother hugs a brother; and to touch the hem of the shabby black coat in awe and reverence. The preacher crouched and gently examined the still unconscious Bartleet. He smiled at Jethro.

'Thanks to you, boy, he's not badly hurt, but we'd best get him to his house.'

Jethro got stiffly to his feet and sharp pains lanced into his head and body at a dozen points. The preacher patted his shoulder.

'Aye! I don't doubt that you're feeling very sore yourself, boy. You'll come to the house also and let Dr Murdoch attend to you.'

Together they carried the Colonel from the common. The last volunteers' resistance had ended, beaten down by the clogs and cudgels, and the grass was strewn with the fallen, some groaning and moving, others ominously still. The crowds of onlookers spread across the open space and did what they could for the injured, while on the far side of the common at the Fox and Goose Inn, the mob used the outside benches to batter in the doors and shutters.

CHAPTER FIFTEEN

Cautiously Owen Treadgold opened the front door of his house which stood in its own grounds enclosed by high walls at the rear of the Crown Inn. From the distance there came screams, shouts and the sounds of fighting, but here all was quiet. The only things that moved were the bees humming among the flowers. Satisfied that all was clear, he stepped out and closed the door behind him. Grunting with the effort, he tore up one of the small boulders that lined the neat gravel pathway and hurled it against the door-catch. The thin metal clasp splintered from the wood and the door crashed inwards. Next Treadgold gathered some stones and clods of earth and smashed the glass and leaded panes of the windows. He stepped back and admired his handiwork, then went quickly up the pathway and opened the gate that led into the alley-way.

He was about to step out when the sound of hurrying foot-steps made him draw back. He closed the gate and put one eye to a crack in the panel. The footsteps came nearer and as they passed Treadgold glimpsed the two men hurrying by. Batten the keeper and Peter Stanton. The watching man frowned in perplexity. They made a strange pair, the pointer who was well known for his antipathy towards the aristocracy and the trusted servant of the Earl.

Their rapid footsteps died away and again Treadgold started to leave, but as he did so another group came running into the alley. Quickly he closed the door and waited for the men to pass. He heard someone giving orders.

'Smith, Tompkins! You carry on along there ... Myers! You check that side. I'll take this one ...'

Treadgold peeped through the crack. Four heavy-set, tough-looking men carrying pistols were in the alley. The one who had given the orders was slightly taller than the rest, his clothes of better quality and on his head he wore a black bicorn hat. It was he who now came towards the gate while the others ran on. Treadgold drew in his breath with sudden terror, then scurried back up the pathway and into the house. In the hall he paused for a second, frantically racking his brain for a hiding-place. The sound of heavy steps crunching over the gravel sent him flying through the kitchen and into the wash-house at the rear of the building. In one corner was the huge wash-copper, half full of dirty water. Uncaring in his dread of discovery, Treadgold slid aside the wooden cover and forced his small frame into the copper, drawing the cover over his head and crushing the tricorn hat over his ears without pausing to take it off.

For what seemed hours he stayed in the copper, biting his lips to stop himself groaning with the agony of the cramp that almost immediately began to knot his twisted muscles. He could hear the clumping boots of the man searching the house and he started when the sound of a sudden exclamation followed by a string of oaths came from the bedroom above. The cold of the water chilled his bones and he began to shiver with damp and fear. As his misery grew more intense, he began to whimper softly. His control ebbed away and the low whimpers deepened to loud sobs. He was not even aware of the wooden cover being lifted and it took the sharp rappings of a pistol barrel on the top of his head to bring him to his senses.

The tall man in the bicorn hat dragged him bodily from the copper and Treadgold stood trembling and crying in the centre of the wash-house, his hat still jammed down over his ears and the water streaming from his clothes to form a large puddle upon the stone-flagged floor.

'Don't you try telling me it was the rioters who did that upstairs,' the tall man said quietly. 'Because I know for certain that it was you.'

The needle master's sobs slowed and, covering his tear-streaked face with his hands, he hiccupped loudly and whined.

'I didn't mean to kill her ... I swear before God and all his saints, I didn't mean to kill my wife, nagging slut that she was ... I only meant to teach her a lesson for once

'. . . She drove me to it . . . I swear to you, she drove me to it . . .'

The tall man used the pistol barrel to lift Treadgold's chin until their eyes met. His hard face, networked by the tiny broken veins of a gin-drinker, creased into something resembling a smile.

'My name is Stone, little man,' he said harshly. 'Jacob Stone! And my heart is like my name.'

'Oh no!' Treadgold begged. 'Please! I'll do anything you want. Anything at all ... Just let me go from here. I don't want to hang ... Please! I beg of you! I'll give you money ... anything ... I don't want to hang!'

Jacob Stone stared at the man in front of him, pondering how best to use the situation to his own advantage.

'Master Stone?' The voice came from outside.

'Now listen, cully,' he whispered harshly. 'One sound out of you before I say so and I'll blow your brains out. Wait here and keep as still as a dead man ... Or, by God, that's what you'll be!'

He hurried from the wash-house, leaving Treadgold huddled shivering by the wall. The man Myers was standing by the front door.

'There's no sign of them, Master Stone,' he said. 'Tompkins says that they've got clean away.'

'God rot their bloody eyes!' Stone cursed. 'Ah well, never mind that now, go and get the others.'

When the three men gathered in front of him, Stone indicated the upper floor with a tilt of his head.

'Come on upstairs, I've got something to show you.'

In the bedroom the furniture was tumbled about and broken. In one corner a chest had been opened and the clothes inside it ripped and strewn on the floor. Lying across the bed, her head hanging over the edge, eyes wide with horror, was the body of a woman. A curved wide-gapped gash stretched round her neck beneath the plump double chins, and the blood still oozed in two sluggish coils, one behind each ear, into the streaming grey hair that hung loose to the floor.

'Jesus Christ!' Myers gasped.

Tompkins gave vent to an hysterical giggle. Jacob Stone pointed with his pistol at the red-smeared carving knife lying on the floor beneath the head.

'We'd best leave that there for the magistrates to see. Come on.'

With backward glances, his men followed him downstairs. He led them through the kitchen to the wash-house. Owen Treadgold was still in the same posture. Stone went to him and put his arm gently round the thin shoulders.

'Now don't fret yourself, master,' he said kindly. 'Do you know a man named Peter Stanton and another called Batten? Do you?'

Treadgold gulped and nodded. Stone smiled mirthlessly, his voice dropped almost to a whisper.

'Now you pay close attention to what I'm saying, master.'

Treadgold's fear-dulled mind sensed that somehow he was going to be saved from the hangman. He nodded vigorously.

'I'm paying attention, Mr Stone,' he jerked out.

'Good!' Stone hugged the frail shoulders. 'Now, master,' he went on slowly and distinctly. 'I want you to tell these gentlemen here about how Peter Stanton and the man Batten broke into your house, knocked you silly and then robbed you of the money you were keeping in the chest upstairs.' He paused as Treadgold looked up at him in shock, and he narrowed his eyes threateningly. 'Oh yes, master, they robbed you of the money that was in the chest ... And tell them as well how Batten held your good wife helpless on the bed while that evil bastard Stanton cut her throat.' He shook Treadgold's shoulders and his voice became loud, commanding. 'Go on, man! Tell them!'

Taking a deep breath, Treadgold haltingly repeated the big man's words.

'Right, you there,' Stone said sharply. 'Have you all understood what this gentleman has told you?'

They nodded.

'Good!' Stone was satisfied. 'Go on now, and make sure that no one comes into the house or garden. Move, curse you!'

They clattered out, leaving Stone and Treadgold alone. Treadgold felt weak with gratitude. He slumped to his knees and, clasping the other round his legs, he poured out a torrent of thanks.

Stone smiled grimly down at him. 'There now, master. I'm sure that someday you'll be able to repay me for what I've done, but there's one thing more we must do. I've got to make you look as if you were attacked.'

He reached down and pushed Treadgold's head back. Then his eyes moistened with intense pleasure, and he began to beat the small man's face with the pistol.

CHAPTER SIXTEEN

'There now. That should leave ye as good as new.' Doctor Murdoch's strong fingers smoothed the last of the ointment around Jethro's bruises and he stood up, straightening his back with a groan. 'Guid God above! This damned English climate will be the finish of me, it stiffens my bones more every year.'

The two men were in the large stone-flagged kitchen of the Bartleet's home, surrounded by a flock of admiring servants.

'Is it true that this young man saved the Colonel's life, sir?' the motherly cook asked.

'Why not ask him yourself, woman?' the doctor snapped. 'He's sitting right here in front of ye ... Or did ye think it was the chair I was spreading salve on?'

Before the cook could reply, Mace, the clerk, came into the kitchen.

'Doctor Murdoch,' he said, 'the Colonel wishes to speak with this young man in the drawing-room.'

The doctor nodded and spoke to Jethro. 'Are you well enough to listen to a load of blethering, young Stanton?'

Jethro got to his feet, he grimaced with the pain, then forced a smile. 'Thank you very much for treating me.'

The Scotsman shook his head impatiently.

'I want no thanks for doing what was my duty,' he snapped, then his face softened and he smiled. 'And what was also my pleasure. Come ... We mustn't keep the Colonel waiting.'

Preceded by Mace the two went along the dark passage to the drawing-room. Colonel Bartleet, his head heavily bandaged, sat in an armchair. At each side of him sat his daughters and standing ranged around the room were many of the needle masters and local gentry, including Clem and Harry

Washford, together with John Mence and the three yeomanry officers.

Emmanuel Clayton was standing just inside the door. When Jethro entered, the Colonel beckoned to him.

'Come here, young man. I want to shake your hand. It's not every day that a man is able to thank someone for saving his life.'

Nervous and embarrassed, Jethro went forward and took the proffered hand. His embarrassment increased when one of the gentlemen began to applaud, clapping his hands. The others joined in and Jethro stood red faced and awkward before the storm of approval.

'Bring this young man a seat,' the Colonel ordered, and a dozen hands pushed forward a high-backed damask chair.

'Sit down, my boy,' Bartleet pressed Jethro's hand. 'Now you'll take a glass of wine ... I'll not accept any refusal, sir.'

In a daze Jethro took the delicate glass and sipped the purple wine.

'There! Is that to your taste, sir?' The Colonel leant forward eagerly. 'I do assure you, it's the very finest I have in my cellars ... Now? Is there anything else you would enjoy?'

Jethro shook his head. 'No, sir, I thank you.' He took another sip of the wine, savouring its heady sweetness.

'Young man,' Bartleet smiled expansively, 'these gentlemen here and myself would like to hear something about you.'

He lay back in his chair and waited expectantly. Jethro swallowed nervously. A vision of his father telling the crowd that he was General Ludd appeared in his mind's eye, and the memory of his father telling him time and time again that the smiling faces around him now were the enemy. Confused, Jethro's gaze went from face to face until he found himself confronted by the dark eyes of Abigail Bartleet, where he saw such warmth and admiration that his doubts left him and he knew what he must say.

But before he could begin, John Mence, standing in a fever of bitter shame and anger, and driven almost to madness by what he had read in the girl's eyes when she looked at the young carter, burst out, 'Yes! Tell us all why the son of a rioting slumrat should have saved the life of the Colonel here?'

After a moment of shocked surprise Bartleet turned furiously on Mence. 'How dare you speak in that manner here in my house, to an honoured guest?' he demanded.

Jethro jumped to his feet. 'I understand why he said that, Colonel Bartleet,' his voice rang out.

The Colonel stared hard at him. 'Then you had better explain young man,' he said sternly.

Jethro nodded. 'I will, sir ... My father, Peter Stanton, a man that I am proud to be son to, is one of those who are known as General Ludd.'

A murmur of shocked anger came from the men present.

'I am telling you no secret,' Jethro went on. 'Indeed, by now, I would think that nearly every man, woman and child in this town knows of it. I myself found out when my father told the rioters who he was in an attempt to persuade them to disperse.'

The yeomanry officer stepped up to him. In a voice trembling with anger, he said, 'Then, Stanton, I shall have the pleasure of horse-whipping you when you leave this house.'

Jethro looked quickly at the angry, threatening faces surrounding him and realized that he felt only contempt for these men. Blusterers like the yeomanry officer, hard man-drivers like Clem Washford, vicious unstable cowards like John Mence. He smiled at the cavalryman.

'Before you try to horsewhip me, I would advise you to lose some of that fat you carry on your belly.'

A clamour of threats greeted his words.

'Enough, gentlemen!' the Colonel roared them to silence. When all was quiet, he went on, 'I would ask you to remember that you are in my house and that my daughters are present ... As for you, young man ...' He stared long and hard at Jethro, who met his stare with steady eyes. 'While I admire the courage that you undoubtedly possess in good measure, I would advise you not to let that courage become the insolence of bad manners while speaking with those who are of a higher station in life than yourself ...' And then the Colonel showed the measure of man that he was. 'Please sit down, Stanton, and take another glass of wine. You are still an honoured guest in my house and in order to understand what lies at the root of the troubles that have come to our country, I would again ask you to tell us something of yourself. Perhaps in doing so, you will enlighten all present as to what has gone wrong.'

Jethro stood undecided. He glanced at Abigail and saw on her beautiful face an expression that pleaded with him to remain. He sat down and picked up his glass of wine.

'If any gentleman present wishes to withdraw, he may do so,' the Colonel said grimly. 'And I'll thank you, sir, to stop your warlike posturings,' he snapped at the fat yeomanry officer.

The man was flustered and stepped back among his fellows. There was a long silence which lasted until Bartleet was satisfied.

'Please continue, Mr Stanton,' he told Jethro.

The young man looked first at Abigail. She smiled encouragingly and he felt suddenly ten feet tall. Confidently he faced the Colonel.

'With your permission, sir, I would like to tell you something about my father Peter Stanton, a man whom I love and admire above anyone I have ever known. He came of a line of tenant farmers in Warwickshire. When he was still a boy, the land was taken from his father as a result of a Bill of Enclosure. Both his parents died shortly afterwards in poverty, leaving my father alone in the world. After years of suffering and wandering, my father took service with John Company's Army in India. In March of 1791 he was a Sergeant and he took part in the assault on Bangalore. During the fighting when the Grenadiers of the 36th had lost all their officers, he led them in the Forlorn Hope. For his bravery Lord Cornwallis himself gazetted him Ensign in the Crown Army. In October of '91 my father led the Forlorn Hope at the capture of Nundydoorg Fort, and to reward him for this the officers of his regiment subscribed the amount necessary to buy him a vacant captaincy. After the capture of Seringapatam my father accused another officer of cowardice during the battle. They fought a duel and the other man was killed. My father was sentenced by court martial to hang; it seems the man he had fought was well connected. But Lord Cornwallis, who greatly admired my father, intervened and instead of hanging, he was cashiered and dismissed the service. After more wanderings he returned to England and at Babraham village in Cambridgeshire he met and married my mother. He worked for her father, who was a tenant farmer.

115

'I was born on the farm and so were my two sisters. I remember that we were very happy there. Then in 1809 my father was balloted for the militia and sent to Ely. While he was there my grandad died in debt and we were put from the farm. My mother took we three children and walked to Ely. When we got there we were nearly dead from hunger and my sisters were very sick. The militia were under marching orders and my father had no money to give my mother so that we would be provided for when he marched ...' Jethro's voice faltered and he swallowed hard. 'I expect that you gentlemen already know what happened at Ely. Led by my father and others, the men demanded their arrears of pay and the Marching Guinea, before they would march ...' His voice became hard and angry.

'That money meant the difference between life and death to my sisters. Without it, my mother had no hope of getting them the treatment and rest and food that they needed. The Cavalry of the King's German Legion was brought in from Bury St Edmunds ... Foreign troops ordered into action against Englishmen on English soil by our own English rulers ... The ringleaders, including my father, were charged with mutiny and flogged almost to death.'

Jethro closed his eyes and was once more the small boy hidden in a tree overlooking the flogging parade. He saw again the German cavalrymen rip the shirt from his father's back and truss him to the triangle of halberds. He heard the supercilious tones of the English officer, entreating his opposite number in the German uniform to make sure that his Hanoverian drummers stripped the skin from the mutinous English backs. He heard again the swish of blood-heavy cords through the air and saw the shredded flesh and soggy blood ripple and fly out under the impact. He glimpsed the white of bone and felt the blackness overwhelming him and knew once more the jarring thud as his fainting body fell from the branches to the ground beneath.

Jethro opened his eyes and drew in great gulps of air, fighting to steady his emotions. When he went on his voice was jerking with strain.

'When they brought my father to her, my mother saw his back and she screamed once only ...' He remembered well that long, long scream that seemed to go on echoing through all the streets of Ely. 'Then she fell to the ground in a fit. She never recovered.'

Anne's eyes filled with tears. 'And your sisters?' she asked.

'They are both buried at Ely,' Jethro said simply. 'In the pauper's grave with my mother.'

He looked steadily at the men standing around him and then at Charles Bartleet.

'When my father was strong enough, we left the poorhouse in Ely and travelled all over the North Country; and everywhere we went we saw the poor people suffering as we had suffered. Hunger, disease, cold, that awful cold. That is the reason my father is numbered among those who are called Luddites and Radicals; and that is why I myself believe utterly in what my father is trying to achieve.'

He got to his feet. 'I thank you for listening to me, Colonel Bartleet,' he said quietly, and left the hushed room.

'Hum!' Clem Washford exclaimed. 'A touching story ... but a most unlikely one.'

His son rounded on him angrily. 'I think that he spoke the truth, father.'

'You would,' the old man scoffed. 'You're too soft to tell the difference between truth and a beggar's prattle.'

Some of the others present voiced their agreement with the needle master.

'Gentlemen, you're a pack of blind fools,' Emmanuel Clayton boomed. He scowled at them in fury. 'You can't distinguish truth from falsehood because of your own prejudice.'

'And you can, preacher. I suppose the Lord shows you the difference,' Clem Washford said with heavy sarcasm.

'In this case, yes!' Clayton was emphatic. 'Because some years ago I saw the terrible scars of the flogging on Stanton's back, and to satisfy my curiosity about the man I made enquiries. I can tell you this, and I would not think any man wise to call me a liar: everything that young Jethro Stanton has told you is the absolute truth.'

The silence that followed the preacher's words was finally broken by Charles Bartleet.

'I must say, gentlemen, that I too thought the young man spoke only truth. His manner carried conviction.'

'Hear, hear!' Harry Washford's slender pale face was animated by his pleasure. 'From my own knowledge of Peter

Stanton, I must echo his son's high opinion of him. He is a fine man.'

While they were speaking the door of the room had opened slightly, and now, as Harry Washford finished, the door swung fully ajar and Jacob Stone came into the room, followed by the badly beaten Owen Treadgold.

'Who the devil are you?' the Colonel demanded.

Stone was unabashed. 'Jacob Stone, at your service, sir,' he said loudly. 'And having heard what this gentleman thinks of Peter Stanton, I'll make so bold as to tell him to listen to what Mr Treadgold here has to say, before he praises that murdering swine of a Luddite any further.'

CHAPTER SEVENTEEN

The news of Mrs Treadgold's murder ended the riot. Men who were not afraid to face volunteers, yeomanry and dragoons now felt ashamed to look into the eyes of their fellows. The terrible crime had soiled them all. There were some, Luke Fisher, the Brights, Doll Greenaway among them, who would not believe that Peter Stanton was capable of slitting a woman's throat, but even they felt all desire to challenge the authorities drain from them. Before the rattle of drums announced the arrival of the Bromsgrove Volunteers, the mob had returned to the hovels whence they had come.

Some of the gentry and masters demanded that the rioters should be punished with the utmost severity, but others, led by Charles Bartleet and Harry Washford, overruled the vengeance-seekers.

'These unhappy and tragic events have shown that the fault for what has happened in our town lies at all our doors,' Bartleet told the stormy meeting held a few days after the riot. 'We shall gain no glory and win no victory by sentencing to death or transportation men and women whose crimes are hunger and want. I propose that those people identified as ringleaders should be bound over to be of good behaviour in the future.'

Clem Washford stood up and leaned across the table, chin jutting out. 'Are you mad?' he shouted. 'These villains have burned and looted shops and inns. They have injured scores of reputable citizens, some of whom lie gravely ill; and all that you can suggest is a mealy-mouthed plea to them to be good children in the future ...'

From the opposite seat, Harry Washford jumped to his feet and confronted his father.

'I don't regard the giving of simple justice as being mealy-

119

mouthed,' he said angrily. 'And as for forgiveness? It is we ... the so-called leaders of the community who should ask the people for forgiveness. It is because of our greed and corruption that they are driven to riot through hunger and hardship ...'

'Why you ...!' In blind fury Clem Washford struck his son in the face.

Harry fell back on to the chair behind him, while others restrained his father. The young man put his hand to his lips and wiped away the trickle of blood which the blow had drawn.

'That is the last time, father, you will ever raise your hand to me,' he said slowly and calmly, then, disregarding all entreaties to make up the quarrel, he left the meeting.

Clem Washford subsided into a sullen silence and slumped down in his chair to remain staring blankly at the green cloth table cover for the rest of the meeting.

When he resumed his speech, Charles Bartleet's tone brooked no further interruptions.

'Very well, gentlemen. I think that what has just occurred is an admirable illustration of what passions can be aroused over this matter. Therefore I say again ... I propose that the ringleaders shall be bound over to keep the peace, this will enable the town to get back to its old happy way of life as quickly as possible.

'A warrant must be sworn for Stanton and Batten on a charge of murder. Lastly, we present shall subscribe generously to a fund which will be used to compensate those who have been injured or whose property has been damaged in the riot ... Is there anyone who wishes to say anything against these proposals, or who has anything to add to them?'

He waited for a reply, his face stern.

'Very well, gentlemen,' he said, when no one spoke. 'So be it.'

The meeting broke up and, after the magistrates had carried out the necessary measures, Bartleet went in search of his gig.

On the way to his home the sound of galloping hooves and his name being called caused him to stop. John Mence came up to him astride a heavily lathered, hard-ridden horse.

'I'm sorry that I was unable to attend the meeting, sir,' the young man apologized. 'The damned hounds picked up the wrong scent and took us clear across the county.'

He swayed in the saddle as he spoke and his blotched skin and bleary eyes were evidence enough of heavy drinking, without the brandy-fumed breath.

The Colonel regarded him with distaste. 'The meeting went perfectly well,' he answered curtly.

'Good!' Mence grinned savagely. 'And how many of the damned rogues are to be sent to the Assizes for hanging?'

'None, sir!' Bartleet snapped.

'But why not?' Mence's face darkened in anger. 'The murdering swine ought to be hung, every last one of them. Blast their stinking hides!'

Bartleet's mouth set in a harsh line. 'Your conduct at the scene of the riot, Captain Mence, does not really entitle you to dictate the punishment.'

'What do you mean by that?' the other blustered.

The Colonel's voice was a whiplash.

'I mean, sir, that you behaved like a coward. You turned tail and fled from the field. If you had been in Banastre Tarleton's Legion, as I was, he would have shot you with his own hand.'

'Who accuses me of running?' Mence shouted. 'My horse bolted out of control ... I'll call out and kill the man who calls me a coward.'

'In that case, sir, you will be fighting duels with every man, woman and child in this town,' Bartleet snapped contemptuously. 'You are no longer welcome at my home, Mence, and in future you will cease paying your addresses to my daughter.'

'And suppose I don't choose to stop courting Miss Bartleet?' Mence sneered.

'Then you will answer to me personally.' Bartleet was icily calm. 'I do assure you that my wrist is still supple enough to handle a rapier, and my eyes and hand steady enough to sight a pistol. Do I make myself clear?'

The younger man muttered angrily, but made no audible reply.

'Very well!' The Colonel flicked the whip at his horse's rump. 'I bid you good day, sir.'

The horse jerked forward and the gig rolled on, leaving John Mence glowering sullenly after its occupant.

CHAPTER EIGHTEEN

Jethro sat alone in his darkened cottage. More than a week had passed since the riot and for Jethro it had been worse even than those dreadful days at Ely. For the hundredth time he read the bold print of the handbill that lay on the table in front of him.

'Wanted for Murder.
Peter Stanton, Needle Pointer
John Batten, Gamekeeper.'

Underneath was a description of the two men and of the crime. At the bottom of the bill in large letters was the promise ... 'A reward of 200 Guineas each is offered for the capture of the murderers. Signed. Clement Washford. Chairman. Needle Masters Association.'

'Damn your black hearts!' Jethro muttered. 'You've condemned my father without even giving him a chance to defend himself.'

A soft tapping at the door attracted his attention. Warily he moved to one side of the doorway and asked, 'Who is it?'

There was no reply. For some moments Jethro waited, listening intently. He had good reason to be cautious, he had already been questioned repeatedly by the magistrates about his father's whereabouts, and although Charles Bartleet had accepted his denials of any such knowledge, others among the gentry had not. Threats had been made and Jethro knew that men like John Mence were capable of bringing in hired bullies to see if information could be beaten out of him. He asked again, 'Who is it knocking? I'll not unbar the door until I know.'

'Please let me in. Quickly! Before I'm seen here.'

Jethro stiffened in surprise, the voice was that of a young

girl. He unbarred the door and opened it. A slim figure, head and shoulders swathed in a shawl, slipped into the room even before the door was fully open. Jethro looked outside, the street was empty. He closed and re-barred the door before turning to his visitor. When he did, his heart leapt. Abigail Bartleet stood by the rough wooden table, the shawl which had hidden her lustrous black hair now draped about her shoulders. She smiled at Jethro's surprise, and although she was flushed and flustered, her voice, when she spoke, was clear and unafraid.

'I felt that I must come to see you.'

Jethro recovered from his shock, and stepped nearer to her until they were only inches apart. He smiled down at the perfect oval of her face, his whole being was suffused with deep happiness.

'Would you think me a fool if I told you that from the very first instant of our meeting I knew ... that some day you would be a wife to me?' he asked her.

For a moment Abigail was silent. Then she laughed delightedly. 'What a match it would be! A match to set tongues wagging all over the county.'

Her gaiety was infectious, and Jethro laughed with her.

'We shall be able to tell our children that the first time we met, our marriage was decided.'

'They would hardly believe us,' she whispered breathlessly. 'Although I know that I am not quite sane, Jethro, yet I had hoped that you were both sane and sensible.'

'Until I saw you, I was,' he told her, then his face became serious and gently he touched his lips to her cheek. She flushed again, and, lifted her hands to take his face between them, gazing searchingly at him.

'Do you really love me, Jethro, and wish to marry me?' she asked softly.

He nodded. 'I love you and some day I shall marry you,' he said with conviction. 'No matter that at this moment there are obstacles that stand like mountains between us, yet I know, as if God himself had told me, that some day we shall marry.'

'I too feel it,' she told him. 'I seem to have known all my life that I should find you. Do you think that strange?'

'No!' he said passionately. 'It is not strange to me. How can it be, when I have the same feeling? My father once told me that when he was in India the wise men there believed that men and women lived many lives in different centuries and different lands; and that those who loved deeply enough were destined to meet again in every incarnation, because the love they bore each other was a bond too strong ever to be broken. Since I saw you that day in Doll Greenaway's house, I have known that those Indian wise men spoke the truth.'

She drew his head down and, at first shyly, then avidly, kissed his lips, his cheeks, his throat while he gently caressed her arms and shoulders and her slender waist.

His passion mounted and quietly he led her with him into the bedroom. There on his narrow cot they kissed again, and his hands began to roam across her soft rounded thighs. At first she responded eagerly to his hungry searching, but when he gently pushed her down upon the bed and attempted to make her fully his, she struggled violently, thrusting him from her.

'No Jethro! No!' She rolled from the bed and stood facing him, her colour high, breathing in short frightened gasps.

'But why not?' Jethro could not understand her reluctance.

Abigail stared at him with beseeching eyes, then buried her face in her hands and began to sob bitterly. Instantly remorse and shame overwhelmed him.

'Oh Abi! What a blackguard I am ...' He rose from the bed and went to her, gently cradling her head against his chest. 'There, my heart, there, my love. Do not weep ... I love you truly ... Do not weep.'

Her sobs slowly stilled and she grew calmer. Jethro felt great pulsebeats of emotion surging through his entire being; he was no stranger to a woman's body, but never had he experienced before the contentment and the sense of fulfilment that he felt as he held her now.

Abigail lifted her head and smiled at him. 'Are you happy, Jethro?'

He leant to kiss her. 'If I were to die at this moment,' he said in deep seriousness, 'then I would be able to say to God that he had never given to any other man such happiness as he has given to me this day.'

'You make me feel the most adored woman who has ever lived,' she told him.

'I think that in all truth you may well be,' he said soberly. 'For if I were to lose you, then I should be no longer a man . . .'

Before Abigail returned to her home, they discussed the future.

'I've lost my employment,' Jethro told her. 'And while my father stands accused of murder it's unlikely that any master in this district will give me work.'

'I will speak to my father,' Abigail said, eagerly. 'I'm sure that he will help you.'

'No, sweetheart,' he said. 'For the time being it's not important. I have enough money saved to live on for a while. No, the first thing I must do is to find my father, it may well be that he doesn't even know he is being sought for this crime.'

'I know that he is innocent.' The girl was vehement. 'It is not possible that someone of yours could do such a thing.'

Jethro took her hands in his and said, 'I swear to you that Peter Stanton could not so much as think of committing a murder. He is a fine and noble person. I believe that if he knew what had happened, he would return here and face his accusers.'

'You are forgetting something, dearest,' Abigail told him sadly. 'Your father is a self-proclaimed Luddite. If he were to come back and prove his innocence of murder, then he would still be arrested and perhaps hung for being known as General Ludd.'

'I had not forgotten,' Jethro answered. 'I know only too well that he could hang,' he finished bitterly.

'I must go now,' Abigail said. 'And listen, Jethro. You must do whatever you feel is the right thing. I know that for the time being that which is between us must be secret, but I also know that some day we shall be able to speak openly of how we love each other.'

Jethro kissed the loving dark eyes. 'Some day, my heart,' he whispered. 'We'll go to the fair, and you shall wear my fairing and show the whole world that you are my true love.'

Gently he arranged the shawl over her hair, half-hiding her face.

'Goodbye love,' he said. 'Trust me.'

'I do,' she replied simply.

Then she was gone, and only the sweet scent of her youth remained with Jethro in the still, darkened room.

CHAPTER NINETEEN

The hot days of the summer passed and slowly the wounds left on the face of the town by the riot were healed. The burnt-out shops and houses were rebuilt, the shattered doors and windows repaired, the barrels of ale and cider refilled, the flasks of gin and rum replenished. An ornate headstone, paid for by popular subscription, marked the grave of Mrs Tread-gold and the surface cuts and bruises of the volunteers and rioters had disappeared. Some of them, it was true, still suffered in various ways, but all agreed that it was God's mercy that no one had died, except for the woman. Trade improved and, led by Charles Bartleet, the gentry and masters tried to bring in a supply of cheaper food and grain.

Life had returned to outward normality, which meant that men and women worked a ten to fourteen hour day in the mills and factories, and children of eight years, in some cases even younger, were taken from school and play, and set to labour at the 'soft' work. The more fortunate people were the self-employed in their cottage workshops who at least received their payment in coin of the realm. The millhands and factory workers were paid in company tokens, issued by the manufacturers, which had to be spent at the company truck shops and alehouses, high prices for shoddy goods.

Saturday was payday and Saturday night was for the majority an orgy of drinking and fighting. Children hung about the doors of the alehouse and watched with enjoyment the drunken antics of their elders. When the alehouses closed, women either screamed and wept under a rain of kicks and blows or lay in fuddled stoic acceptance while their drink-sodden menfolk eased their hungers on their childworn bodies.

On Sundays, the Wesleyans went to their chapels morning,

127

afternoon and night to renew their covenant with God. A curate rode over from Tardebigge Parish Church to minister to the Anglicans at St Stephens, while the few Catholics in the district made their own arrangements. For the swarms of the ungodly, Sunday meant the long lie in bed until, if a man was lucky enough to have some money left, he would once more join his mates in the alehouse and there spend the remaining hours of his precious freedom.

Sometimes there were other entertainments. Cock-throwing, badger-baiting, dog-fighting, prize-fighting, bull-baiting and cock-fights were frequent, while travelling fairs and strolling players occasionally came bumping up the hilly town approaches in their gaily painted wagons. Twice a year, the grand fairs were held, the Horse Fair at the beginning of August and the Hiring Fair the week before Michaelmas, when the farmworkers and servants would journey to Redditch to find fresh masters and enjoy themselves. As Peg Whittington said, 'Life's hard, but you 'as to take your fun wheer you finds it ...'

'Knives Oooohh ...! Who'll buy knives? Sheffield knives! Finest knives!'

The pedlar's shouts echoed along the street, and Sammy Merry, a labourer in Bartleet's needle mill, stopped his work to listen. Merry, a squat gnomelike figure, grinned and ran to the pointing shop which occupied the ground floor at the end of the courtyard.

'Tom!' he shouted. 'Quick! There's a packman coming up the road.'

Tom Bright lifted the needles he was dry-grinding and touched the points. Satisfied, he laid them in the workbasket at his side and pulled the protecting rags from his mouth.

'Goo and get him, Sammy,' he shouted back. 'We'll 'av us a bit o' fun.'

Merry waved his hand and capered out into the road.

The pedlar, a dark tough-looking gypsy, wearing velvet clothes and a wide-brimmed slouch hat, his pack of wares strapped to his back, was leant against the mill wall, puffing at a broken-stemmed clay pipe.

' 'Ere, gippo,' Merry beckoned him. 'Cummon in 'ere. Me mates wants to see your knives.'

The gypsy grinned at the ragged little man. 'They'm the

128

best knives that ever come out of Sheffield, little master, are you sure your mates can afford to pay for them?'

Merry spat upon the ground. 'If you don't want to sell, then bollocks to you!' he growled.

The gypsy laughed at his display of temper. 'All right, master, lead on,' he said, and followed the little man into the courtyard.

In doorways and leaning from windows, the millhands were watching expectantly. The pedlar felt a sense of unease then mentally shrugged it away and went with Merry to where Tom Bright and a crowd of pointers stood waiting at the entrance to their workshop.

'Let's 'ave a look at what you'm selling, gippo,' Tom Bright shouted.

The pedlar smiled ingratiatingly, showing good white teeth. 'No offence meant, master, but let's see the colour of some rhino. These knives are the finest and they comes dear.'

Bright laughed. 'Bugger me! You'm a hard-necked un, an't you,' he swore, and pulled out a handful of silver coins from his pocket. 'There now, you saucy bugger, will that buy one of your knives?'

The pedlar's smile widened. 'May God bless you, master, and may you be lucky and have seven fine sons, for I see that you're a true gentleman.'

Dexterously he swung his pack from his shoulders to the ground in front of him. His nimble fingers loosened straps and in seconds an array of knives were laid out on strips of velvet.

'Here's a fine shiny bright working knife for a fine shiny bright working man.' The gypsy half-sang the patter, demonstrating first one knife then another, turning and twisting the blades causing them to shine in the sunlight.

The pointers waited until there was a pause in the rapid patter then a couple of them picked up knives and enquired, 'What does this one cost?'

When they heard the price, they threw down the knives in disgust.

'Too bloody dear by far, pedlar,' one snarled.

The gypsy persisted in his efforts to make a sale and concentrated on Tom Bright.

'Come on, master ... Here! Look at this for a fine kitchen knife, I could get five shillings for this easy. But because I likes the look of you, then I'm agoing to let you have it for two shillings only ... Come now, master ... only two shillings ... What do you say?'

Tom Bright held his hand out. 'Give it here, gippo, let me have a look at it.'

He took the knife and turned it in his large work-scarred hands.

'There, master, an't that a fine blade? An't it a beauty?' the gypsy urged. 'Fit for the King's kitchen, so it is, and I'll tell you what I'll do ... You can have it for eighteen pennies ... One shilling and sixpence ... How does that sound, master?'

Bright grinned wickedly at the pedlar. 'I reckon it sounds as if you'm trying it on, gippo,' he said. 'Why, this knife is just a bit of tin.'

The pedlar tried to placate him. 'Now master, I know you're only joking. That's a fine Sheffield blade, that is. It's not tin.'

Deliberately Bright held the end of the blade in one hand and the haft in the other. He gave a sudden jerk, grunting with effort and the blade snapped in half. He brandished the broken pieces under the pedlar's nose. 'No, gippo, it's not tin, it don't bend. But it an't steel neither.'

Before the man could react to this, half a dozen other knives were snatched up and broken by the men around him.

'You'm a bloody cheapjack, you am!' one man bellowed in mock indignation.

'Ahr, coming here to take the money away from poor silly chaps like us for rubbish like this,' his mate shouted.

The pedlar's temper flared. 'You dirty bastards!' he hissed, and whipped out a curved dagger from under his jacket. 'I'll cut your tripes out,' he threatened.

'Gippo!' A shout from above made him look up. As he did so a deluge of filthy liquid grease cascaded over him. From the windows above, the women hurled bucket after bucket full of the stinking waste dotment, while the pointers scattered hooting with laughter. Blinded by the grease, the pedlar struck futile blows at the empty air with his dagger, until one of the pointers knocked it from his hand with a billet of wood. Another pointer ducked under the swinging arms and tripped the pedlar, sending him rolling across the ground. Roaring with enjoyment the men grabbed the gypsy by his hands and feet and dumped him head-first in a butt of rainwater. The sight of the furiously kicking legs protruding from the top of the butt caused the whole millyard to erupt in an explosion of delight.

The uproar brought Owen Treadgold running from his office to see what was happening.

'What's going on here? And who is that man?' he shouted.

'It's a bloody cheapjack, gaffer,' a woman screeched.

Treadgold looked at the kicking legs and began to laugh. He waved his arms. 'Get him out before he drowns.'

Led by Tom Bright, two or three men pushed the barrel on to its side, the water gushed across the yard and splashed Treadgold's shoes.

'Get that man out of the mill this instant,' he shouted in sudden annoyance.

Sammy Merry had a fresh idea. 'Somebody get a hammer and nails. We can send his lordship away in style, in his own carriage.'

Before the half-drowned pedlar could crawl from the barrel his legs were stuffed inside and slats of wood were nailed across the open top. Jeering and shouting, the millhands trundled the barrel with the luckless man inside it across the yard and out into the street. Eager hands rolled it along, until they came to the top of a long steep slope.

Tom Bright took a deep breath and yelled, 'Have a nice journey, cully, and Godspeed.'

The barrel was carefully aimed and then pushed bouncing down the hill. Faster and faster it rolled and above the clatter of its metalled hoops on the cobbles could be heard the high-pitched screams of the pedlar. At the bottom of the hill it twisted, changed course and smashed into a wall, disintegrating on impact. The gypsy rolled away from the wreckage and lay dazed and groaning, blood seeping from a dozen cuts and grazes. The millhands gave one last thunderous cheer and returned laughing and singing to their work.

Jethro was strolling aimlessly down the hill when he heard the tumult and saw the barrel go bouncing past him. By the time he reached the bottom of the slope, a crowd of small children had gathered and were amusing themselves by throwing stones and mud at the prostrate man. At first Jethro started to walk on past, roughly handled cheapjacks were a common sight in Redditch. But then he heard the man groan in pain as a stone hit him and he turned to help. After chasing the children away, Jethro knelt by the pedlar.

'Any bones broken, cully?' he asked.

The man gingerly moved his arms and legs then shook his head. 'No, master, leastways I don't think so.'

'You'd best come to my house and get cleaned up. They've made a proper mess of you,' Jethro told him.

When they reached the cottage, Jethro busied himself lighting a fire and putting water to heat. The pedlar squatted by the fire, shivering with the after-effects of his ordeal. He held out his hands to the warmth.

'By God! I thought those mad buggers would do for me,' he said.

'Here!' Jethro gave him a glass of rum. 'Drink this, it'll make you feel better.'

The man's gratitude showed without words as he gulped the liquor.

'Ahh! That's good, that is ... really good. Tell me, master? Do they always treat the travelling people like they served me today?'

'Sometimes,' Jethro told him. 'You were foolish to let a bunch of pointer lads get you inside the mill like that.'

The man's spirit was returning, aided by the rum. He grinned and said, 'I know now that it was daft, master, but this is the first time I've been in this part of the world. Normally I travels the Welsh country. You don't earn much rhino with the farming Welsh, but at least they don't try to kill a man if they don't like his wares.'

'What brings you here then?' Jethro asked.

'Oh, I'm by way of doing a favour for a friend,' the man replied vaguely, and stared into the fire.

Jethro took the hint and did not press the question. He gave the pedlar more rum and they sat in companionable silence until the pot of water hanging over the fire was boiling. Jethro took the pot and emptied the water into a wooden tub. He fetched cold water and topped the tub up, then handed the man a strip of rough towelling.

'Here, get yourself cleaned up. I've some clothes here that will fit you well enough, those that you're wearing are ruined. While you're washing, I'll get a bite of food ready.'

132

'By God, master, you'm a friend in need all right.' The pedlar grinned and, stripping off his grease-soaked clothing, he noisily ducked himself in the tub.

Afterwards, cleansed of blood and filth and dressed in some of Peter Stanton's clothes, the gypsy sat and shared Jethro's supper of bread, cheese and onions, washed down with ale. Satisfied, he leant back in his chair and belched loudly.

'That was good, master,' he said, smiling. 'And I want you to know that Solly Lee, that being my name, will never forget your kindness.'

Jethro nodded. 'Don't speak of it,' he said quietly. 'Hayhap some day you'll be able to do the same thing for me.' He looked out of the tiny window. 'It's getting dark. If you wish, you can sleep here for the night. There's a spare cot.'

The gypsy shook his head. 'Thank you kindly, master, but I must finish my business here and then head on to catch my tribe. They'm on the road to Gloucester.' He paused then went on. 'Do you know whereabouts I can find a man called Stanton ... Jethro Stanton?'

Jethro laughed aloud. 'He's sitting a yard from you, man.'

'What's your father's name?' the gypsy asked, his face impassive.

Jethro caught the question's hidden connotation. 'Well,' he said slowly, 'he's known as Peter, but at the moment in this town they call him Ned Ludd. I'm told the Romanies call him Peter the Friend.'

'Ahr, that's right,' the man replied. 'But begging your pardon, young master, and I mean no offence ... What are the names of your Mam and your sister? And where are they now?'

'I had two sisters, not one,' Jethro told him. 'My mother's name was Rachel and my sisters were Sarah and Ruth. They all lie in the potters' field at Ely.'

'Well, that's a lucky thing in finding you this way, Master Jethro,' the man grinned. 'I've got a message from your Da to you.'

'Where is he?' Jethro burst out. 'Is he well? What's he doing? Does he know he stands accused of murder?'

The gypsy held up his hands. 'Steady, master, I can only answer one question at a time. First, let me tell you that I've known your father for a good many years, ever since we served

133

together in John Company's Army. He was a good friend to me and he always has been, there's not many Gorgios that the Romany can say that of. Never mind that now ... I've to tell you that he's well and he's travelling in the border country, over Salop way. He was heading to Tipton for the Wakes, when I saw him. He didn't mention any murder, so I doubt that he knows of it.' The gypsy stood up. 'Now I must go, young master. My woman has our caravan waiting for me near here and we've a long journey ahead.'

Jethro also stood. 'Thank you for your message, Solly Lee. Do you need money or anything else for your journey?'

The man shook his head and clasped Jethro's hand.

'No thanks, Master Stanton. But I wants to tell you that the travelling people will hear about your goodness to me when I was just another cheapjack lying bleeding in the gutter. Goodbye, and may you have many fine sons.'

Alone again Jethro sat for long hours until he had decided on his course of action. Then he stretched out on his narrow cot and slept.

CHAPTER TWENTY

In the bar parlour of the Crown Inn, Jacob Stone tilted his head and drained the last dregs of brandy from the glass. He took it from his lips and sat at ease in the wooden armchair, momentarily sated. On the round table in front of him lay the remnants of a saddle of mutton; the empty dishes and bottles around it were a testimony to the prodigious appetite of the man. He wiped the grease from his mouth and chin with a soiled napkin and hammered on the table with his fist.

'Will!' he bawled. 'Send that damned slut in here.'

The fat white-haired landlord came to the serving hatch. He smiled obsequiously, running his podgy hands up and down the sides of the hatch.

'She'll only be a moment, Mr Stone, sir. She's just dealing with an order. Will you be wanting anything more, sir?'

Stone ran his tongue across the front of his teeth, sucking loudly at a shred of meat trapped there. Finally he told the landlord. 'She can bring me a quartern of gin, after she's cleared this mess ... Good London, mind you, none of your local rubbish, and make sure that I'm not disturbed.'

'Yes, Mr Stone, I'll make sure of that, sir.' The landlord bobbed his head and withdrew.

'And Will?' shouted Stone. The man popped back into the hatch frame. 'If any of my men come in, tell them to wait in the bar for me, and give them whatever they want to drink.'

The landlord bobbed his head and again disappeared. Stone relaxed and sat reflecting ... At the moment, life was sweet for Jacob Stone. His mother a prostitute, and his father any one of a hundred men, he had entered the world one stifling hot June night in the very midst of the Gordon Riots. His mother had given birth prematurely, lying in a Moorfields gutter, out of her mind with gin while the gimcrack houses of Irish labourers burned fiercely around her. Somehow Jacob Stone had survived his birth, just as he had survived as an infant disease, starvation and cold. In the brothels and thieves' kitchens of St Giles, he spent his childhood and at the age that other children were lisping over their first lessons, he had already mastered his, and was an adept and hardened thief. By his twelfth birthday he was acting as pimp and bully to ten-year-old whores, and by the time he was fifteen he knew all that could be known of vice and depravity.

His body grew tall and strong and his intelligence and worldly cunning kept pace with his body. He soon realized that the path he was on led only to transportation or the gallows, even if he managed to survive the savage brawls, the treacherous knife thrusts and the gaol fevers that decimated the criminal ranks. So, at eighteen he changed his alliances and became a professional informer and thief-taker, acting in concert with the Bow Street Runners and magistrates. From this he graduated into still higher fields and now, under the office of the Home Secretary, Lord Sidmouth, he was an agent of the government, 'a provocation man', employed to spy on, hunt down and provoke into actions leading to their own destruction all political enemies of the State. He felt no great personal animosity for his present quarries, the Luddites and their counterparts. To him they were merely another species who inhabited the hostile jungle of life in which survival went to the fittest; and at thirty-odd years of age Jacob Stone, whose favourite jest was that he was the bastard son of a riot, was one of the very fittest. Tough, intelligent and fearless, he was a formidable opponent for those who cared to challenge him.

He smiled to himself and blessed the good fortune that had brought Owen Treadgold to him. Stone was already benefiting from his hold over the inventor, a tidy supplement to his income was assured for the future and he wasn't prepared to show any mercy to anyone who might pose a threat to Treadgold, such as Stanton and Batten.

The small serving-girl came into the parlour to clear the table. Stone watched her working and lust tightened his loins. This was his one serious weakness, an uncontrollable desire for very young girls. He reached out and drew her to him, one large hand rested warningly around the thin childish throat while the other lifted her skirts and cruelly mauled and kneaded the immature flanks and buttocks and the private recesses of her slender body. She opened her mouth to protest but he tightened his grip on her throat and she remained silent in fear.

He clamped his mouth on hers, his tongue probing between her soft lips. Her squirming attempts to pull away only served to increase his excitement. He got to his feet lifting her with him and pushed her down across the edge of the table, fumbling with his breeches and using his thick thighs and trunk to force her thin legs astraddle. Then, mouth still clamped on hers, gazing straight into the wide terrified eyes of the girl, he brutally thrust into her. Her screams of pain and horror were stifled by his searching tongue and her fragile body could not fight off his animal strength.

When he had satisfied his lust, he took a golden guinea from his pocket and held it for her to see while he covered her mouth with his hand, smothering the sobs.

'There now, my pretty,' he whispered. 'This is for you if you're a good girl. Listen to what I say very careful now. If you speak of what's happened here between us, then I'm going to break your neck ... Believe me!' He released her.

Between her sobs she told him. 'I'll say nothing, sir. I promise on my mother's grave, I'll say nothing. Only let me go now ... please let me go.'

'Good!' He smiled at her. 'You know my room, don't you?'

Mutely she nodded.

'Well, you'll come there tonight after the inn closes.' He grabbed her throat once more. 'You'd better come,' he said threateningly.

She nodded, too afraid even to speak.

'Good girl!' He grinned and released her. 'When you come tonight I'll give you this gold guinea. That's a promise.'

He lifted himself from her body and rearranged his clothes. When he spoke again, his voice was harsh.

'Now clear this mess up and bring me my quartern of gin, and be quick about it, or I'll kick your arse through the top of your head, you little trollop.'

CHAPTER TWENTY-ONE

The night after his talk with the gypsy, Jethro went to the Bartleets' home. He stood beneath the shadow of the trees that surrounded the house and watched for a sight of Abigail. He saw a maid come into the drawing-room and light the lamps, then Abigail and her sister came into the room and sat facing each other. Anne busied herself with embroidery while Abigail leafed idly through the pages of a book. Jethro waited patiently, happy to be this close to his loved one, happy to watch the play of emotion on her expressive features; even her petulant frown, as she closed the book and dropped it carelessly on the floor, he found charming.

He marvelled afresh to himself that this beautiful girl should have given her love to him. It was like a passage from Lord Byron's poems, he thought. The love of a highborn lady for a baseborn peasant. He chuckled at his fancies.

The room door opened and Charles Bartleet entered. He spoke to the girls and they both went to him, he kissed them and left the room. Jethro heard the hooves ringing on the cobbled yard as the boy Abram led the Colonel's horse to the front entrance. The Colonel mounted and spurred out of the driveway, not noticing the man crouched in the undergrowth as he cantered past. When the hoofbeats died away, Jethro resumed his vigil.

At last he was rewarded. Anne took her embroidery and left Abigail alone in the room. Quickly but stealthily, Jethro moved from the shadows and crossed to the window. He tapped on the glass and called softly, 'Don't be alarmed, sweetheart, it's me, Jethro.'

Apprehension changed to delight on Abigail's face and she ran to open the casement.

'Jethro.' She kissed him eagerly, running her fingers through his thick hair and over his muscled neck and shoulders.

Gently he held her away from him. 'I've come to say good-bye for a time, sweetheart,' he told her, his voice low. 'I must go to my father right away.'

Her eyes were worried. 'How long will you be gone?'

'Only a few days,' he assured her. 'Don't worry, my love, I won't be parted from you any longer than I have to.'

She kissed him again. 'Take care, Jethro ... take care, my love. Tell me where you are going so that I can imagine myself there with you.'

He smiled at her intensity. 'I'm going to a place called Tipton. It's in Staffordshire, across in the Black Country. Listen!' He paused. 'I think someone's coming ... Goodbye, my love.' One hurried kiss, and he broke away and ran back to the shadows to melt from her view.

She stayed at the window, her face a study of serene content. She hugged herself.

'It's so romantic,' she told herself. 'Like a novel about doomed tragic lovers.'

Upstairs, in the bedroom which was directly above the window, Anne heard the voices from below. She went to the window and looked out just as Jethro ran back across the lawn. The moon moved from behind the clouds as he ran and she recognized him. Her lips tightened in anger and she ran downstairs.

In the drawing-room, Abigail was gazing contentedly out at the moonlit night. Anne grasped her sister by the arm and swung her round to face her.

'Are you truly mad?' she shouted. 'Keeping lovers' trysts with that Luddite's son? Do not deny it, I know that you have been doing so for weeks now.'

Abigail flushed deeply and she answered defiantly, 'No, I am not mad. I love him and he loves me. Some day we shall marry.'

Anne's hand flashed out to strike the girl's cheek.

'You little fool!' she stormed. 'You don't know what love means. For you it is moonlight and forbidden passions, Sir Lancelot and Queen Guinevere. What in Heaven's name possesses you that you should imagine yourself to be in love with a labouring man; and if that were not bad enough, you choose to weave your silly foolish dreams about the son of a rebel and murderer.'

Tears welled out of Abigail's eyes. 'He is not a murderer's son,' she protested. 'He's fine and good and could well be of noble birth. It has happened before that a nobleman masquerades as a beggar. History is full of such happenings.'

Anne was scathing. 'There you are again, talking like a retarded imbecile, a serving girl who listens to trashy broadsheets and believes them ...' She paused then attacked from another angle. 'And pray tell me, what has become of the grand passion that you had for the gallant Captain Mence?'

Abigail's face became ugly in temper. 'You're hateful!' she screamed. 'You try to spoil all my love affairs ... You're jealous, that's all! Just a jealous old maid! You wait until Jethro returns from Tipton, I shall elope with him ... That is what I shall do, and you may all go to the devil!'

Anne's anger died away. She shook her head sadly and regarded her lovely sister with something close to pity. She was her father's daughter, while Abigail was her mother's and possessed in full measure all the flightiness and immaturity that her mother had shown.

'What do you think would happen if I told father about this new love of your life?' Anne asked quietly.

Abigail tossed her glossy black hair. 'You may do as you wish,' she snapped petulantly. 'But I know that I shall always love Jethro Stanton, and if I am prevented from marrying him, then I shall die ... Yes, that's it! I shall die. Then you will all be sorry for your cruel treatment of me.'

'I shall not tell father,' Anne said wearily. 'But let us hope and pray that he does not find out for himself.'

'I do not care if he does,' Abigail shouted, and flounced from the room.

Anne could not help but smile. 'I know you too well, miss,' she murmured. 'By this time next month you will imagine yourself to be madly in love with Napoleon Bonaparte.'

She followed her sister up to their bedroom.

In the corridor below, still hidden behind the door from where she had listened to what the sisters had said, the parlour maid quietly repeated to herself what she had heard. 'It'll be worth a few shillings from Captain Mence,' she murmured.

CHAPTER TWENTY-TWO

Jethro set out for Tipton on the Friday night. He waited until the town was still and quiet, all the alehouses closed and the last drinker safely in bed and asleep. The night was wild and windy and the July moon rode through stormy seas of cloud. All through the night he strode over the rutted roads, through Bromsgrove and Halesowen, past the workshops of the Cradley chain-makers and over the line of the Netherton Tunnel, until in the early hours of Saturday morning he saw the ruined walls of Dudley Castle towering above him on its limestone crag. He climbed the hill and fumbled his way into the castle keep. There he lay down, pillowing his head on the small canvas bag he carried and fell into a deep sleep.

When he awoke, the sun was high and, feeling hungry and thirsty, he made his way down the hill into the town. After slaking his thirst from a horse trough, he bought bread and cooked sausage from a stall and, munching happily, continued on his way.

The afternoon wore on and the road to Tipton grew busier and more crowded with people heading towards the town for the wakes. Wagons, carriages, farmcarts loaded with people and produce, all driving in the same direction. On foot, gangs of coal-blackened colliers, smoke-grimed nailers, clay-stained navvies with red neckscarves, pushed, jostled and sky-larked with the young men and girls who were dressed in all their bits of finery, embroidered shawls and aprons. Arrogant yeomanry cavalrymen forced their thoroughbred hunters through the throng, while dotted here and there the blue, red and green uniforms of the humbler foot volunteers could be seen, walking with the mass.

Jethro sat on a convenient garden wall to rest and watch the passing scene. He spotted a troupe of gypsies leading shuffling dancing bears, and a haycart passed with a blind fiddler sitting perched on top of the load playing a sea-shanty. A tap on the shoulder made him look round.

'Hello, young Jethro, am you gooin' to Tipton Wakes?' It was a man from Redditch.

'Hello, Will. Yes, I'm going to find a friend there.'

'Ahr, it ull take a deal o' lookin'.' The man laughed and went on towards Dudley.

Jethro sat on and after a time there came a rattle of drums and the shrilling of fifes from the distance. Dragoons mounted on huge black chargers came cantering along the road leading from Tipton. They swung scabbarded sabres as they rode and shouted, 'Clear the way, goddam you! Clear the way!'

Jethro stood up to watch the drum and fife band come into view, followed by officers on horseback leading files of scarlet, white and gold uniformed men. The road in front of the band cleared and the crowds pressed each side to see the spectacle of a marching regiment. The drums thudded past and the fifes shrilled out the tune, 'Over the Hills and Far Away'. The crowd sang the words of the old song as the band passed.

> *'Oh, it's over the hills and over the plain,*
> *To Flanders, Portugal and Spain,*
> *The King commands and we'll obey,*
> *Over the hills and far awaaayyy.'*

'Three cheers for the lobsters,' a collier bellowed, and the crowd roared the hurrahs. The soldiers marching past jeered and whistled, winking at the women and making lewd gestures with their fingers.

'They'm off to America,' an excited man shouted in Jethro's ear. 'That's our kid's regiment and they'm off to America to give the bloody Yankees a kick up the arse.'

'Don't talk like a fule!' a collier told the man. 'They'm away to Spain to fight the French, we ben't fightin' the Yankees now. That wor all finished years sin.'

'Hah!'. The first man snatched a scrap of newspaper from his pocket and flourished it under the collier's nose. 'That just goes to show how stupid and ignorant you bloody pitmen are. Read this, if you knows how to, and I doubt that you does ... We bin at war wi' them Yankee sods sin the end o' June.' He laughed in triumph at the collier's discomfiture.

'Still, let um all come, that's what I says. We'em the lads to gie it to um. Sod the whole bloody boiling lot o' the foreigners!'

The collier grew indignant. 'A fat lot yow'd gie any bogger, blubber guts! I know who yow bist now. You keeps the tommy shop for the anchor works at Netherton.'

'So what?' the man challenged.

'So this!' the collier shouted, and hit the shopkeeper squarely in the jaw, sending him reeling into the ranks of marching troups. They immediately grabbed him and began to tumble and twist him along with them, laughing at his frantic attempts to break free from the scarlet lines. The last Jethro saw of him was his upraised arm, still frantically waving the scrap of newspaper, being borne helplessly along in a sea of black shakoes and long bayonets.

When the last troops had passed, a crowd of exhausted-looking women followed in their wake. Many carried babies in their arms while weeping infants clung to their long skirts and were dragged along. The collier who had hit the shop-keeper turned and spoke to Jethro.

'Poor boggers!' he swore. 'It's the women and nippers I feels sorry fower. Theer's no glory for them when they follows the drum, only a lot o' grief an' pain.'

Jethro nodded and walked on to Tipton Wakes.

The market square was a boiling crowd; pushing, jostling, surging around. Stalls and booths of all types were erected in long lines, and the gaily painted caravans and carts of the fair people cluttered up the surrounding streets. Jethro decided to stroll around and see the sights. The Wakes did not begin, traditionally, until the following day, Sunday, but already everything was in full swing. Cheapjacks and packmen wheed-led and heckled the crowds to buy their wares; showmen stood on platforms outside their wood and canvas booths and boasted of the marvels to be seen behind the garishly decorated facades.

A long blast from a post-horn followed by a tattoo on a kettle drum attracted Jethro's attention. The musician was a little man dressed in the flowing black robe and tapered coni-cal hat of a mediaeval wizard, complete with gold and silver tinselled zodiacal signs. He capered about in front of a large pantechnicon with two donkeys slouched dejectedly in its shafts. Jethro joined the throngs pressing about the van. On its side he saw painted in large yellow letters the words 'Doctor Dick's Antilocapharmacuragoria.'

The little man blew another blast on the horn, then put the instrument on one side with the drum and mounted the crude plank and barrel platform in front of the yellow sign and sang out in a high-pitched tuneful voice:

> 'I'm Doctor Dick, who comes quick,
> I have a pill, cures every ill,
> It cures bad temper, and empty pockets,
> Who'll try it, who'll try it, who'll try it?'

The onlookers laughed and applauded noisily, Jethro joining in. On the platform was an upright stall lined with shelves crammed with medicines, tonics, boxes of pills, powders, lozenges, and turkey rhubarb, herbs and twisted roots, but pride of place was held by a giant glass jar packed solidly with a writhing, churning mass of red, black, grey, white, brown and green worms.

'Lissen to me, and I'll tell thee a tale,' Doctor Dick sang, and the crowd hushed, craning forward to hear the quack's patter. He lifted a box of sickly looking yellow pills and took one from it. Holding it between black-nailed finger and thumb, he displayed it to his audience.

'Dost thee see it?' he demanded. 'Dost thee see it? Answer me, blast you!'

'Ahr, we con see it,' the crowd bawled in unison.

The little quack grinned at them, looking like a red-faced monkey, his minute button nose flattened in his face and his ears tiny and tight to his wispy-haired head.

'Well, if thee con see it, thee doon't need it,' he cackled. 'Cos it's a pill that makes the blind for to see.'

'Boo! Gerroff!' the crowd hissed, and abused him in great good humour.

With a flourish Doctor Dick lifted another pill, this time coloured purple, and displayed it in the same manner.

'Dost thee see it? Dost thee see it? Answer me, blast you!'

'Ahr, we con see it,' the crowd rejoined.

'Well, open thy bloody lugs and lissen.' The quack waved both arms above his head. 'Larst week, a little gel in Warwick was cured o' the consumption by two boxes o' these 'ere pills.'

'Be that jannock?' a hulking collier questioned.

144

The quack drew himself majestically to his full height of five feet. 'Dost thee dare to doubt the word o' Doctor Dick?' he challenged.

'Ahr, that's about the strength on it,' the collier told him.

'Shut thy gob!'

'Goo on about thee business!'

'Aye, put a rock in thy 'ole, afore we does it for thee!'

The crowd turned on the collier, resenting his interruption. The man subsided into silence and the little quack swaggered on the platform, arrogant in victory.

'Cummon, Dicky!'

'Ahr, cummon. Tell us the story.'

The little man glared in triumph at the embarrassed collier, then shouted, 'The bloody surgeon towld the gel thit her left lung was gone. Then he towld her that her right un was gone. So when her come to me, her'd got no bloody lungs at all ... I gi'ed her a box o' these pills, and does you know, in a week her left lung come back. So I gi'ed her another box, and does you know, may God strike me dead if I lies, in a week her right lung come back as well!'

Somebody in the crowd laughed raucously.

The quack took an affront. 'Did I 'ear somebody laugh? Does you not believe it? Yow con please thy bloody sen. But, when thee'st got no lungs, thee'll be pleased to come to Doctor Dick and try his pills ... bollocks to it!'

In a fit of temper, he pitched the box to the back of the stall.

'What con thee gie me to bring this loony bogger back to sense?' An old woman came forward to the platform, pushing in front of her a shambling, idiot boy.

Doctor Dick made a great show of examining the drooling, wall-eyed idiot, and then smacked one hand noisily on his thigh.

'I 'ave it!' he exclaimed. He rummaged in the depths of the stall and sorted out a mortar and pestle. Opening the jar of worms he burrowed into the squirming mass with long stained fingers and extracted several juicy specimens. He dropped them wriggling into the mortar and added powders from various boxes, then vigorously pounded the mixture into a glutinous mess.

'These 'ere worms,' he told the crowd, 'has bin specially

145

catched for me on the Isle o' Java. They cures bladder stones, gall stones, stomach stones, liver stones and stones in the bleedin' 'ead. That's what this lad 'ere has got ... a stone in 'is 'ead.'

He snatched at the idiot's lank hair and turned his head so that the boy's vacant eyes rolled at the crowd.

'Theer! Thou sees that? 'Ere, missus, howd this gormless bogger's mouth open, 'ull thee?'

The old woman did as she was bid and Doctor Dick scooped up piles of the crushed worm meat on his fingers and crammed it into the boy's gaping mouth. The idiot gulped the mess down with every appearance of enjoyment.

'Uughh!' A man next to Jethro turned and ran, retching helplessly while his neighbours scoffed at him and mouthed their pleasure.

'Ahr, that's my good lad.' The quack patted the boy's head and beamed at him benevolently. 'Thee's not so barmy, bin thou. Thee knows what's good for thee ... That's a shillin', missus,' he said to the old woman. 'And if he's not as clever as an Oxford scholar by this time next week, then bring 'im back 'ere and I'll gi' thee money back ... Is that fair?' He appealed to the crowd, who laughed and cheered him. 'Now we comes to the part that thee'st bin waitin' fower,' he went on. He lined up some bottles and poured from one a generous measure of bright red scarlet cordial into a grease-thick glass. ' 'Ere it be, me own magic Sarsaparilla. The secret recipe of which was gid to me forebears by the priests of Egypt and 'anded down from feyther to son.' He pointed at a navvy in the crowd. 'Dost thee know why Methuselah lived so long?'

The navvy grinned sheepishly and shook his head.

'Well, I'll tell thee.' Doctor Dick lifted the glass so that the sunlight sparkled on its contents. 'Methuselah lived so long becos' the King o' the 'Ebrews, Solomon 'iself, gid Methusalah this magic Sarsaparilla, brewed from the secret recipe and made wi' the holy waters o' the Sea o' Galilee.'

'What's that made wi?' Horse piss?' a man shouted.

'No! Owd Dick's piss,' another called, and the audience hooted good-humouredly.

The quack grinned and sneered. 'My owld 'ooman allus said that if thee talked long enough to donkeys, they ull answer thee, and that's proved her right, ennit?'

The crowd roared at his sally and the two hecklers retired.

'This is the stuff to put new life into thee,' Doctor Dick proclaimed, and took a long swig from the glass. 'Ahhh!' he breathed in satisfaction. 'Do thee mower good than a glass of owld ale, that ull. It'll make the owld boggers jump like Pardoes pony, and as for appetite, they'll need a truss o' hay to ate.' He glanced from under his lids at the crowd and grinned knowingly. 'Now theer's only a few bottles, so who wants to take a dram ... It's the best thing in the world for a man's third leg and your 'ooman ull not be gettin' any sleep o' nights, I can tell thee.' He winked suggestively. 'Not that they'll complain, every 'ooman likes a stallion between her legs, and that's what this stuff ull turn thee into ... Cummon then ... A tanner a dram! Who's fust?'

Many old and young men came to the platform and for a while trade was brisk. Then Doctor Dick noticed a well-dressed man scoffing at the customers. He beckoned him to the platform.

'Will thee have a dram for free, marster?' the quack offered. 'I con see that thee thinks it's not what I says it is.'

'No, I thank you,' the man refused politely.

The quack was piqued. ' 'Ave it,' he urged, 'it wunt poison thee.'

'No, thank you, I don't want it,' the man demurred once more.

The quack's face hardened. 'Thee'll ha' to 'ave it!' he shouted.

The well-dressed man shook his head. 'No, I shall not.'

'Yes, you ull! I'll make thee ... Theer!' Doctor Dick threw the liquid into the man's face. In a second the man had reached forward and, grabbing one leg of the rickety stall, he wrenched it off. Even as the stall tilted, the man, cordial streaming down his face and neck, began to sweep the contents from its shelves with the wooden spar. Boxes of pills, powders, turkey rhubarb, herbs, roots, bottles of cordial and the huge jar of worms smashed on to the ground bursting out in all directions.

'Goo on, toff!' a collier bawled encouragement.

Doctor Dick hurled himself at the destroyer of his stock-in-trade. Together they rolled across the debris, biting, punching and scratching, while the crowd, bellowing its enjoyment, scrambled to see them.

Jethro pushed clear, chuckling at what had occurred, and went on.

'Hello, my handsome, dost thee want for company?' A dark-skinned gypsy girl smiled up at him and twitched her hips provocatively. 'Dost thee want me to warm thee bed for thee ... it ull only cost thee a crown.'

Jethro smiled back. 'No thanks, my pretty "Buy a Broom", I've urgent business to attend to.'

She pulled a face and swayed on, her eyes searching for other prospects.

'Just one penny! Just one penny piece, my masters and fair pretty maids. For one penny you can see the Tallest Man in the World, and for another you can see his son, who's the Smallest,' a showman cajoled in front of his garishly illuminated booth, while at his side another offered the Original Fat Lady plus the Six-legged Pony.

'Come and buy, come and buy me before I go my way, just a paltry penny for the news of all the town.' A broadsheet seller sang into Jethro's ear.

The deep rich dark smell of hot meat pies and plump black puddings wafted from the wheeled ovens and the sharp tang of Spanish onions cut into his nostrils.

'Sithee, Isaac, look at this, the 'uman ape!'

'I doon't need to spend to see that, ower kid, I only 'as to look at you,' half-drunk nailers joked at Jethro's side. And a gang of youths suddenly enveloped him, linked arms, carrying him along with them for some paces, chorusing at the tops of their voices, 'We'em the Dudley Lads am we, clear the way 'fore we stops thy tea ...'

'Johnny? Johnny, wheer bin thee?' a distraught woman screeched for her missing child.

'Here, marsters, here's the finest cloth that e'er was wove, and I'll sell it to thee chape,' a packman offered.

'Come buy my beads and buttons, all fresh from Brummagen,' another promised.

'Stop the bogger! Stop 'im!' A runaway mule came battering through the crowds, sending men, women and children jumping cursing, squealing, drunkenly laughing from its path.

'Wilt thou buy me a fairing, Billy?'

'Ahr, that I ull, Keziah.'

A gay-smocked ploughboy and his sweetheart clung together lovingly, while from an alleyway a sharp-featured gentleman invited all and sundry to 'Find the pea, good sirs. Find the pea. Which thimble is it under? Is it there? No? Is it there? No! Ah! Here we have it ... Never mind, good sir, try again. You pays your money and takes your choice. Come now, who'll find the pea? Who'll find it?'

'Brandy snaps, loverly brandy snaps! Brandy snaps?' The old crone held a bag of her crisp oily wares under Jethro's chin. He shook his head.

'Watch who thou art pushing,' a drunken soldier threatened truculently.

'Sorry, lobster, sorry. It were an accident ... Put that bayonet away,' a respectable-looking artisan apologized.

'Jasus Moichael! ' 'Tis a long hard pull, this.'

'Faith! Ye'll not see the loike o' this ivery day though, will yea.' Irish bogmen, shillelaghs under their arms, wandered open-mouthed with their clay-pipe smoking women lugging squalling babies, while their nimble-witted city-bred brethren from Dublin, Belfast and Cork gloried in the tumult and bustle and kept sharp eyes open for the main chance.

'Roll up, roll up! See the monkey wi' the babby's face! See the Living Skeleton! ... Roll up, me bonny boys, and see the Seven Wonders o' the World!'

'You are all acurst, and shall be cast down into the bottomless pit!' a cadaverous, black-visaged, black-clothed hellfire and brimstone preacher threatened. 'Oh, ye whores of Babylon! Oh ye spawn of Sodom and Gomorrah! Repent! Repent! Turn from your sinful, evil ways before it is too late!' He ranted and raved.

'Goo on! Gie it to um!' Jeering, grime-covered colliers encouraged him.

'May God's curse fall upon all ye that mock the righteous. You, sir?' he accosted Jethro. 'Are you washed in the Blood of the Gentle Lamb?'

Before Jethro could reply, a young whore came to his side.

'Gerroff, wi ye ... You owld black crow!' she screamed at the preacher, who glared insanely at her.

'Jezebel! Scarlet woman!' he screeched.

She laughed at him and lifted her breasts until they nearly spilled from her low-cut blouse. ''Ere, black crow! Take a suck. It might sweeten yer.'

'It ud take a barrel o' treacle to sweeten that 'un,' an old man cackled.

Jethro walked on and a swarthy, tarbooshed man caught his arm, babbling promises of visions of paradise with belly-dancing houris. A small herd of cows came stumbling and slipping over the cobbles, mooing plaintively and dropping huge pats of dung whose odour filled the air, momentarily overlaying the perfumes of the women, the scented macassar oils of the dandies, the reek of beer, gin, rum and brandy, the clean fresh smell of young bodies in new linen, the stench of unwashed flesh in musty rags, the appetizing, tantalizing vapours of broiling beefsteaks, mutton chops, frying sausages, roasting pork, baking bread and piled fruits—the reeking morass of rotting ordure beneath the feet of the crowds.

'Goddam my eyes! I've been robbed. My bloody pocket's been picked, God rot me!' a rotund, puce-complexioned hunting parson shouted indignantly, the mud spattered thickly on his riding boots and breeches and the stains of spilled port wine discolouring his clerical coat.

'Well, pray to Gawd to send yer the bleedin' rhino back agen,' a cockney sneak-thief, who had marked the parson for his own prey, remarked disgruntledly.

From all sides voices assailed Jethro's ears.

'Stop thee weepin' and wailin', wench. O' course I loves thee.'

'Amos Barton? Wheer's that money you owes me?'

'You drunken useless cow! I'll larn thee thy lesson.'

'Stop gawping at that bloody wench, wilt thou, Charlie! Her's young enow to be thy daughter.'

'I wished her was, I'd show her a few tricks, I'll tell thee.'

'Yow dirty bogger!'

'Theer now, child. Is that nice?'

'Oh, bless his little face.'

'Mam, Mam, I wants a toffee apple!'

'Mammy, gis some money for a ride on the hosses.'

'Shurrup werritin'! I'll tell thee feyther.'

'Will you ...'

'Roll up! Roll up! Roll up! Just a penny piece, only a penny piece! See the Three-Legged Chinaman. See the Siamese Twins. See the Welsh Wizard. See the Irish Giant. See the English Unicorn. See the Scottish Dragon . . .'

'Look theer, Dad, they'm awrestling.'

'I'm the champion wrestler o' the kingdom and I challenges any man to the Cumberland style . . . to the Greek-Roman . . . to the Cornish . . .'

Muscled colliers, chainmakers, nailers, navvies, rushed to accept the challenges and men grunted, groaned, heaved and twisted sweatsoaked bodies and won or lost their bets.

The wooden horses of the carousel turned tirelessly round and round, the big four-armed dipper went over and over, and the seesaws and swingboats went higher and higher. Strong-men wielded mighty hammers which sent iron billets flying to ring brass bells. Drunken men spewed and groaned and wiped lips free of vomit before staggering back into the packed beer tents and taverns to fill their bellies once more. Young men bought brightly coloured fairings of ribbons and presented them gallantly to young girls who blushed and giggled and gloried in this their moment of romance . . . And all around the fairground swarmed the beggars and the fiddlers and the one-man bands. The tambourine players, the ballad singers, the tumblers, the acrobats and the children . . . Hundreds and hundreds of delighted, frightened, laughing, crying children, shrieking with joy, screaming with anguish. And in the midst of all this chaotic commotion, Jethro found his father.

CHAPTER TWENTY-THREE

Chappell's Boxing Booth was the largest sideshow at the fair and was erected in the middle of the ground, on a site best calculated to attract customers. Any objections by other stall-holders to Old Chappell taking this spot were quickly silenced by his string of boxers. When Jethro came to the booth, Chappell was haranguing the spectators gathered in front of the platform on which his six bare-chested fighters were stand-ing. They were dressed in their fighting rig of kneebreeches and stockings. They wore light dancing pumps on their feet, and a different-coloured sash was tied round each man's waist. They flexed their muscles and glowered at the crowd.

Old Chappell was almost seventy and had once been a noted fighter. Even now his leathery body was sparse and hard and he repeatedly offered to fight any man over sixty years of age in the kingdom.

Now, his battered face red and sweating with effort, he hoarsely shouted out his challenge. 'Come on, you Tipton men, who'll step up to scratch with one of my boys? Are there only women and lily-livered Nancies left in the Black Country these days? Who's got spunk enough to meet the Black Terror?' He pointed at a well-muscled Negro heavyweight, standing slightly in front of the other boxers. 'Look at him well, my buckos ... Bill Richmond! Born in Ameriky ... His patron was none other than General the Earl Percy, which noble Lord brought Bill here to England when he'd beat everything there was to beat over there ... And he's met and beat the best here as well.'

'Like who?' a man shouted.

Old Chappell grinned, showing snags of broken discoloured teeth.

'Like George Maddox, Young Powers, Ike Wood, Jack

Carter and a whole boiling of others ... that's who!' he answered.

'Ahr, but what did Tom Cribb do to 'im?' the same man shouted back.

'It took Cribb one and a half hours to beat the Black Terror,' Chappell growled. 'And let me tell you, the great Tom is not too eager to have another bout. He found Bill here a tougher nut to crack than the nigger Molineaux!'

A chorus of jeers and boos greeted this last statement.

'Goo on wi' yow! That black bugger's too old to fight any-body now,' a collier bawled. 'Tim Cribb would eat him for dinner these days.'

Richmond turned his grizzled head and glared at the pit-man. 'Ah's onny fowerty-nine,' he shouted.

The crowd hooted with laughter at the Negro's outlandish accent. Richmond's eyes reddened with murderous hate and he went to jump from the platform and tackle his tormentors, but Old Chappell and the other fighters grabbed him and held him back. Jethro was struck by the beauty of the black and white oil-gleaming bodies writhing together, the muscles standing out in sharp relief.

When the Negro quietened, Chappell turned again to the crowd. He shouted at the man standing beneath him. 'If you'll open your mouth a bit wider, cully, then I'd like the privilege of jumping down it.'

The crowd laughed its appreciation of the sally. Jethro could not see the man from where he was standing, but he heard the reply.

'You're not capable of jumping into my mouth, old man, and never was nor could be. You wasn't even a good cudgel fighter, never mind using the mauleys.'

Jethro could have sworn he recognized the rustic burr of that voice. He tried to move through the crowd to see who the man was, but the half-drunk nailers and colliers roughly resisted his efforts to make progress and he was forced to stay where he was.

Old Chappell leant over the platform railing and pointed his forefinger, stabbing the air to give emphasis to his words.

'By the look of that ugly mug o' yourn, there's bin a few men capable of shutting your gob, and if I was ten years younger I'd do it meself in two shakes of a mare's tail. If

153

you're such a fighting buck as you seem to think you are, why not try and stand up to the Black Terror for three minutes ... or haven't you got the stomach for facing a real fighting man?' He appealed to the crowd, stretching wide his arms. 'How does that sound to you, gentlemen? Let's see if Slack-mouth here can stand up to my man for three minutes? If he can, I'll give him half a crown and a glass of the finest brandy that can be bought. How does that sound to you?'

The crowd noisily applauded the suggestion.

'Oi'll do better than that!' The rustic burr was more noticeable as tempers rose. 'Oi'll fight the best man in your booth for twenty guineas stake a side. We'll fight under prize ring rules and do the job proper.'

The crowd roared approval.

Old Chappell was momentarily shaken by the challenge, but recovered himself and sneered, 'If you wants to put the mauleys up with the Terror, then you'd best show us the colour of your rhino, for he don't fight with no vagrants.'

The challenger moved up the platform steps to stand facing Old Chappell, and for the first time Jethro was able to see him. It was Batten, the keeper, bearded now and wearing the clay-covered clothes and boots of a navigator. A broad-brimmed hat was pulled down low over his eyes but there was no way of disguising the immense width of the shoulders under the rough donkey coat, or the huge fists with which he had battered young Jos Boswell. Batten held out a closed fist so that the crowd could see and slowly unclenched the thick fingers, revealing a handful of gold coins. 'There's twenty guineas there, old 'un,' he said. 'Now bring on your man.'

Chappell nodded. 'Fair enough! The Terror here will fight you. What name do you go under?'

Batten grinned. 'You can bill me as the "Battling Navvy",' he said.

The old man held up both arms for silence. When the racket died down a little, he bellowed, 'In half an hour's time, there will be a contest held here in my booth between Bill Richmond, the Black Terror, and the Battling Navvy. The stakes are twenty guineas a side. My boys will keep the ring. Anybody here knows how to read a turnip?'

A soldier held up his hand.

'Righto, lobster,' Old Chappell said. 'I'll give you a shilling and free entrance and you'll be timekeeper; and to keep it all fair and square I'll do the referee meself. Is that all right by you, navvy?'

Batten indicated his agreement.

'Have you got seconds?' Chappell asked next.

Batten nodded.

'Right you are,' the old man went on. 'You be ready in half an hour, there's a tent at the back you can strip and get ready in.' He paused only to shout, 'The pay office is now open,' then bustled to watch the old woman taking the entrance money, while his boxers went to prepare the ring and to get Richmond warmed up for the bout.

Batten stepped down from the platform and Jethro was now able to force his way through the crowd as they pressed forward to enter the booth.

Jethro smiled when he saw Batten's companion. 'Hello, father,' he said quietly.

Peter Stanton swung round, the shock on his face fast overlayed by delight. The two embraced each other, then Peter Stanton held his son away.

'Let me have a glimpse of you, boy ... yes! You're looking fine ... fine!' he said, love and pride in his voice.

Jethro grinned at the man in front of him. Dressed in the navvy rig, his face half-hidden by a beard, he looked fit and sun-tanned.

'The navvying trade suits you, Dad,' Jethro laughed.

Batten held out his hand. 'Hello, young Jethro ... Well, we meet again.'

Jethro hesitated before taking the proffered hand.

'Yes, so we do,' he answered, his voice carefully neutral.

The keeper cocked his head to one side and he regarded the young man quizzically.

'You still hold it against me for what I did to your friend, don't you?'

Jethro nodded. 'Yes, I do,' he replied evenly. 'Jos Boswell was my very good friend and you served him worse than you would have served a mad dog.'

'I know that,' Batten told him. 'And let me tell you that I didn't enjoy doing what I did to that young gippo. But I'd a part to play and I'd no choice in the matter.'

Peter Stanton intervened. 'It's true what John says, boy, and

155

don't be forgetting that the Boswells were good friends of mine also, but John had no choice. He was already under suspicion.'

'That may well be,' Jethro said stiffly. 'But it takes a lot of forgiving.'

'Ah well!' Batten sounded resigned. 'At least perhaps now you'll have a chance to come to know me better and you'll see that I'm not really such a brute ... Let us hope so.'

Peter Stanton hugged his son again. 'It's good to have you here again with me, Jethro. We've a lot to talk of, but first we've got to get this fight over and done with.'

'But why do you thrust yourselves into the forefront like this, when there are warrants sworn out for both of you?' Jethro asked.

His father smiled. 'I'm an old fox, son, and I found out long since that there's nothing so well hidden as that which stands in plain sight, if you understand my meaning. And judging by your face, you don't,' he laughed. 'Come now, and help me to second John here.'

'Don't ask the lad to do what he may not care to,' the keeper said.

Jethro considered for some moments, then said, 'I'll be happy to second you, Master Batten.'

The man's hard, battered face softened in a grin. 'Thank you, boy. But don't forget now, my name is the "Battling Navigator".'

Jethro returned the grin. 'I won't forget, Master Navvy.'

As they went to the tent at the rear, they could hear above the noise and hubbub of the fairground the touting of Chappell's barkers as they went through the crowds, broadcasting the news of the challenge match. Jethro felt a twinge of doubt.

'Do you not think that there is a risk of someone of the Fancy recognizing Master Navvy?' he asked.

'It's no use worrying about that, boy,' the fighter said, 'we need the money too badly.'

'But you've got twenty guineas!' Jethro exclaimed.

'That's not enough for our purpose, son,' Peter Stanton said grimly. 'There's good lads lying in the cells of Nottingham Castle at this moment relying on us to help them. Mayhap if we can get enough money together, we can save a few of them from the gallows.'

'Do you mean the Luddites that were captured?' Jethro questioned.

'That's right,' Batten said gravely. 'Things have been going very badly for our cause. We've lost much support. Anyway we've made contact with a couple of the turnkeys there, and for the right money they'll maybe help to get some of the lads away. If not ...' he stopped speaking, and drew his hand across his throat.

CHAPTER TWENTY-FOUR

The hammering on the door grew louder and more insistent.

'Stone? Are you deaf or dead? Open this damned door, man! I must speak with you.'

The heaped blankets on the fourposter bed in the best guest room of the Crown Inn moved abruptly, and Jacob Stone's gin-bleared eyes focused on the door.

'Who the hell wants me?' he roared.

'I do, Captain Mence, and it will be greatly to your advantage to listen to what I have to say.'

'Well, say it then,' Stone told him in a surly voice.

'Don't be a fool man! I can't bawl private matters through a locked door.'

'Oh, very well then!' The agent threw the bedcovers back disclosing the small immature body that lay beside his hairy strength. The girl whimpered in sleep and curled herself into a ball. Stone padded on bare feet across the room and, naked, opened the door to his visitor.

Ignoring Mence's surprised stare he said brusquely, 'State your business quickly, Captain Mence, for I've many matters to attend to and cannot waste time in idle chatter.'

Mence smiled sardonically and held out a heavy purse which clinked richly.

'Cannot you spare the time even to earn yourself a great deal of money, Master Stone?' he asked.

The man's manner changed immediately. 'Please to step inside, Captain Mence, sir, forgive my rudeness, but the night was a long and wild one.'

He went to the bed and, catching the girl by her ankle, he dragged her thudding on to the floor. She came awake protesting shrilly until his heel ground into her stomach, winding her. 'Cut that bloody rattle, you little slut, and get out of here,' he ordered harshly.

The girl hurriedly snatched up her clothes, holding them to shield her budding breasts from Mence's interested eyes. Then, head downcast, she scuttled from the room. Stone sat on the bed and ran his hand across his stubbled chin.

'Don't mind her, Captain,' he said casually. 'She's the serving wench here, and I've made sure she keeps a still tongue in her head when it comes to me and my affairs.'

Mence nodded. 'No matter,' he answered. He checked to see that the corridor was empty before shutting the door and coming to the bed where Stone waited.

'I've good reason to believe that Peter Stanton and Batten are at Tipton. Now this is what I want you to do,' he began.

Within the hour, Mence, Stone and the agent's men were spurring their horses towards the Black Country.

CHAPTER TWENTY-FIVE

The big marquee was packed with spectators. So dense was the crowd that only by using their knees and elbows could the Stantons clear a passageway for Batten to come to the ring, which had been set up in the centre of the hard-stamped earth floor. Around the marquee, tiers of plank-benches, now lined with excited, expectant faces, stretched up to the roof. The air was blue with tobacco smoke and thick with the stench of unwashed bodies.

Batten ducked through the ropes and rubbed his shoes on the dirt. Stripped to the waist, the crowd was able to see for the first time the enormous muscular development of the man. He really did appear to be built like a bull. Some of the knowing gamblers who stood at the ringside began to offer evens and there were many takers.

The Black Terror made his entrance, preceded by the booth boxers clearing the way. Taller than Batten, the Negro had a superbly proportioned body, but somehow seemed to lack the elemental strength of his opponent. Old Chappell came next and used his cane to draw a line in the dirt at the centre of the ring. 'My Lords and gentlemen,' he shouted hoarsely. 'This is a finish fight for stakes of twenty guineas a side between, in the blue corner ...' he pointed at the blue sash which the Negro had taken from about his waist and tied to the post, 'the Black Terror! Bill Richmond, the undefeated champion of Ameriky!'

The crowd cheered lustily.

'And in the ...' Chappell stopped speaking and peered at the unadorned post in Batten's corner. 'Where's your fogle?' he asked Batten.

A navvy standing next to the corner pulled his red kerchief from his neck and handed it through the ropes to the boxer.

'Here, matey,' he said. 'If you'm a navigator, then you'd best fight under our colours.'

'My thanks to ye.' Batten grinned, and tied the kerchief round the post to a wave of cheering from the navvies in the audience.

Old Chappell, satisfied, began again. 'And here in the red corner ... the Battling Navigator!'

'I'll give three to one in guineas on the blackie,' a prosperously dressed man shouted.

'I'll take that,' the navvy who had given the kerchief answered.

All round the ring, bets were laid and taken before Chappell shouted, 'Clear the ring!'

The seconds stepped outside the ropes.

'Come to the mark!' the old man instructed.

The two fighters advanced into the centre and each placed his left foot on the line scratched into the dirt. The crowd fell silent, and the tension grew. The fighters lifted their hands in the classic fighting stance, left fists pushed out, the right held back on the chest under the chin.

Old Chappell looked across at the soldier who was acting as timekeeper. 'Now then, lobster!' he growled.

The soldier nodded and lifted the tiny hammer to bring it down sharply on the bell he held in his other hand. 'Briiiiinnnnnggggg!'

'TIME!' the crowd roared, and the fighters stepped off in their deadly dance.

They circled each other, fists weaving, then in a black blur the Negro struck. Jethro winced as the iron-hard knuckles thudded once, twice, three times into the white body of the keeper. The force of the blows sent Batten shuffling back across the ring, the Negro went after him, his left stung the other's face and he threw a tremendous right. Batten moved his head a fraction only, to let the blow whistle harmlessly past, then he stepped forward and for the first time let fly. A left, a right, exploded almost simultaneously under the Negro's ribcage right in the solar plexus, lifting him bodily off his feet and dropping him face downwards on to the dirt.

The navvies in the crowd who had all bet on Batten, bellowed their pleasure. Batten grinned his acknowledgement and went back to his corner. The Negro's seconds rushed to drag him back and while one man acted as a chair the others worked desperately to bring the agonized fighter up to the mark in time.

The American came to scratch for the second round, grey-faced with pain and moving with difficulty. Wisely he kept his distance, using his left to keep Batten out of range of his stomach.

'Goo on, the navvy!'

'Finish him! Finish the black bogger!'

'Finish the bloody nigger!'

The crowd urged Batten on, but each time he tried to get inside the longer reach of the Terror, the black's left fist whipped into his face, three and four jabs finding their target in lightning succession. Each punch brought roars of encouragement from Richmond's backers.

'That's it, Terror!'

'That's the way to do it, boy!'

'Cut the bogger to pieces!'

The round wore on, the American's face lost its grey undertones, his breathing eased and it was plain that the strength taken from him by the terrible stomach blows was rapidly returning. His steps became springier and suddenly he went over to the attack. Two slashing lefts brought blood from Batten's lips, then a roundhouse right caught him flush on the side of the jaw. Batten dropped to both knees and the round was over. In the corner, Peter Stanton massaged the thick neck muscles.

'How does it feel, John?' he asked anxiously. 'Did it catch you badly?'

The keeper grinned. 'That nigger couldn't knock the wings from a fly, lad,' he said, and added with complete confidence, 'The next round will be the last one. I only wanted to see what he could do, and he can't do enough to put me away.'

Jethro stared at the man, trying to judge if the words were only bravado. He surprised himself by finding that he believed them.

Time was called and the two men toed the line. The Negro was up on his toes now and smiled confidently as he came to the mark. When the bell went, Batten said, loudly enough for the ringsiders to hear, 'This is your last round, blackie.'

He dropped his head on to his chest and bulled forward.

The Negro's left stabbed out, one, two, three, four times, but Batten shrugged off the blows as he bustled his man against the ropes. On the ropes he let go his right and left, thudding into the pit of Richmond's stomach, then, before the man could drop, Batten ducked and twisted bringing his opponent over his hip in a cross-buttock throw and crashed down to the dirt on top of him.

The crack of breaking ribs was clearly audible and the Negro screamed aloud in agony.

The crowd fell silent and waited tensely. Only the sounds of heavy breathing and the groans of the semi-conscious Negro could be heard. In spite of all the frantic efforts of his seconds and his own courage, Richmond could not come to the scratch for the next round. Batten's backers went berserk with delight and swarmed into the ring. It took nearly half an hour to clear the tent of the delirious men. When the last shouting, cheering man had been bodily ejected by the booth boxers and the tent flaps securely laced against interruption, Old Chappell came to the tent where Batten and the Stantons were waiting.

'Here!' the old man growled. 'Here's your twenty guineas' stake and another twenty from me ... I never imagined you could fight like that, navvy,' he grumbled.

Batten took the money. 'My thanks to you, Master Chappell. Here!' He counted out five guineas from the heap. 'That's for your man, Bill Richmond. He's a game fellow.'

'Ahr, but he can't fight like he used to ... not like some that I'm beginning to recall,' Chappell said meaningfully.

'What do you mean by that?' Batten asked.

'Oh, I means nothing!' the old man said airily.

'I think Bill Richmond was one of the best in his day,' Peter Stanton put in. 'But he's getting too old for it.'

'You'm right there,' Chappell agreed. 'Listen to me, lads, I've got a proposition to make to you ... Seeing as how you've finished my best man for the rest of the fair, how about stopping on for a couple of days in my booth here?'

'Do you mean you wants me to fight for you?' Batten asked.

'Well, be fair, cully! Tomorrow is the Wakes Day and there's good business to be done; and the way you fight, I reckon we could make a fortune in side bets, I do really; and I've played fair with you 'aven't I? I paid you the stakes with

163

no arguments, and good as you may well be with the mauleys, navvy, I doubt that you could 'a done much against all my fighters together iffen I'd said I wouldn't pay ... Come now, what do you say? You can sleep in one of my vans and we can make a fortune tomorrow.'

After a moment's hesitation, Batten nodded.

'I'm your man,' he said.

CHAPTER TWENTY-SIX

Wakes Day dawned bright and sunny, the cool night air already changing to the hot stillness of a full summer morning. Jethro woke and lay for a moment, remembering where he was. By his side on the floor of the caravan was his father, and beyond him lay Batten, snoring heavily through his flattened nose. At Jethro's feet was the doorway of the van and behind his head were another two rows of sleeping men.

Jethro sat up and rummaged in the pile of old clothes that covered them, searching for his boots which was all he had removed before sleeping. He found them and strapped them on. Then he went out into the clean air.

The camping field was quiet, only a few early risers moved across the ground. Some carried buckets and pots of water which they had drawn from the stream crossing the bottom of the field, others busied themselves in lighting fires and preparing food for breakfast. Jethro sniffed the air appreciatively, enjoying the scented tang of wood smoke, then drew a deep breath and ran across the field to the stream.

At the stream he stripped naked and plunged into the cold, clear water. The chill shocked the breath from his body, but he struck out against the swift-flowing current and his muscles began to generate their own heat as his steady beating heart fed the fresh blood to them.

When he tired, he stopped fighting the current and allowed the flow to carry him back to where he had left his clothes. He dried the water from his hair and eyes with his shirt before putting it back on his body. After he was dressed, he ran up and down the banks of the stream until he was dry. His body glowing with well-being, he trotted back to the camp site. By now Old Chappell and the rest of the troupe were at breakfast, sitting on planks each side of a long trestle table.

'There you are, boy,' the old man growled. 'Ah me! If I was only ten years younger, I'd be doing what you bin adoing.'

His string of fighters began to make ribald jokes at this until he silenced them by belabouring the nearest with his stone drinking jug. Jethro took his seat next to his father and Batten. The old woman who acted as cook put a huge dish of hot mutton chops in front of him and poured him ale from a mug she carried. Old Chappell passed him a round loaf of warm new-baked bread.

'Here, boy, eat hearty,' he growled, and winked at the others. 'If you eats this, then you've got the making of a pug.'

Jethro felt ravenous. He tore the bread in two and begun to cram chunks of it in his mouth together with the tender meat, swilling the mouthfuls down with the rich ale. He thought it was the finest breakfast he had ever eaten. After the meal, the men smoked clay pipes of strong-smelling tobacco, talking and spitting contentedly. Then without warning, Old Chappell produced his bombshell.

'Tell me, navvy,' he asked Batten. 'Why is it that a fighter who I saw a few years since going seventy-nine rounds with the great Jem Belcher, a man who is thought by the Fancy to have a good chance of being the champion one day—why is it that that fighter should change his name and fight in a boxing booth against poor old Bill there?' He pointed with his pipe stem at the strapped and bandaged Negro.

Batten made no attempt to prevaricate. Looking at the old man steadily, he replied, 'I thought last night that you'd recognized me. Well, I changed my name because there's people in this county that don't like the politics that me and my friend here preaches. Also our young matey, Jethro there, told us last night before we slept that we'em being accused of murdering some poor woman back in our home town of Redditch. Now I'm telling you what is the truth when I says that the first time we heard about any murder was when he told us. If you doubts me, old man, then you'd best get the constables here and now. The politics is another story and I'll not try and tell you any different. We'em Luddites, and a lot more besides and proud of it.'

The old man smiled. 'It's not my intention to call the constables, nor my boys' intention either. I believe what you say and I'll tell you in return that we all agrees with General

Ludd. So we'll say no more, except that if you needs help at any time, then you'll find it here.' He turned his head and shouted to the old woman. 'Nellie! Fetch the mufflers to me.'

The old woman came from the caravan with two pairs of what resembled leather pillows and brought them to Chappell.

'Come on, cully.' The old man passed one pair to Batten. 'Shove these on your mauleys, I wants you to show me that corkscrew hit that you closed Jem Belcher's peepers with!'

Batten grinned. 'Gladly, old un ... But you've got to promise that you'll go steady with me ... I'm not getting any younger.'

The men around the table laughed and the whole of them formed a circle in which Batten and the old man began to spar. Jethro watched with the others for some time, then feeling restless he told his father, 'I'm away for a stroll, Dad. Are you coming?'

'No, son,' Peter Stanton replied. 'I'll stay here and take it easy. You go on and enjoy yourself ... here!'

He pushed a guinea into Jethro's pocket, in spite of the young man's protests.

'Take it,' he insisted. 'I won a great deal on John last night.' Jethro's surprise showed on his face. His father winked at him. 'I've told you before, boy, I'm an old fox.'

CHAPTER TWENTY-SEVEN

The streets of the town were thronged with shoppers and the stalls and stores were doing good trade. It was still too early in the day for the drinking and brawling to have begun and the respectable artisans and tradespeople's womenfolk made a gay picture in their bonnets and fine dresses as they sauntered along.

Jethro attracted many demure glances from bright young eyes as he strolled, and not a few blatantly inviting looks from the older more experienced women. But, in love as he was with Abigail Bartleet, the smiles made no impression on his consciousness. The ribbon and lace-sellers, flowergirls, hot-pie vendors, ginger-beer sellers, gypsies with performing dogs and monkeys, fiddlers and singers, street conjurors and acrobats absorbed his interest. He stood for a long time watching the straining efforts of a cursing man to free himself from a cocoon of ropes and chains. Billed as the 'Greatest Escaper since the Immortal Jack Shepheard', it was unfortunate for the man that some wild young nailers had waited until he was loaded with chains, then rushed in with pieces of rope and trussed him until he could hardly move a finger. Jethro joined in the howls of amusement at the Great Escaper's indignant protests and curses.

In one side alley he came upon two small boys squaring up to fight. Their fathers came out into the alley, drawn by their children's argument.

'You'll fight French and English?' one man asked.

'Ahr, that's right,' the other agreed.

They each took their son on their shoulders astride their necks and grasped the boys' legs securely. The men then stood face to face, a foot apart.

'Two shillings enough for you, Bart?' the first asked.

Bart agreed. 'Who'll give the word?' he added

A youth lounging against the wall held up his hand. 'One to be ready ... two to be steady ...' he shouted. 'And three's away!'

The small boys began to windmill their arms at each other's heads. Crying out in pain as small fists found their target, one boy's nose started to bleed and he screamed to his father to let him down.

The father ignored him. 'Keep gooing, you little bogger! Keep gooing!' he urged.

But the child only cried louder and cowered back, trying to shield his head and face. Eventually his father put him down in disgust.

'Gerroff out of my sight, or I'll gie thee belloil!' he shouted and cuffed the boy's head.

The child ran off down the alley still crying and his father pulled out two shillings and gave them to the other man.

'Ne'er mind,' the winner said. 'Yow're other nipper is a proper game 'un, an't he.'

'Ahr, but he an't got the size to take on yow're little bogger yet,' the loser grumbled.

Jethro walked on, scenes like this did not disgust or anger him. It was a violent age and he was a man of it. As a small boy he had himself fought French and English. He came to a small market place where three rows of terraced hovels formed a triangle. In the open space between them a silent crowd had gathered, engrossed in what was happening.

A young collier, wearing his candlegrease-streaked leather skull cap, unwashed and unshaven, staggered drunkenly round and round the edges of the triangle. Over his shoulder he was dragging a long rope, the other end of which was tied about the neck of a young woman, hardly more than a girl judging by what could be seen of her features under their covering of coal-dust. She was badly lame and periodically the collier would tug viciously on the rope causing her to stumble, limping painfully in an effort not to fall. Jethro moved through to the front of the watchers.

'What's happening here?' he asked a middle-aged man next to him, also a collier, from his dress.

'That's young Moey Elliot,' the man told him. 'He's come to sell his missus.'

'Sell her?' Jethro was incredulous.

The man looked sideways at him. 'Yow'm a bloody furriner, I take it?'

Jethro nodded. 'I'm from Redditch way.'

The man hawked and spat. 'Ahr then, yow uddent know about our ways here. Them bloody needle men don't know nuthin' else but fighting, drinking and burning down houses, I'm towld. They don't know how to handle a ooman.'

Jethro sensed the man's aggressiveness.

'Look, master,' he said evenly. 'I'm not here to quarrel. If I've upset you by asking what's happening here, then I'm sorry for it. I meant no offence.'

The man's truculence disappeared in an instant.

'Then there's no offence took, young 'un.' He grinned and held out a grimy hand. 'Onny a lot of furriners comes by here and not knowing our ways they acts as though we'em a load o' savages.'

Jethro shook hands. 'No, I don't think that. I was only surprised because I've heard of this custom, but I've never seen it before.'

'I've sin it dozens o' times,' the man told him. 'Ahr, and to tell yow the truth I should have sold my owld ooman years sin. Onny no bogger would have bought her.'

He laughed and Jethro could not help laughing with him.

'What's he selling her for?' he asked. 'What has she done?'

The man hawked and spat once more before replying.

'It's a bloody shame! Her's a good little wench, her is. I've known her ever sin her feyther brung her ower from Salop way, her feyther took the fever and died and left the wench all alone in the world. Her married Moey Elliot three or fower years sin, and I reckon her's cursed the day her did many and many a time.'

'Does he serve her badly?' Jethro asked, his sympathy roused.

'Ahr! Wuss than bad,' the man said. 'We all gis our ooman a bit of hammer now and again, I know, but I've heard that poor wench screaming for her life night after night. Her's lost two babbies through him akicking her when her was carrying, and he makes her work like a dog for him down the pit, no matter what state her's in; and now that the coal's had her and her legs um no good for the heavy work . . . Why then, the bogger wants to get rid of her. Before now when her wanted to leave him, his brothers nigh on killed anybody who tried to help her get away, but now the poor little wench is crippled ... Why they just wants her sent off.'

'But if that's the case, why insist on selling her?' Jethro asked.

The man laughed mirthlessly. 'I see you don't know the bloody Elliots. There's none of um would gie the time to a blind man ... no! Not if they'd got two watches in their hands they wouldn't gie the hour ... Grabbing boggers, they bin.'

By now the young collier had finished dragging the girl around the triangle. He shortened the rope until she was next to him then wrapped his hand in her long hair and forced her on to her knees.

'What am I bid for this prime cow?' he shouted, and swayed, spittle frothing at the corners of his slack mouth. No one answered and the collier's temper worsened. He dragged his wife's head back until she was staring up at him, then lifted his boot and drove it into her buttocks. 'You see! Nobody wants you, you gowky-legged bitch!' he bawled.

'I'll gie thee three ha'pence,' a youth shouted, and the crowd laughed, scoffing at his meanness.

'Thee won't,' the collier told him. 'I'll see thee dead fust ... Ahr! and thee as well!'

He shook the girl's head from side to side by her hair, ignoring her moans of pain.

'I'll gie thee a tanner and risk being robbed,' another youth jeered.

The collier swayed again and nearly fell, he opened his mouth to reply, but could only belch.

'Here's a shilling offered,' an elderly man quavered. 'I needs an 'ousekeeper.'

'A bloody shillin'?' the collier finally managed to blurt disgustedly. 'Get up, you.' He kicked the girl to her feet. 'Look!' he shouted. 'I know that her's gowky-legged, but her's still able to be ridden. And look at these, they'm the best pair o' tits this side o' Brum.' He hooked his fingers in the neckline of her ragged dress and brutally ripped the rotting fabric. It fell to the girl's waist and when she tried to cover her full, well-shaped breasts, her husband beat her hands down with the coiled rope. He lifted the breasts and squeezed them cruelly.

'Look at them udders,' he bawled. 'Show me another pair as good as them in Tipton . . . yow bloody can't!'

Some people in the crowd protested strongly at this display of sadism, but there were others who pressed closer to get a better view and called to the collier to strip her completely.

One great hulking brute of a man waved a five shilling piece above his head.

'I'll offer a crown,' he bellowed. 'Just so as you sells her tits with her.'

The laughter rang out, and Jethro saw the tears of shame running down the girl's cheeks. Impelled by the deepest pity he had ever known in his life, he stepped forward and shouted, 'I'll give you a guinea.'

There was a hush and the collier swung to face Jethro.

'What didst thee say?' he slurred.

'I said I'll give you a guinea.' Jethro took the money his father had pressed on him and held it out to the collier. 'Is it a bargain?'

The young collier laughed delightedly. 'I'll say it is. Her's all yours.' He pushed the girl and sent her tumbling at Jethro's feet.

Jethro looked around him, trying to gauge the temper of the crowd, then said, 'Here's your money.'

The collier snatched the coin.

'And here's what you get for being such a bloody animal,' Jethro hissed, and stepping forward another pace he hit the collier straight between the eyes. The man's nose crunched flat beneath his fist and the blood spurted in a torrent. He went over, as if hit by a cannonball, and crashed senseless on to his back. The crowd cheered good-naturedly.

'He deserved that,' the middle-aged man said, and slapped Jethro's back. 'Now you'd best pick up your woman and be on your way, matey, before his brothers come to find you.'

It was a moment or two before the import of the man's words penetrated. When they did, Jethro could only stand helplessly looking down at the sobbing girl. 'My woman?' he murmured in dismay.

CHAPTER TWENTY-EIGHT

In a small alehouse not far from the triangle where Jethro was watching the wife auction, John Mence sat moodily drinking, waiting for Stone to report back. Over and over again, the news that the Bartleet's maid had given him went through his mind, fanning his jealous anger until he felt that he wanted to smash the very table in front of him into splinters. The door of the room opened and Stone entered, followed by two of his men. Mence scowled up at him. 'Well? Have you found them?' Jacob Stone shook his head mockingly. 'Now, Captain, sir. Give a man a chance to sit down and take a drink. It's been hot and thirsty work I can tell you ... Especially thirsty, aye lads?'

The men chuckled agreement.

'Answer me, goddam you!' Mence shouted.

Jacob Stone's voice became menacing. 'Don't use that tone to me, Captain,' he said warningly, his hard eyes boring into the eyes of the seated man. 'Jacob Stone is not a man to be shouted at by bully boys, no matter what their station in life may be.'

The other dropped his gaze. 'I'm sorry, Mr Stone,' he apologized grudgingly. 'It's only that I'm overwrought and impatient to get on with the business.'

'As we all are, Captain.' Stone smiled, then shouted for the alehouse keeper to bring drink and food.

Oblivious to Mence's fidgeting, Stone and his men made a leisurely meal. When the food was finished, Stone poured himself a large glass of gin and sipped it slowly, smacking his lips in appreciation. Over the rim of the glass, his hard eyes regarded his employer's barely concealed anger with amusement. When he tired of this diversion he placed his glass on the table and said, 'I think we've found them.'

173

Mence jumped to his feet, sending his chair crashing to the floor.

'Where?' he questioned excitedly. 'Why didn't you arrest them and bring them here? Let's go now and get them.'

Stone held his hand up, palm facing his interrogator.

'Now hold hard, Captain, I said I thought we'd found them. I've left Myers watching and as soon as he's sure, then he'll report here.'

'Well, tell me man,' Mence almost pleaded.

Stone took another gulp of gin.

'Ahh! That's good stuff that,' he breathed. 'Would you care to take a glass, Captain?'

'No.' Mence brushed the offer aside. 'Master Stone, I beg of you, release me from suspense and tell me what you have found out.'

Stone was satisfied now that he had forced this arrogant man to plead. He began to speak rapidly.

'Well, Tompkins here has done a bit of prize fighting in the past and he heard tell of a bout that took place here yesterday between a nigger called Richmond, who's a handy man with the dukes, and some navvy who wandered up out of the blue, so to speak. From the description of this navigator, Tompkins thought that it could be Batten, who's one of the top fighting men round these parts, and the way that this navvy served the nigger, then he'd got to be a top pug. So I sent Tompkins to the camp where the boxing boys got their vans. When he gets there, he sees this navvy sparring. Now the navvy's got a beard and Tompkins daren't go too close, in case he was spotted, but he reckons the navvy is none other than Batten himself.'

'And the Stantons?' Mence broke in.

'He saw no sign of them, Captain, but at the fight last night Batten had two seconds and from what I hear they could well be the old man and his son.'

'Why didn't you take the man Batten?' Mence asked.

Stone placed his two hands on the table and assumed an expression of incredulity.

'Suppose we had, Captain, the other two would have scarpered, wouldn't they?'

Mence realized that he had made himself appear a fool. He felt his anger rising as Stone's men sniggered. With an effort he mastered his anger and forced himself to speak calmly.

'That was a foolish question of mine, Mr Stone.' God rot you! I'll make you pay for it some day, he promised himself silently.

'Yes, Captain, it was foolish,' Stone sniggered, then went on. 'I'll tell you in all seriousness, Captain, it's not going to be an easy job to take those three. That Batten is a hard man and all the travelling people stick together like glue. If he's part of that boxing troupe, it'll take a regiment to arrest the three of them, because whoever tries to will have to fight the whole bloody fairground; and if you were to fetch a magistrate and call out the constables here on a Wakes Day, why you'd have a riot on your hands. These people here are as bad as those bastards in Redditch for kicking up rows.'

'Then what do we do?' Mence asked.

Stone nodded at his men, who got to their feet. 'We watch and we wait, Captain,' he told Mence, and rose to join his men. 'We wait until we see our chance, and then . . .' He patted the small pistol that he carried concealed in a hidden pocket of his coat. '. . . and then we takes that chance, even if the Devil himself should try to bar the way to us.'

Away on the other side of the town, along the old road from Wednesbury, a string of brightly painted caravans, drawn by raw-boned horses, rattled and lurched over the ruts. On the driving seat of the lead caravan, a huge old man sat erect and proud. A pack of tough-looking well-built young men drove the other vehicles or walked at the horses' heads, while a swarm of women and children rode in and on top of the vans and gambolled by the side of them.

The Boswell tribe had come to the Wakes.

CHAPTER TWENTY-NINE

In Redditch town the service at St Stephen's Church was over and outside in the churchyard friends and acquaintances met together in small groups to chat and exchange news.

Anne and Abigail Bartleet, for once wearing bonnets on their glossy heads, stood demurely beside their father as he chatted with his fellow magistrate Adam Milward. In appearance Milward was a prototype John Bull and a fervent patriot and monarchist. Today he was holding forth about the fall of Badajoz which had occurred in April.

'God dammee!' he boomed. 'Have you heard the lying rumours that those damned anti-war Radicals are spreading? They accuse our gallant soldiers of committing all manner of outrages against the civilian population in Badajoz. Their lies should be hurled in their teeth, sir! And by God, I would be happy to do so, if I were to hear one in person. I'd kick him for the cur that he would be!'

'What sort of outrages are the soldiers accused of, Mr Milward?' Abigail asked, wide-eyed.

The choleric magistrate coughed and reddened.

'Why ... burning, killing, looting and so forth, missy,' he told her.

'What does the "so forth" entail?' Her twinkling eyes belied the innocent expression.

Milward looked stern. 'Outrages against womanhood which are not fit for your ears, young lady,' he said pompously.

'It may well be true, Adam,' Charles Bartleet said pleasantly. 'In the heat of battle, men become like wild animals; and from all accounts the assault on the city was a very bloody affair. It cost the lives of many of the finest troops in the army.'

'Dammit all, Charles!' Milward spluttered. 'I refuse to believe that British soldiers could ever act in that manner.

176

Besides, unlike the damned Frogs, our officers are gentlemen and would not permit the troops to get so out of hand. Although that fellow Wellesley is only a Sepoy General, yet I have it on very good authority that he maintains a strict discipline at all times.'

'Yes, Adam, I realize the truth of what you say, but there are occasions when it simply is not possible to maintain discipline. Even Sir John Moore found that on the retreat to Corunna,' Bartleet insisted.

Anne Bartleet bit her lower lip worriedly. Her fiancé Mark Purcell had been wounded at Badajoz and was at present convalescing in Lisbon. She found it hard to visualize her gentle lover pillaging, burning and raping, and yet, as her father said, in the madness of combat men did become like wild beasts.

'Dear God, I pray that he did not take part in such terrible excesses,' she thought.

'Good morning, Harry,' Charles Bartleet called out.

Harry Washford came up to the group and lifted his high-crowned hat. 'Good morning,' he smiled at them.

'And how is your father?' Milward asked the young man.

Clem Washford had been ailing for some days.

'I fear, sir, that my father's indisposition does little towards sweetening his temper. However, he seems to be recovering very well,' Harry joked gently.

'Good! I'm pleased to hear that he is improving, in health at least.' Charles Bartleet laughed. 'And it also pleases me that you have made up your quarrel with him, young man. He is getting old and has great need of you.'

Harry smiled again, showing beautifully formed white teeth. 'I hope that the present amicable relations between my father and myself may continue,' he said. 'But at times we act like flint and steel upon each other.'

Abigail looked at the tall, slender young man with interest.

'He's really grown very handsome,' she told herself, examining him from head to foot. His face was sun-tanned and although his cutaway coat and breeches were dark and sombre, yet his white shirtfront and warm-coloured waistcoat and cravat set them off to perfection. 'He has a most pleasing manner,' she decided.

With a smile, Harry made his goodbyes and walked away.

Abigail watched his easy strides and graceful erect carriage.

'He really is a most charming eligible young man,' she thought warmly, and into her mind there crept speculation.

During the days that followed, her thoughts of the absent Jethro became increasingly overlaid by fresh romantic fancies —provoked by the attentions of her newest admirer, Harry Washford.

CHAPTER THIRTY

The girl's sobs quietened to whimpers and Jethro gently lifted her to her feet.

'We must go,' he said, and led her away. She glanced to where her husband still lay flat on his back. As she looked he stirred and lifted one knee.

'What about him?' she asked Jethro. Her voice was country-soft and seemed cultured compared with the uncouth speech of the Black Country.

'Are you concerned for him?' Jethro asked.

She shivered and drew the rags of her dress close about her.

'I'm afraid of him,' she said simply.

'There's no need to be afraid any more,' he told her. 'You're free of him now.'

'Lord, I hope so,' she answered.

The crowd at the edge of the triangle parted to let them through and as they passed a haggard, toil-worn woman stroked Jethro's sleeve.

'You'm a good man,' she told him. 'A good man.'

Jethro nodded to her and inwardly felt anything but good. Now that he had rescued this crippled girl, he didn't know what he was going to do with her. When they had left the triangle far behind, he led her into a wayside field and sat down with her on the sun-warmed grass.

'Where will you go now?' he asked her.

Her eyes were velvet brown, and her hair, when washed, would be the same colour. Her face, though thin and marked with her sufferings, was sweet and gentle. She glanced timidly at Jethro, then dropped her eyes, and her small, delicately fashioned hands, calloused and broken-skinned from her work in the pits, plucked at the blades of grass.

179

'I don't know,' she whispered. 'You see I didn't know that I was to have any choice.'

Pity filled Jethro's heart and he asked gently, 'Have you no family or friends?'

Mutely she shook her head.

They sat for long minutes in silence, and Jethro began to resent the appeal that she made to his emotions. In a sudden spurt of anger he got to his feet; she looked up at him, fear darkening the soft brown eyes. 'Well, I can do nothing more for you,' he said, his voice hard. 'You'll have to make your own way. I've troubles enough of my own without adding you to my burdens . . . I'm going.'

She made no answer, only dropped her head once more and stared at the ground.

'Don't you understand?' he shouted. 'I've got enough of my own worries, I can't shoulder yours as well. Can't you understand why I can't help you further?'

Without looking up she nodded her head. 'Good! Well, goodbye to you.' He spun on his heels and walked away. As he neared the gate that led on to the road his footsteps slowed.

'I can't leave the poor girl like this,' he thought. 'Yes, you can,' his other half said firmly, and he strode out again. But inevitably he stopped just before the gate and looked back.

She was sitting in the same position he had left her in. While he watched she lifted one hand to her eyes, as if to wipe away tears. For a moment he thought that he was going to burst into tears himself.

'Damn and blast it!' he cursed. 'God strike me for a weak, stupid bugger!'

He went back across the field.

He reached her and stood looking down at the bowed, submissive head. He put out one hand and gently touched her hair.

'Come on,' he said, and walked slowly away.

She got to her feet and limped after him.

Back at the camp, Jethro went in search of his father and Old Chappell. When he found them, he explained what had happened and asked the old man if the girl could stay with them.

Chappell smiled when he saw her pathetic appearance.

'God rot me!' he spat out, with mock ferociousness. 'I've seen better things crawl out of a midden . . . Nellie!' he bellowed. 'Get this little wench washed, dressed, fed and watered, she'll be helping you for a time.'

He turned to Jethro and looked at the young man with kindly eyes.

'What will you do with her after the Wakes are finished?'

'I'll take her back to Redditch with me,' Jethro told him. 'I think that I might be able to find her a place as a domestic with some people I know there.'

'And if you don't find a position for her?' the old man persisted.

Jethro grinned ruefully. 'Well then, I've got a sister to support, I suppose.'

Chappell clapped him on the back and spoke to Peter Stanton.

'Mind you love this son of yours well, and always be proud of him,' he instructed. 'For he's worthy of it.'

'I know that well,' Peter Stanton said fondly. 'Young fool that he is.'

Old Chappell decided that the best way to use Batten was to send criers through the town challenging anyone to a finish fight for a hundred guineas stake a side. 'That way,' he explained to the Stantons, 'we'll only get some pug who is good enough to attract plenty of backers. We'll put our rhino on John and we'll make ourselves a fortune.'

'But what if the pug who fights John, beats him?' Jethro asked.

'What? It's not possible for that to happen,' Chappell stated flatly. 'You listen to me, boy. I saw Batten when he was just an up-and-coming fighter, and it took Jem Belcher himself seventy-nine rounds to stop him; and Batten's twice as good now as he was then. You saw him with the Terror last night, he treated him as if he was a babby, and the only men in England who have ever beat the Terror were George Maddox in 1804 and the great Cribb, the champion himself, in 05; and it took Cribb an hour and a half to do it . . . No! The old man shook his head. 'There's not a man in these parts that has the measure of Batten.' He rubbed his hands together gleefully. 'We'll make a fortune,' he chuckled. 'A bloody fortune.'

During the afternoon, the remainder of Chappell's string of boxers fought a succession of local fighting men. Rugged colliers and nailers, hardy navvies and farmworkers bulging with muscles. The bouts were of three rounds' duration and a lot of blood was spilt and hard knocks given and received.

At last it was time for the big event. Old Chappell went out on the platform and addressed the crowd gathered outside the booth.

'My Lords and gentlemen! A challenge was issued this day on behalf of the 'Battling Navigator' that he would meet the finest man in the Midlands for a side stake of one hundred guineas each. Now I'm waiting to see who will accept the challenge, and please, gentlemen, I know that there are plenty of lion-hearted lads present who would be only too happy to lift the mauleys with my man, but I must insist that whoever accepts the challenge deposits the rhino with me here. And, gentlemen, you all know my reputation for honest dealing and fair play, I want you to choose from among yourselves the referee and the timekeeper. But they must be men of good standing and repute with the Fancy.'

'Bring out your man,' the crowd began to chant. 'Let's see your man, Chappell.'

The old man held up both arms for silence. 'My Lords and gentlemen, I give you . . . the Battling Navigator!'

The navvies massed in the audience roared their welcome as Batten stepped on to the platform. He was a magnificent specimen in his boxing tights and stockings, light leather pumps on his feet and the red kerchief of the navvy knotted loosely about his waist as a fogle. He folded his arms and stood gazing over the heads of the crowd.

'Who takes up the challenge?' Old Chappell shouted. 'Or is there no man here today good enough to meet the Battling Navigator?'

'I take the challenge.' From the side of a tent where he had been concealed, a huge grey-bearded man, his hair hanging to his shoulders and a gold ring glinting in his ear, stepped into view.

'And here's the rhino, Chappell.'

He poured a glittering cascade of gold coins from one great hand to the other. He was recognized and his name flew through the crowd. 'It's Old Boswell . . . the fighting tinker.'

With his pack of half-wild sons flanking and preceding him, Simeon Boswell moved majestically to the platform. He mounted the steps and stood towering over Chappell. 'Do you accept the challenge?' His dark eyes glared hatred at Batten.

The keeper was unperturbed. 'Surely I will, gippo . . . All right Chappell?'

Old Chappell nodded doubtfully. 'Do you know the navvy then?' he asked Boswell.

The tinker nodded. 'We know each other,' he said grimly.

The old man turned to Batten. 'Do you want this fight, cully?'

Batten smiled. 'If this bloody gippo wants his head broke, then I'm happy to oblige him.'

Chappell shrugged and addressed the crowd.

'The match is made!' he shouted. 'Pay your entrance now, the bout starts in thirty minutes. Where's the referee and timekeeper?'

Two of the local gentry who fancied themselves as Corinthians offered their services.

'Is that satisfactory to you?' the old man asked the fighters.

They concurred and the two gentlemen went inside to inspect the ring.

When Batten and Boswell came to the mark there were murmurings of surprise at the obvious fitness of the old tinker. The mat of grey hairs covering his broad chest was the only indication of age on his body. His skin was as smooth as a young boy's, and the long muscles that ran over his torso were sharply defined and supple. He carried no fat around his middle and the pectorals under the grey hairs were like two plates of armour. Some of the gamblers who had bet heavily on Batten now had second thoughts and tried to cover some of their wagers by backing the tinker as well.

The bell rang for the first round and the fighters moved around in the familiar circling movement. Simeon Boswell's seconds were Jos Boswell and an elder brother. Jethro caught Jos's eye and smiled at him, lifting his hand in greeting. Jos stared at him as if he were a stranger. Jethro, after the initial hurt, thought that he understood the reason for his old friend behaving as he did. He promised himself that as soon as possible he would go to Jos and explain why he was in Batten's corner. Until the fight was over, however, there was nothing could be done, so Jethro concentrated on the ring.

The crowd were silent, seeming hypnotized by the fists weaving to and fro as each of the combatants waited for an opening to present itself. Surprisingly to Jethro, it was Batten who made the first attack. The keeper feinted at Simeon's head with the left, drawing the old man's guard up, then swung his hammerlike right to the body. The right found only empty air as the tinker twisted sideways causing Batten to miss badly.

'Pretty, sir! Very pretty!' a spectator shouted appreciatively.

Batten's face stayed impassive, but Simeon Boswell smiled tauntingly.

'You're not fighting a boy in the woods now, keeper.'

He jabbed the left, catching Batten high on the cheekbone, then moved back to avoid the counter punch. Batten followed him trying to crowd him against the ropes but with almost contemptuous ease the old man evaded the trap. His left came again, this time flush on Batten's nose, halting the keeper in his tracks. The blood began to trickle from the shorter man's nostrils and the tinker's backers screamed out their joy.

'First colour to the tinker!'

'Good lad, tinker, that's tapped the claret all right!'

Batten now retreated, trying to draw the older man after him, but Boswell refused to be drawn, instead he concentrated on peppering Batten's damaged nose with his left. Batten again bored in doggedly, soaking up the left jabs in an effort to get inside the big man's extraordinary length of reach. Boswell, finding the left jab could not keep Batten at a distance, let go his right. Unfortunately for him, Batten half ducked and the tinker's knuckles bounced harmlessly off the side of the smaller man's skull. Batten seized his opportunity, he sprang in and sent his terrible right hand hammering into the tinker's stomach. The whoof of expelled breath could be heard all over the marquee, but even in that instant of agony, Simeon Boswell's fighting brain still functioned and he threw himself sideways to the ground, preventing Batten catching him with a cross-buttock throw.

The two sons helped their father to his corner, while the Stantons wiped the blood from their man's face and chest with a wet rag, and tried to stanch the flow from his nose.

'He's a tricky bugger,' Batten remarked.

'He always was in the ring,' Peter Stanton said. 'I think he must have taken lessons from Mendoza.'

Batten grinned. 'Ah well, it's understandable, them both being of the same colour nearly.'

BRIIINNNGG!

The bell sounded and the fighters came to scratch for the second round. This time, both men scorned to use ringcraft. The hatred the tinker felt for his opponent overcame him, and they stood toe to toe at the mark, slugging it out until Batten dropped the old man with another crushing stomach punch.

When he came up for the third, Boswell slipped back into his old tactics, jabbing with the left and moving away from the counter-punch. Batten's nose began to bleed again and the flesh of his cheekbones started to swell under the constant tap tap tapping of the remorseless left hand. Both men were now beginning to pant for breath and the sweat ran down their bodies. Neither wasted any energy in useless taunts and the round stretched into five, then ten, then fifteen minutes; always that left fist rapped into Batten's face, until at last, maddened by the persistent drumming, he dropped his guard and went in swinging both fists. Old Simeon rocked back on his heels and then let go his right. It crashed into the side of Batten's jaw and dropped him stunned to the ground.

This time it was the Stantons who had to drag their man to his corner, while Boswell sauntered to his, acknowledging the thunderous applause of his supporters.

Batten was still dazed from the blow when he was called to the mark and the tinker immediately slashed into the attack and dropped his man again. 'God rot my bloody eyes!' Old Chappell bellowed. 'Get that bogger up to the mark with some sense in his noddle, or I'm a ruined man.'

The interval wore on and still Batten's eyes were vacant and rolling. Peter Stanton stepped back and studied the fighter for a moment then told Jethro, 'Hold his arms, son.'

'Why?' Jethro wanted to know.

'Just do as I tell you, boy,' his father snapped, and as Jethro held Batten's arms, Peter Stanton placed his mouth on the fighter's ear and bit the soft lobe until he fetched blood. Batten came to with a jerk and Peter Stanton completed the recovery by throwing a pan of water over him. There were only seconds left before the bell, and Batten shook his head and rubbed the water from his eyes.

'The gippo ull not catch me like that again,' he grunted, and went back to the mark.

Now he changed his tactics. Each time the tinker jabbed the left Batten took it, slipped to the tinker's left and smashed his right into his opponent's upper arm. At first the keeper's supporters in the crowd demanded to know if he had lost his reason.

'Has he knocked all the sense out of thee pudden head?' a nailer bawled.

'Bist thee mad?' a navvy wanted to know. 'You'm supposed to punch his head, not his bloody arm.'

But the tinker knew well what Batten was doing to him. The blows smashing into the muscles of his left arm were slowly but very surely paralysing it.

'You crafty bastard!' he snarled pantingly at the keeper.

Batten made no reply, indeed it was doubtful if he was able to do so. The tinker's left hand had smashed his lips to a pulp and turned his face into a grotesque red mask. Periodically he spat out the gobs of blood that kept forming in his mouth and at the back of his throat. But he knew from long experience that these were not injuries serious enough to impair his ability to fight, no matter how bad they might appear to a bystander. The heavy bone structure jutting over his eyes guarded them sufficiently to save them from being swollen completely shut and he had years past stopped worrying about the loss of his beauty.

By this stage the bodies of both men were plastered in sweaty mud and blood and hardly a clear patch of skin could be seen. The ground they fought upon was liberally spattered with blood and phlegm and trampled into a mushy greasy porridge of earth.

In the next half hour Batten went down three times under the massive right fist of the tinker, which caught him as his attentions were centred on that left arm. But each time he

186

came back to the mark and doggedly persevered in his chosen course of action, which by now was visibly succeeding. The tinker's left arm drooped lower and lower and at last was hanging uselessly at his side. Again he caught Batten with his right and again the man dropped to his knees, shoulders heaving with the effort to draw breath into the furnace of his lungs. Old Simeon went unsteadily to his corner and slumped dejectedly against the ropes while his sons tried fruitlessly to massage some strength into his useless left arm.

'I'm sorry, Jos,' the old man gasped out. 'But if that bugger comes up to the mark this time, then he's beat me.' He shook his lionlike head despondently. 'And the worst of it is, boy, I'm finding myself admiring the bastard for the way he can fight . . . He's a real bulldog! God's curses on him!'

In Batten's corner, Peter Stanton was urging the fighter to throw in his colours and concede the bout.

'John, John, John,' he crooned the name. 'Your head isn't recognizable. You don't even look like a human being. Throw your colours in, you've done enough for ten men. Good God above, man! He's a human giant, that Simeon Boswell. No man alive could have stood up to him the way you have today, he's fighting as if the Devil himself were helping him.'

Batten lifted his battered caricature of a face, swollen beyond belief, blood oozing from a score of gashes quicker than it could be wiped away. He spoke, and the sentences could hardly be understood, so mangled were his mouth and lips.

'Peter, my friend, you'll never make one of the true Fancy . . . I've won the fight . . . It's all over now. I've won!'

Peter stared at his friend with real alarm.

'Has the tinker knocked you into madness?' he asked unbelievingly. 'You haven't won at all. The fight hasn't finished yet.'

The fighter tugged on Jethro's hand. 'Look over at his corner, look at his right hand. Can you see it?'

'Yes,' Jethro told him. 'Old Simeon is holding it by his stomach and looking at it.'

'Is it badly swollen?' Batten asked, pointing to his own eyes which were mere slits cut into bruised balls of flesh. 'Only I can't see that far.'

Jethro nodded. 'Yes, it's badly swollen and it looks almost black.'

'Ahr!' Batten wagged his head from side to side. 'I knew it. I heard the bones go when he downed me the last time. He's finished! That right hand of his is no more use to hit with now than a wet feather duster; and I've put paid to his left myself.'

BRIIINNNGGG!

The bell summoned them once more and to a storm of cheering Batten went to the mark. Old Simeon toed the line with him. And the slaughter began.

His right hand smashed, his left hanging useless, the tinker could only duck and weave, and try to catch Batten and throw him with a cross-buttock. Once, twice, three times, four times, five times, Batten's terrible hammer of a right sent the old tinker crashing to the dirt; and at last, unable to watch their father's fighting heart dragging him up again and again to be beaten to death, the Boswells ripped his colours from the corner post and hurled them into the ring.

The crowd exploded into frenzy with Old Chappell hung on to Batten's neck, tears streaming down his face, shouting over and over again, 'The greatest fight I ever did see . . . The greatest fight I ever did see . . . You should be champion of England . . . Champion of England.'

When there was a lull in the hysteria, Jethro went to look for the Boswells, but they had disappeared and no one knew where they could be found.

CHAPTER THIRTY-ONE

The Wakes came to an end and the Fair broke up, leaving behind it the yearly debris of brawl-injured men, and love-pregnant women. Old Chappell had won so much money on the fight between Batten and the tinker that he insisted on them all staying with the troupe in Tipton, drinking and feasting to celebrate his good fortune. The days passed and the orgy came to an end on Friday. Chappell pressed the three to travel with the booth, offering to train Jethro as a boxer, but they all refused.

'Well, if you must go, then you must.' The old man shook them by the hand. 'But you remember now, if you ever need a friend, then come ye and find Old Chappell.'

'We will, and thank you,' Peter Stanton answered for them all.

The string of wagons and caravans moved off and the Stantons with Batten and the cripple girl waved the troupe goodbye.

'Come with us to Nottingham,' Peter Stanton urged his son. 'It's no good for you to be alone in Redditch.' Jethro shook his head. 'No, Dad, I'm going back. I think that whoever killed the Treadgold woman is to be found there. Besides, I have to see to the girl here.' Peter Stanton smiled at him.

'All right, boy, I understand, but John and I must leave now.'

'I'll walk some of the way with you,' Jethro said. He turned to the girl. 'You wait here for me, Bron, I'll be back in an hour or so.'

The girl, Bronwen Elliot, as they now knew her, smiled at him. 'I'll wait, master Jethro.'

A week's good food and rest had changed her greatly. Her

brown hair shone richly from constant brushings and her skin, cleansed of the grimed-in filth of the pits, was pale, her colouring delicate. Her eyes had lost the pain of a trapped creature and the lines of suffering etched around her mouth and on her brow were fading fast. She was not beautiful, as Abigail Bartleet was beautiful, but her face was sweet and very gentle and she had a quality of serenity that was comforting to a man.

The three men walked through the streets of the town and headed north. It was evening and the country road was deserted. They were walking through a patch of thick woodland when the attack came.

There was a shout and from the bushes at each side of the narrow road hooded men burst out wielding bludgeons and iron bars. It was over in seconds. Batten, still suffering from the after-effects of his fight, knocked down one attacker but then was battered to the ground. Peter Stanton fared no better, and Jethro's shout of warning was cut short by an iron bar thudding into the base of his skull. There was a shock of blinding pain, then he tumbled into a black pit of nothingness and knew no more.

It was the rain falling gently on to his face that brought him to consciousness. Night had long since fallen and the darkness was almost impenetrable. Jethro opened his mouth, letting the soft rainwater moisten his parched tongue and throat. He felt mildly surprised that he could feel no pain. The mild surprise became acute fear when he realized that not only could he feel no pain, he could feel nothing at all, his body was numb from the neck down.

He tried to move his arms and legs but could not. A clammy sweat of sheer terror broke out on his forehead as desperately he willed his body to move. He screamed for his father and from his mouth came only a guttural croak. For what seemed to him an age, he lay in a stupor of horror, uncaring of anything other than the fact that his fine, well muscled body was useless. Then little by little, he began to regain some control over his emotions. He tried to push the horror and fear into the recesses of his mind and to plan a course of action. When he called for his father once more, he found to his overwhelming relief that his voice now functioned. He called and listened for a reply, but none came.

Again and again he called and at last he was answered.

'Jethro? Where are you, boy?' His father's voice was weak and strained.

'I'm over here, father, I think I'm in a ditch, only I can't move.'

'I'm coming, son, I'm coming.'

Jethro could hear his father's progress, it sounded as if the older man were dragging himself over the ground.

'Father?' he shouted. 'Are you injured?'

As he shouted he heard his father cry out in pain.

'What is it? What's the matter?' he questioned anxiously.

'It's my knee, boy, I think they broke it with their damned clubs.'

'Stay there,' Jethro shouted. 'Don't try and come to me, wait until someone comes to help . . . Where's John? Can you see him?'

There was silence for a while, then his father replied, 'He's down the road a piece, it looks as if he's still senseless. I'm going to go and have a look at him.' For long minutes Jethro could hear the scraping of his father's body against the road and the muffled grunts of pain when the older man's injured knee twisted awkwardly. Then he heard his father gasp out. 'Jesus Christ! What have they done to you, John? What have they done?'

'What's happened?' Jethro almost screamed the question.

From Peter Stanton's lips there dribbled a stream of curses.

'What's happened, for God's sake?' Jethro pleaded to know.

'It's John's hands,' his father shouted back. 'They're lying on the ground beside him . . . Those filthy bastards have chopped them off.'

At first Jethro could make no reply, the horror of what had happened to the prizefighter left him speechless. When he recovered sufficiently, he shouted, 'Is he alive?'

'He's alive now,' Peter Stanton told him. 'But I doubt that he'll live much longer, he's lost a bucketful of blood and he needs attention from a doctor. I can only tie his wrists and stop the bleeding.'

As he finished speaking, there came carrying on the wind the sound of horses' hooves drumming along the road.

'Do you hear that?' Jethro shouted. 'It sounds like horsemen, and they're coming fast.'

'Thank God for that!' his father exclaimed. 'Perhaps we can save John after all.'

The hoofbeats grew nearer and nearer and suddenly Peter Stanton hissed urgently. 'Keep quiet, Jethro, whatever happens. They're provocation men.'

Jethro heard the slithering clatter of horses being reigned in at mid-gallop and the curses of the riders.

'Rot my bloody eyes!' he heard a man shout. 'It's them, Captain, and lying down waiting for us as promised.'

'I'll finish the job now,' another man shouted. 'It'll save the hanging guinea and it'll give the young bastard something to remember me for until we catch him.'

'Now you, where's your son?' the man shouted. 'All right, you can be silent, this is far better. He'll grieve all the longer.'

There came a long drawn-out scream of terrible pain which was ended abruptly by the sharp crack of a pistol. Jethro gnawed his lips to bloody shreds, knowing that the only intervention he was capable of making would lead to his discovery and death, and would serve no purpose other than that. He knew who had screamed and his anguish burgeoned until he felt that his heart and head would split with the agony of his father's death. Through his raging torment, he heard the first speaker giving orders.

'Myers! Hold those bloody horses still. We'll have to sling these buggers across their backs . . . Jesus, Captain! That was a messy shot, it's took the back of his head clean off.'

'Check that the pug's dead,' the man addressed as Captain ordered.

Jethro knew with certainty who the Captain was, just as he knew also who were the others with him. What he was not completely sure about was the identity of the hooded attackers, but when his father had told him about Batten's hands, a chain of thought had begun in his mind which led inevitably to one suspicion and one name . . . Boswell!

'The pug's about dead, Captain,' a voice said.

'Good!' Mence replied. 'It'll save wasting a ball on him.' He sniggered.

'Dammee, but I'd like to reward our friends with a King's Ransom for this.'

192

'I'll second that, Captain,' Jacob Stone chuckled. 'It was thoughtful of them to lop them off for us. If they hadn't he might have been able to knock one of our heads off, before we could finish him . . . Give us them hands here man, you're acting as though you'd never handled a pig's trotters before. I think I'll hang these on the wall of my parlour back in London as a memento,' he joked.

By now the bodies of Peter Stanton and Batten had been slung over the rumps of the horses and secured.

'All right, men,' Mence said. 'Let's take these carcasses back to Tipton, and keep it clear in your minds that they had both been set on by footpads and were dead when we found them.'

'But that might mean that we won't get the reward . . . You don't get nothing for finding dead meat, do you?' Myers protested.

'Don't worry about that,' Mence answered. 'I'll see that you don't lose by it.'

'Surely you will, Captain . . . surely,' Jacob Stone chuckled.

The sound of the horses' hooves slowly died away and left only the soft weeping of the wind to lament the deaths of brave men. Jethro at last gave way to his torment and sobbed as bitterly as a heartbroken child.

Gradually he drifted into a coma of anguished grief, as the rain began to fall once more.

CHAPTER THIRTY-TWO

Bronwen Elliot smiled at the backs of the three men as they walked away from her, and settled herself comfortably on the ground to wait for Jethro's return. As his tall figure passed from her sight, she fancifully blew a kiss in his direction.

'Come back soon, love,' she murmured. 'But if it takes you till the Day of Judgement, I'll still be waiting for you.'

Understandably, she had fallen utterly in love with her rescuer, but did not dare to show even a hint of it, believing as she did that he was not, and never could be, destined for her. Alone now, she entered her private world of dreams, a world which she had created during the long purgatory of her marriage to Moey Elliot. Into this world she would retreat whenever the burden of her life grew too great to be borne and there she would become whatever she chose to be. Now she was, in her fancies, the dearly loved wife of Jethro Stanton, and she smiled contentedly as she indulged her harmless pleasure.

'I bin looking all over the district for thee!'

The harsh voice shattered her dream bubble. She looked up in terror. Standing over her, legs astride, arms folded, was her husband, Moey Elliot.

He grinned savagely. 'Well now, gowky-legs! You'm looking very clean and presentable, I see that the bloke what bought you has bin caring for thee well.'

His eyes and nose were still puffy and discoloured from the blow that Jethro had given him, and he lifted a finger and pointed at the injuries.

'Where is he? The bogger that done this? I've got a score to settle wi' him.'

'He'll not be long,' she retorted in a burst of spirit. 'He's only gone along the road aways to see his father on his journey.'

The next moment she could have bitten her tongue when she realized just what she had told her husband.

Moey Elliot laughed his satisfaction. 'So he'll be coming back alone, will he? That's fine, that is ... Fine and dandy.'

She went to struggle to her feet but he lifted his iron-shod boot threateningly.

'Yow'd do better to sit quiet if yow don't want this on yow're neck,' he warned her.

She stayed quite still, knowing so very well that he would not hesitate to carry out his threat. The silence lasted for a considerable time and then her anxiety for Jethro overcame her and she asked, 'Why do you want to settle a score with him? He bought me from you fair and square.'

'So he did, gowky-legs,' Elliot agreed. 'But not content wi' that, he lifted his fists to me didn't he.'

'I think that he'll do so again if he finds you here,' she said defiantly.

A spasm of murderous rage crossed his face. Then he relaxed and told her, 'Take a gander over at the edge there, outside the Colliers Arms. What do you see?'

She stared at the place indicated and what she saw made her draw her breath in sharply. Moey's four brothers were sitting on the benches, drinking and paying careful attention to what Moey was doing. As she stared, one of the brothers lifted his jug of beer to her in a mocking salute. Her voice cracking with fear, she began to beg and plead with her husband to let Jethro alone. With growing impatience he listened, then silenced her by simply backhanding her brutally across the mouth, knocking her flat to the ground. Her breasts heaved under the thin fabric of her dress and she saw the lust come into Moey's eyes. He dropped to his knees straddling her body and with one strong hand he held her fragile wrists over her head against the ground. When he spoke his voice was thick.

'You'm looking and smelling very sweet, Bronny,' he told her, and with his free hand he undid the laces that held closed the bodice of her dress.

'Let's see if your tits am still as white and tender as before.'

He pulled the dress back from her full swelling breasts and

195

bent his head, taking the hard brown nipples in turn between his teeth and biting them sharply.

'Nooo!' she screamed, and twisted her body, trying to throw him off. He straightened and whipcracked his leathery hands backwards and forwards across her face raising ugly red welts on the delicate skin and causing her eyes to fill with tears of pain.

'You just lie quiet, you little bitch,' he snarled.

Powerless to fight him off, she subsided and lay still. For long minutes she endured his slavering over her breasts, then driven by the fear that she would lose the new hope of life that had been given to her she resorted to the age-old weapon of her sex.

'Moey?' She forced herself to say the name lovingly. 'Oh, Moey, do you really want me again?'

In a fever of desire, her husband panted into her ear, 'Yes, I wants you, my pretty.'

'Well, let's go somewhere quiet,' she pleaded. 'We can't really pleasure ourselves with half the town watching, can we?'

Releasing her trapped hands, he began to fumble under her long skirt, fondling her soft thighs, then reaching higher.

'Why not,' he panted. 'Others ha' done it here.'

'I know, Moey,' she steeled herself to open her legs and accept his caresses. 'But if we was to go somewhere quiet, then we could do it properly, I mean take off our clothes and that ... You used to like to have me like that, didn't you, Moey? And I could do all the things that you used to make me do, only this time I'd try and do them nicely, not like before.'

He drew back to stare at her face and grinned happily at what he saw there.

'Yow still loves me, don't yow,' he said.

She nodded.

'Come on!' He stood up and pulled her to her feet. He turned and waved to his brothers, indicating that everything was all right, then said impatiently, 'Come on, Bronny, we'll goo to old Knacker's stables, he's got a pile of straw in his loft.'

She picked up Jethro's canvas bag which he had left with her and followed her husband across the open space to the stables which stood some distance beyond. Moey put one arm around her waist pulling her against him hungrily while with the other he cupped her breasts, squeezing the soft white flesh until she moaned with pain.

'I'll gie thee summat as ull make thee moan, when I gets thee in the stable,' he promised and crushed his mouth on hers. She surreptitiously hefted the canvas bag, it was weighty; inside it there were some leather-bound books and a spare pair of heavy iron-shod shoes. She began to nerve herself for what lay ahead. When they reached the stables all was still and quiet and the main gate was chained and padlocked.

'Bollocks to it!' Moey cursed, and led her round to the side. 'I know where there's a hole in the fence.'

They scrambled through the fence and into the yard. Bron took a deep breath and summoned up all her reserves of courage. When Moey stepped away from her and turned his back, she grasped the bag in both hands and swung it as hard as she was able. It thudded against the man's head. He staggered and half-spun to face her, his expression one of stupefied amazement. She struck again and this time he fell stunned, grabbing the bag in his hands as he did so. Terrified, she let him drag it from her and she ran hobbling through the fence and along the lanes until she came to the road north that Jethro had taken. Gasping in fear, she struggled on, expecting every moment to hear her husband pounding after her. Finally, unable to take one step more, so exhausted was she with fear and strain, she crept into a wayside ditch and crawled deep into the roots of the thick brambles that filled it.

For many hours she stayed there, shivering with fright at every sound from the roadway. Night fell and intermittently rain gusted down. She lost all track of time but could not bring herself to move. Then there came a horror which almost unhinged her mind.

The moon slipped out from behind the clouds and shone on a party of horsemen trotting towards Tipton. In the bright moonlight she saw clearly, bounding upon the rumps of two of the horses, the limp bodies of Peter Stanton and Batten. As Batten's body was borne past her the horse jolted into a pothole, causing Batten's handless arms to fly up as if in greeting to the hidden girl. She thrust her hand into her mouth to stop herself screaming aloud. Then she realized that Jethro was not with them.

'Dear God!' she begged. 'Let him still be alive, let me find him.'

The instant the party had gone from sight, Bron left her cover and went north. Hobbling across the rutted tracks, stumbling and falling, bruising and cutting her hands and knees, but always disregarding these and the other pains that knifed through her chest and lungs, she forced her body onwards through the night.

CHAPTER THIRTY-THREE

The man in the green coat trudged up the hill leading to Redditch Common from the east and cursed bitterly under his breath, as he cursed each and every Friday that he made the long climb from Henley in Arden to Redditch. He shifted his leather bag, with its metal badge of the buglehorn surmounted by the royal cipher, to signify that this was the official mail-carrier, from one sore shoulder to the other; and at the same time changed from one hand to the other his long trumpet horn.

As on every other Friday, those urchins of the town who had managed to escape from work or school swarmed around him shouting excitedly.

'Gi's a blow on your trumpet, postie ...'

''As you got a packet for me, postie ...'

'Postie, postie, limping on your wooden legs ... Daft old postie ...' one morsel of humanity sang to him.

'You'll see if my legs are wooden or not when I puts my boot up your backside, you cheeky young jackanapes,' the post messenger threatened.

At last he saw in front of him the welcome sight of the stocks and pillory which occupied a triangle of land directly behind St Stephen's Church. The stocks had a doleful occupant sitting uncomfortably on the wooden seat-bar, his single leg locked securely in the stock itself.

'What cheer, Peg?' the messenger greeted, when he stopped to catch his breath, hanging his heavy bag on one arm of the pillory.

Peg Whittington, the prisoner, let fly a mouthful of vile abuse.

'It's no good your acursing of me, my lad,' the messenger admonished him. 'It's not my fault that you'm in your favourite resting place, now is it?'

Peg grumblingly acknowledged the truth of that.

'What you bin doing to get yourself in there again?'

'I tapped me old woman across the head for being saucy to me when I come back from the pub.'

'Ahr, I see,' the messenger commiserated. 'Where's your wooden leg?'

'That bloody Methody pisspot, Salter Allday, unstrapped it and took it off with him. He said that if he didn't I'd only take it off myself and chuck it at some bugger.' Whittington spat in disgust. 'A pox on all bloody constables, I says.'

'Ahr well, it's only fair, Peg.' The messenger was reasonable. 'After all, you did throw it at a chap and nearly brain him last time you was in here, didn't you?'

'I should bloody well think I did!' Peg spluttered indignantly. 'Why, the bugger whose head I broke threw a half-brick at me, so he did.'

'Ahr well, never mind, Peg. You always got your crutch to manage with,' the messenger grinned at him.

'I aren't', the prisoner snapped.

'Why not?'

'Because it's broke, you bloody daft yokel.'

'How did you manage that?' The messenger was mystified. 'That was a lovely crutch, that was, best blackthorn! I should know, since I brought you the wood myself.'

Peg grinned wickedly. 'That just goes to show, don't it, postie, there's nothing good comes out of Henley ... 'Cept the road to Redditch, of course.'

The mailman grew angry. 'Don't you try telling me that that wood was no use,' he shouted. 'I cut it meself from the finest old blackthorn tree in the whole of Warwickshire.'

'Ahr! And I broke it on the thickest old skull in Worcestershire,' Peg answered. 'My old woman's! Which just goes to show the truth of what my grandad always said. . . Worcester bone is a damn sight tougher than Warwick wood any day of the week.'

The messenger snatched his bag from the pillory and stormed up the road in a huff, leaving Peg cackling with laughter behind him.

When he reached the main crossroads at the centre of the town, the messenger placed his horn to his lips and blew a long blast. Turning to all four points of the compass, he repeated the signal and continued to do so until the entire population knew that His Majesty's Mail had arrived.

Anne and Abigail Bartleet were trying on new bonnets in the shop of Madame Ferrand, a French emigre who had escaped from revolutionary France and settled in Redditch. Her exotic and worldy manners had ensured her an instant success with the fashion-conscious ladies of the town, when she had opened her millinery store.

Abigail was examining the effect of one high-poked, feather-decorated bonnet in the mirror when the post horn's blast sounded through the streets.

'Ah *Mademoiselle*, if I dare to say so myself, that creation is *très mignon*; *C'est parfait! You look charmante! C'est vrai, n'est ce pas Mademoiselle Annie?*' Madame Ferrand gushed.

Anne nodded absently. She seemed preoccupied, and when she heard the horn, she started and said to her sister, 'Quickly, Abi, the post is come. Let us go and see if we have any packets.'

She hurried from the shop, followed by Abigail who was still wearing the new bonnet.

'Mademoiselle Abi! You have forgotten ze bonnet,' the Frenchwoman called anxiously.

Abigail shouted over her shoulder. 'I'll keep it, madame. You may send the bill and my old bonnet up to the house.'

A small group had gathered around the post messenger and he handed out mail to some and received in return packets and letters for other parts of the country.

'Hello, Miss Anne,' he smiled at Anne Bartleet. 'There's a a very special one for you. The guard on the night coach was very particular about this one. He said the gentleman who give it to him in London had brought it all the way from Portugal. The gentleman treated him very generous like, if you get my meaning.'

Anne fumbled in her reticule and handed the man a florin. 'Then I must also be generous, postie,' she said, smiling.

He pocketed the coin and knuckled his forehead in salute. 'Thank you kindly, Miss Anne, thank you kindly. I always says to my good wife that I can rely on the good heart of at least one lady in Redditch, because this job do get awful hard at times, I must say, and I'm not getting any younger. Why at times these old bones do positively groan so they . . .'

'Yes, yes man! I know that . . .' she broke in impatiently. 'Now give me the letter if you please . . . thank you!' She snatched it from his hand and quickly made her way to Abigail who was waiting a little distance down the street.

'Abi, you read it for me . . . please!' Anne Bartleet entreated. 'I have not got my spectacles.'

Her younger sister took the wax-sealed, oilskin-wrapped letter from her. She broke the seals, unwrapped it and quickly scanned through the single sheet of notepaper that it contained, while Anne bit her lips anxiously. Abigail finished reading the letter, refolded it and without a word handed it back to her sister.

'Well?' Anne demanded.

Abigail's face was serious, but lurking deep in her eyes was the familiar devil of mischief.

'Well what?' she asked, as if surprised at the question.

'Well, what was in the letter?' Anne burst out.

'Oh nothing of any importance really . . . Come! Shall we go and look at the new gowns in Mitchell's windows?'

'Ah, Abi!' Anne entreated, half-angrily. 'You know that I do not see well enough to read without my spectacles. Tell me, please! What was in the letter? Was it from Mark?'

'Yes, it was from Mark Purcell,' Abi said off-handedly, and began to walk away from her sister, saying as she did so, 'Really, Anne! Hurry up. I want to see the new gowns. I do wish you would not lag behind so.'

'Abi! I swear that if you do not tell me this instant what was in the letter then I . . . I . . . I will do something that I will be sorry for afterwards.'

Abigail laughed with delight at her sister's outburst and said between giggles, 'If you insist upon it so strongly, then I suppose I must tell you. Mark expects to be home within a month or two . . . Oh! . . . and he also sends his fondest and most sincere love.'

Anne's mouth opened in surprise. 'Mark?' she uttered incredulously. 'Here? In a few weeks?'

Abigail laughed and hugged her sister.

'Yes, here! La! Look how much in love the foolish girl is. It has quite scattered her wits to find that her beau is

202

returning to her, safe and sound from the wars,' she teased.

Tears of happiness began to stream from Anne's eyes.

'Oh, how silly you are,' Abigail said fondly. 'You should be laughing, not crying. If he sees you looking like that, he will probably turn tail and run straight back to fight the French again. Here!' She handed the elder girl a scrap of wispy lace. 'Dry your eyes, for mercy's sake.'

'Is anything wrong? Can I be of any assistance?' Harry Washford stood in front of the girls, his approach unnoticed, so intent were they on each other.

'Oh no, nothing is the matter,' Anne assured him, wiping her tears away. 'It is only that I have received the most wonderful news.'

He laughed easily. 'My word, Miss Anne! I would hate to see you if your news were bad,' he joked.

Both girls laughed with him.

'My fiancé, Mark Purcell, is coming home very soon,' Anne explained.

'What? Old Mark? Well, I am pleased to hear it,' Harry Washford said warmly. 'He has always been a most dear friend of mine, it will be good to see him once more. Though I must confess, I am a little apprehensive as to what his opinion will be of civilians like myself who have been living safely and comfortably in England, while he and other gallant fellows have been fighting the King's enemies in Spain and Portugal.'

'Did you never wish to become a soldier yourself, sir?' Abigail asked.

He turned to look at her and his dark eyes softened at the sight of her beauty.

'Once I did, Miss Abigail,' he answered gravely. 'But I fear that as I grew older my martial propensities gave in to my natural timidity, and I lost all notion of wearing the scarlet coat.'

'I can't believe that you were afraid, sir,' Abigail smiled at him. 'Our father spoke most highly of the bravery you displayed during the riots.'

His face became serious. 'I assure you that I was merely an onlooker and I do not believe that it is a praiseworthy thing when one has to face poor starving wretches driven to desperation and madness. It is a waste of bravery that could be displayed to better advantage elsewhere, Miss Abigail,' he said quietly. 'But I would imagine that the soldiers of Napoleon Bonaparte would indeed terrify me, if I were to see them charging towards me.'

'Perhaps then, sir, you are really made to be a poet,' she answered, with a touch of malice.

He smiled at her and she felt a tremor run through her body.

'Perhaps I am indeed meant for that, Miss Abigail,' he said gently. 'And if you will forgive my boldness, then I would like to invite your father and yourselves to a musical entertainment at my home this evening. Some other ladies and gentlemen will be there and I shall cast my modesty to the winds and read you some of my own verse. Please say that you will come,' he begged.

'Why, he really is a poet,' Abigail thought. 'I've always wanted to meet a real poet and now I have, and a most charming and handsome one too.'

'Well?'

Anne was hesitant, but Abigail met and held his dark eyes and with her own answered the message that she saw written there.

'Oh, let us accept Mr Washford's kind invitation, Anne,' she urged. 'I'm sure that father will be delighted.'

Anne's happiness was so intense with the news of Mark Purcell's return that she could not refuse.

'Very well, Mr Washford,' she told the young man. 'I shall accept for all of us.'

'That is wonderful ... I shall expect you at eight o'clock, if that is convenient?'

On their way home, each girl was immersed in her own thoughts. Anne indulged her fond imaginings about the return of Mark Purcell, while Abigail examined her feelings for Harry Washford. For Jethro she now had only a passing thought.

'Poor dear Jethro, it was so romantic and tragic, our love for each other. But after all, one grows older and wiser, and I see now that it would be impossible ever to think of marrying him ... But Harry? That is altogether different ...'

CHAPTER THIRTY-FOUR

When Bron Elliot found Jethro it was only by the merest chance. She reached the patch of woodland where the murders of Stanton and Batten had occurred and slumped down to rest. She could hear the trickle of water in the roadside ditch and decided to bathe her blistered feet. It was nearly dawn and the first light had appeared in the eastern sky. Carefully she edged down the steep bank of the ditch and with a sigh of relief she slipped her hot sore feet into the ice-cold water. She bent to wash the dirt from between her toes and screamed in fright. There only a few feet away from her was the dark mass of a sprawled body. Even as she saw it, she heard a snatch of song come from the body.

'Said Martin unto his man, Fie, man, fie! Said Martin unto his man, who's the fool now?'

A wave of thankfulness flooded through her. It was Jethro's voice singing a song she had often heard him humming during their time in the boxing booth.

'Jethro, it's me, Bron. I'm here, sweetheart, don't fret now.'

She splashed through the water to him. He was delirious and his mind was wandering. At first she didn't realize that he was paralysed. It was only after she had tried in vain to get him to move out of the stream which was flowing over and around his body that it dawned on her.

'Oh my good God!' she moaned, and wept helplessly. While she wept, Jethro muttered about Luddites and Ely, spoke to his parents and sisters, laughed at unheard jokes, sang snatches of songs and called over and over again for a girl named Abigail.

From somewhere Bron summoned enough strength to pull his inert body from the water and settle him against the side of the ditch. The sky lightened into full day and she sat by his side, stroking his face in an effort to soothe him. Little by little, her abject despair left her and the iron of determination crept into her soul.

'I'll not let you die here, like a helpless babby,' she whispered to him.

She searched his pockets, but could only find a couple of shillings, then remembered that the bulk of his money had been in his bag which she had left with Moey Elliot. At that moment of realization, black hopelessness threatened to overwhelm her once more, but she fought it down and forced himself to think of a way out of these troubles. Firstly, she must get medical care for Jethro. During her years in the pits she had seen and experienced many dreadful accidents and had acquired enough rudimentary knowledge to know that the bleeding lump at the base of Jethro's skull was probably the cause of his paralysis.

She explored the area of the wound gently with her fingers. The memory of the treatment she had endured from the local doctors at the time of her own injury convinced her that they would be able to do nothing for Jethro. Then she remembered how the Stantons and Batten had praised a certain Doctor Murdoch at Redditch for his skill.

'I'll take him to Redditch,' she decided.

But how to get him there safely was another problem. The jolting of a cart or litter over a long distance on country roads would aggravate the injury, possibly beyond repair. Casting about for an alternative, she suddenly thought of a solution.

'I'll get a ride on a canal barge,' she thought. 'It'll be the smoothest passage that could be wished.'

The lack of money to pay a bargee for a ride or men to carry Jethro to the canal side she refused to think about. Unconsciously her hands went to her full firm breasts.

'Maybe I'll be payment enough,' she thought.

Arranging Jethro as comfortably as possible, she next washed herself in the stream and tidied her appearance as well as she could, using a puddle of water for a mirror. She then went on to the road and settled herself to wait. One hour passed, then two, and the road remained deserted. The sun by this time was pleasantly warm and in spite of herself her eyes dropped shut and she dozed. The sound of iron-hooped wheels trundling over the stones broke her sleep and she came awake with a jerk. Coming from the direction of Tipton was a huge hay wain, drawn by a pair of massive oxen. The driver of the wagon was slouched drowsily on the seat and nearly fell off with shock when she spoke to him.

'Are you going anywhere by a canal?' she called.

A large, fat, red-faced man dressed in smock and gaiters, with a round straw hat perched on his head, the driver blinked his eyes at her in puzzlement.

'Why dost thee ask that?' he wanted to know.

'Well, I'm looking for a ride for me and my brother,' she told him.

He reined the oxen in. 'Whoaa up there, you silly daft buggers,' he ordered. 'Wheer's yowr brother?' he asked Bron.

She pointed. 'He's in the ditch there, master. He fell last night and hurt himself when we was coming along the road.' She thought it best to lie.

He grinned at her, revealing gapped teeth. 'Yow bain't one of them highway robbers, bist thee?' he questioned jokingly.

She laughed back at him. 'Not I master, and neither is my brother, I do assure you.'

'Ahr well, that's all right then.' The driver puffed and grunted down from his seat and went with her to look at Jethro. His broad red face was sympathetic.

'Yon poor lad's had a bad crack by the look of 'e.'

Sensing the man's goodness of heart, Bron told him why she wanted to go to Redditch and her reasons for going on the canal boats.

'Theer now, little wench.' He patted her shoulder with one large red paw. 'Don't ee fret theeself. I'll take thee to the canal. I knows a pub wheer a lot of the boatmen drink. Thee'ull find a passage easy enough from theer, I'll warrant.' He waved away her thanks. 'Never mind that. You just gie me a hand wi' Surry here.'

Gently they carried Jethro to the wagon between them and laid him on the new cut hay. The carter whipped the oxen up and the wagon lurched on.

It was noon when they reached the canalside alehouse and, before leaving them, the carter went inside the alehouse and bought bread, beer and cheese.

'Here thee bist, little wench.' He thrust the victuals and jug of beer into Bron's hands. ' 'Tis really sorry I be that I can't take thee and thy brother into Redditch but my master's a hard bugger and he watches me like a hawk on my time.'

This further unasked-for kindness brought a lump to Bron's throat. She could only wave to the kindly driver as the wagon lurched away.

The alehouse was nearly deserted and there were only three narrow boats alongside the wharf and a couple of old horses grazing on the sparse grass in the field next to the wharf. She fed Jethro with broken pieces of bread and cheese and lifted his head so that he could sip the beer from the jug. He was silent now and when she lowered him back on to the ground his head rolled from side to side and he stared up at her with vacant eyes. She felt his body and head with her hands and although he was still hot she didn't think his fever had increased dangerously.

She hobbled into the dark low-ceilinged taproom and looked about her. There was only one person in the room, a dirty-looking hard-faced man of about forty years, who was sitting dressed in his greasy shirt, waistcoat and breeches with a kerchief knotted loosely around his neck, sucking loudly at a long clay churchwarden's pipe.

He stared at Bron then said, 'What dost thee want here, young 'ooman?'

She faced him boldly. 'I want to get a ride on a barge as far as Redditch town,' she told him.

He pulled the pipe stem from his mouth and, leaning forward, he spat into the dead ashes of the fireplace. When he had settled himself comfortably once more in the high-backed chair, he sucked on the pipe a little longer, then he removed it from his mouth again and said, 'Then thee bist bloody daft!'

For a moment her surprise at his bluntness held her silent. Then, recovering, she said, 'Why do you say that?'

He chuckled. 'Because there is no cut that goes as far as Redditch. The nearest waterway to that town is at Tarbick, wheer they'm cutting the tunnel . . . that's about three mile from the place.'

'Then that will have to do,' she said. 'Do you know of anybody that takes a boat there?'

'I might ... Why dost thee want to go?'

Again she told her story. When she had finished he said to her, 'Hast thee any money?'

She showed him the two shillings.

'Ahr, I see,' he nodded. 'That's not a lot for a passage of that length, is it?'

'I can work as well,' she answered defiantly.

'Could thee foot a boat through a tunnel? Because I see that thee's got a gowky leg,' he observed brutally.

She nodded. 'I can.'

'Well then, you'm a lucky young 'ooman.' He grinned at her and measured her body speculatively with his bloodshot eyes. She noticed the particular attention he paid to her breasts jutting out against the bodice of her dress.

'Can this brother of you'rn move at all?' he went on.

She shook her head.

'Ahr, I see.' He nodded, then held his hand out palm uppermost.

'Gi's thy two shillings. We'll have a few jugs of ale afore we starts our journey.'

'Do you mean that you'll take me to that place, Tarbick?' she questioned unbelievingly.

'I said you'd dropped lucky,' he told her. 'I've got to take a load of tools up to the Tarbick cutting, and my 'ooman got drownded a while ago in the Dudley Tunnel. So I needs somebody to give me a help legging the boat through the tunnel. Don't you worry though, my wench, we shan't be seeing my 'ooman in the tunnel, I got her body out of the water a few days sin. My bloody oath, she didn't half look a mess, I can tell you,' he said, grinning.

CHAPTER THIRTY-FIVE

'Get those bloody legs o'yourn moving, or you'll have us into the side.'

The bargee's shouts echoed in the pitch darkness, bouncing off the rough-cut walls. Bron clenched her teeth to stop herself crying out from the pain burning through her awkwardly twisted hips and rammed her feet doggedly against the rocks, levering the boat on through the blackness. For what seemed an eternity she had been lying on her side on a platform of planks laid athwart the bows of the barge, her head and shoulders inward to the deck, her feet against the sides of the tunnel, 'legging', pushing with all her strength to maintain the forward motion of the heavy barge. Across from her on the opposite end of the planks the bargee, half-drunk, carried out identical actions.

Down in the filthy, evil-smelling cabin, Jethro lay in a coma upon a bunk and in the waist of the vessel the spavined old towing horse, head drooping, stood in its own ordure. At last the gloom lightened and the bargee shouted, 'Keep gooing, gowky-legs . . . we'em nearly through.'

The rocks gave way to brick linings and the barge glided out into the early dusk. For precious moments Bron rested her tortured body, dragging great draughts of the cool fresh air into her straining lungs.

'Come on, wench! There's work to be done.' The bargee's raucous shout was loud in her ears.

She rolled over wearily and got to her feet. The bargee used a long pole and pushed the boat against the towpath. Using the planks as a bridge, they got the horse on to the path and re-harnessed it to the barge. The man took the rudder and they went slowly on their way.

'When will we reach Tarbick?' Bron asked.

'About tomorrow noontime,' he told her, and appraised her closely.

In the dim light, with her face flushed by the work and her hair tumbling about her shoulders, she looked beautiful and the bargee ran his tongue across his lips.

'We'll tie up for the night about a mile ahead,' he said. 'You goo on into the cabin and get a bite to eat ready for us. You'll find a skillet and some eggs and ham in the cupboard there, and the charcoal's in the brazier.'

As she passed him she could smell the acrid sweat of his unwashed body, but she had become accustomed to worse during her years in the pits and it did not offend her greatly, only made her appreciate more the clean man scent of Jethro's body.

In the tiny cabin with its two bunks, she first rearranged Jethro's coverings and gave him water to drink, then set about preparing a meal. By the time the barge had been moored and the horse haltered and set to graze, the ham and eggs were ready.

The bargee gulped his food down, smacking his lips and belching noisily, wiping the grease from his mouth with the backs of his hands before swilling beer from the flagons he had brought with him. He watched Bron feeding Jethro and asked her, 'Am you sure that he's your brother, gowky leg?'

'Why do you ask?' she countered.

'Well, he don't much resemble you in the face, does he?'

'He's my brother,' she stated flatly.

She finished feeding the helpless man and made her own meal from the scraps left over. Then she picked up a blanket and started to leave the cabin.

'Hold hard now! Wheer dost thee think thee's gooing?' the bargee questioned. In the flickering light thrown off by the smoky lantern, his face was wolfish.

'I'm going to sleep on deck,' she told him.

He shook his head.

'Oh, no,' he said, his voice thick and husky. 'You'm agoing to share my bunk. That was part of the bargain.'

She looked at him steadily. 'That was no part of the bargain,' she answered, her heart thumping and her hands sweaty with sudden dread. 'And I don't choose to lie with you.'

'All right then,' he said. 'Let's put it this way. I'll chuck your brother here over the side and he can find lodgings in the fields and you with him.' He paused, then went on. 'And you listen to that wind arising and the rain starting to come on the roof, it's going to be a rough old night, by the sound on it. What state is he going to be in tomorrow? After a night in the wind and rain?'

Bron sighed and turned away from the ladder. She pulled her dress over her head then went to the bunk and lay on it. As the bargee's shadow loomed across her and the stench of his body filled her nostrils she closed her eyes and told herself, 'This is for you Jethro . . . and please God, you'll never know that I did it . . .'

At first light next morning, they continued their journey and made rapid progress. At the locks where there were queues of barges waiting to get through, the bargee's reputation amongst his fellows as a fighting man ensured that he went through first and just after noon they reached their destination.

The bargee helped Bron to place Jethro in a field where the canal ended, some distance from the tunnel workings, then said to her, 'You'm not a bad little wench, despite the gowky leg; and you makes a rare sweet pillow for a man to nestle on of a night time. Why don't you stay wi' me on board? You can keep your brother wi' you.'

She ignored the question and busied herself with Jethro, not even looking up at the bargee.

The man hawked and spat. 'Ahr well, suit yourself,' he told her, then threw a shilling on to the ground by her side.

'Here!' he said gruffly. 'That's all the money I got until I goes back to Dudley. At least it'll get you a bite to eat.'

He turned on his heel and walked away.

Bron sat gazing at the shilling, then lifted her head and called, 'Thanks for your help, master.'

He waved and shouted. 'I'm sorry for what happened last night, little 'un. But it's bin a long time sin I had a 'ooman, I couldn't help myself . . . If ever you changes your mind about my offer, then send word to me . . . Scummer's the name.'

'I'll not forget,' she called. He grinned at her and went on his way.

She left Jethro asleep in the field and made her way towards the tunnel working. As she neared the gaping cavern into the green hillside, she saw to one side of her the navvy encampment, a vast sprawl of shanties, tents and wood and turf bothies and leantos.

Knowing as she did that it was too dangerous for Jethro to be taken into Redditch, where his enemies might attempt to finish what they had begun, Bron had decided to try and find work and shelter for them here, until she could contact Doctor Murdoch and ask for his help. Also, she desperately needed money to buy Jethro the things he would need until he was well again.

Near to the camp a group of well-dressed men were standing talking to a large figure wearing the navvy rig. A little distance away was a second group of ragged men, women and children, all of them worn and hungry-looking.

Bron heard one of the well-dressed men saying, 'Now look here, Mortimer, we need more labour if we are to push this damned tunnel through on schedule. What is your objection to taking on these fellows?'

Mortimer, the big navvy, spat contemptuously in the direction of the ragged group.

'We want no damned Irishers on this job,' he growled in a thick Gloucestershire accent. 'Apart from them bringing their bloody ills into the camp and their damned papish priests, they're no good for the work. We need skilled men to drive shafts and all they're good for is to scrat a bit of peat from a bog. No, Mister Anderson, I'm telling you straight, my lads won't work with the buggers. If you wants to use them on another job, then that's your privilege, but we'em not having them on this one, and that's final.'

A tall lean man left the ragged group and came up to Mortimer.

'For Jasus' sake, sor! We've walked from Liverpool to get here, and we've not felt food in our bellies for two days now. All we're asking you for is some work. We're not begging! We're ready and willing to work for any wages at any work you want to give us to do.'

Mortimer swung to face the Irishman. 'The best thing you can do, Paddy, is to walk to Liverpool again and get a boat back to where you came from. I'll not have a load of bog-trotting bastards like you undercutting the wages of Englishmen on this job.'

Anderson, who was the engineer, intervened. 'Look here, Mortimer, I'm the engineer and it's my responsibility to see that the work is finished in good time.'

'And it will be finished!' Mortimer shouted. 'But you remember that I'm the contractor for labour and I want no rebel scum on this job. I only want English, Scots and Welsh, with beef in their guts. I'll get the labour that's needed, I've already sent for a gang to come from Shropshire off one of Telford's jobs.'

He pushed the Irishman roughly. 'Now you get on out of here, Paddy, afore I puts my fist in your earhole and gets my lads to run your mates off.'

The Irishman stood his ground, his temper rising, but then a haggard-eyed young woman, with a torn threadbare shawl over her head and shoulders and carrying a sickly baby in her thin arms, pulled his arm.

'Come on, Con ... There's nothing to be gained here. Come husband, let's go, please.'

Her man's mouth was white and pinched at the edges with his anger. 'All we're asking for is work,' he exclaimed bitterly. 'It doesn't matter how bad paid the job is. For the love of God! Give us work so that we can put some grub into the bellies of our women and children.'

Anderson seemed truly saddened for the man. 'I'm sorry, believe me. Truly sorry! But there's nothing I can do if the contractor does not agree.'

Mortimer bellowed to the men who were working around the shaft entrance. 'Get over here, you lot, and run these bloody papishes off.'

'Don't bother to shout at them, we'll go,' the Irishman said dispiritedly, and he led his ragged band away.

When they had gone the argument broke out afresh.

'Good Lord, Mr Mortimer!' the engineer said. 'It would have done no harm to give those poor people work here, there are many jobs they could have done.'

'You listen to me, Anderson.' The big contractor clenched his fists. 'I'm a loyal subject of King George, God bless him, and I want no damned rebels on my contracts, not while there are loyal Englishmen crying out for bread. Besides, I

214

lost a brother at Vinegar Hill back in '98 when those bastards were in rebellion.'

The engineer looked shocked. 'I didn't know that, Mortimer.'

'Well, you know now,' the contractor said, and the argument ended.

Bron had heard everything and felt that this was not a good time to ask for work. Instead she turned aside and went into the camp.

The ground around and between the tents was littered with rubbish and empty bottles. Mangy dogs trotted among the offal and gnawed at bones, while dozens of dirty half-naked children ran hooting and shouting in play. Tough, sun-bronzed women busied themselves with domestic chores or sat laughing and gossiping or playing cards. Some smoked rank-smelling tobacco in short clay pipes and drank from bottles of beer and gin, others haggled and rowed in a hundred varied disputes.

From a doorway of a large shanty, an old woman, wearing a ragged sackcloth dress over torn petticoats, which showed her dangling shrivelled dugs, beckoned to Bron.

'Have you new come to the camp, hinny?'

Bron went to her. 'I have, and I'm looking for work.'

The old woman looked her up and down. 'There's nae work here for women on the cutting, hinny. That black-hearted devil of a contractor will not let women on the cutting.' Seeing Bron's crestfallen expression, the old woman said, 'Come in here for a wee while, we might think of something.'

Bron followed her inside. The far end of the shanty was dominated by a great brick-built oven and fireplace on which a huge iron cauldron full of liquid was bubbling greasily. From a rafter over the cauldron, lengths of string with wood and bone plaques attached to them hung down to disappear into the bubbling mess. The old woman cackled with glee at Bron's reaction.

'It's arl right, hinny. That's nae a witches' brew. It's the lads' vittles cooking. I ties the meat to the different bits o' string and they makes their marks on yon bits o' wood. Then there's no argifying over who the meat belongs tae.'

Bron nodded in understanding and stared about her. On

each side of the room was a row of double-decked bunks, empty now, for all the men were working; and down the centre of the room was a continuous trestle table, with wooden benches placed each side of it.

'Here, hinny!' The old woman rummaged beneath her layers of rags and pulled out a dark green bottle. 'Here, take a drop of the cratur. It'll do you good.'

Bron sipped the fiery spirit carefully, suppressing the urge to cough it out of her mouth. The old woman replaced the bottle and asked, 'What sort of work was you looking for, hinny?'

'Anything I could have got,' Bron answered. 'I've been a pit lass, so I know how to work.'

'Hmm.' The woman considered the answer, then asked, 'Have you no man with you?'

Bron told her about Jethro.

'That's bad, hinny ... very bad ... Well now, hinny, to my way of thinking, you'll have to jump the broomstick if you wants to stay here. You'll be able to pick your man, mind, a pretty cratur like you. But if you don't jump the stick, your life will be a misery with a dozen lads fighting to get into your bed at nights.' She grinned, showing toothless gums, and spittle flecked her sunken mouth. 'They'm some lusty sods, these navvy lads, I'll tell you. Why, when they's got a skinful, there's some of the buggers even takes their pleasure using me.' She cackled with laughter. 'Still they do say as how the older the nut the sweeter the meat, don't they.'

Bron felt a spasm of revulsion for the old crone, but then told herself that she had been no better, behaving as she had with the bargee.

'Is my grub cooked yet, you filthy old bat?' A young navvy came into the shanty smothered from head to feet in wet clay and mud.

'Here's my favourite sweetheart,' the old woman cackled.

'Young Jos, they calls him . . . Ahr, he's the lad to tickle a woman's fancies an't you, boy?'

The young man cuffed her across the head. 'Just get my grub and less of the nonsense, you old crow,' he told her roughly, and seated himself at the table. While the old woman fetched his food and ale, he eyed Bron.

'And who are you, my pretty?' He grinned at her, showing strong even teeth which gleamed whitely from the mask of mud and clay covering his face.

'Bronwen Elliot,' she told him.

'Bronwen? That's a Welsh name?' he asked.

She nodded. 'My mother was from Wales.'

'Ahr, I knows that country well. Me name's Jos Boswell, I used to travel all over those parts with me Dad.'

The old crone fetched him a chunk of beef, steaming hot from the cauldron. Beside it, she placed a loaf of bread, with cheese and onions and a jug of ale which she tapped from a barrel behind the fireplace.

'This maid's looking for a man to jump the broomstick with,' the old woman told Jos. 'I told her that she's bound to jump the stick if she stays here.'

Jos regarded Bron carefully as she sat, head bowed, blushing with embarrassment, and indicated the meat.

'Would you like a bite of food?' he asked, and using a sharp knife he cut a thick slice of the tender beef, and, breaking bread from the loaf, he handed the food to her.

'Go on . . . take it.' He smiled. 'There's no charge for this, and it ain't going to poison you.'

Her stomach clamoured for the food and with a word of thanks she took it from him and began to tear at it with sharp need.

'Give us another jack here,' Jos ordered the old crone, and when she gave him the leather drinking jack, he filled it with ale and pushed it across to Bron. 'There now, my pretty. You just get that down you as well, it'll do you good.'

After they had eaten, Jos lit up a clay pipe and then began to question Bron. She told him about Jethro, not giving his name but merely saying that he was her brother.

When she had finished her story, Jos pondered over what she had told him for some minutes, then said, 'Well, Bron, what the old un here has told you is the truth. If you stays here, then you'll have to become somebody's woman, you know what I mean, you'll be sort of his wife. Now I likes the look of you, and I needs a woman. You stop here for a few days and then if we finds we gets on all right together, why, we'll jump the broomstick, and I'll help you all I can with your brother. I'm not a bad-hearted chap, you'll find, al-

217

though I knows I'm a bit rough and ready in me ways. So you just think about it. You can sleep here meanwhile and I'll feed you and your brother, and you can do me washing and that. There'll be no trouble for you here, because I'm the cock navvy in this hut and I doubt there's a man in the whole camp as can stand to the mark with me ... So? What do you say?'

Bron only hesitated for seconds, then she nodded agreement.

He smiled. 'Good on you, pretty. You won't regret it. Let's goo and have a look at your brother, shall us?'

'There's one thing you should know first,' she said, and getting to her feet she hobbled up and down the room in front of him. 'I'm gowky-legged.'

Jos, after his initial shock, laughed it off. 'Well, I'm gowky in the head, so that makes us even starters, don't it.'

His laughter died when he saw Jethro. He grabbed Bron by her long hair and brought her face to within inches of his.

'You're a bloody liar!' he shouted. 'Now you tell me the real story. I knows this cove well, and he aren't got a sister ... So what's the truth of it?'

To save herself from his threatening fists, Bron told him everything. When she told him of seeing Batten and Peter Stanton's corpses, and about Batten being handless, he paled beneath his mask of mud and clay and released her abruptly.

'Damn my bloody eyes!' he breathed. 'That was my brothers did that to him, as sure as there's a God above ... It was them that done this to 'im, then ... I bin working here for months,' he told Bron. 'Only I took a few days' holiday to meet up wi' my family for the Tipton Wakes.' He went on to tell her about the fight, and the wild threats his brothers had made to kill Batten after the defeat of their father. 'If my old Dad knew what they'd done, he'd kill um,' he said. 'It would break his heart, so it would. Batten beat him fair and square in the fight, and the Stantons were always good friends to us. Jethro here was my best mate.'

He squatted at the side of Jethro who only gazed vacantly at him. Jos reached out and tentatively touched the sick man's cheek.

'I'll goo t'Hanover, Jethro boy! It fair grieves me, so it does, to see you like this and to know that it was men of my

218

blood who did it to you. Well, don't fret, boy! Jos will look arter you, like you was my own babby.' He looked up at Bron. 'The first thing I'm going to do when I get some money is to go and get Doctor Murdoch,' he told her, and smiled. 'Don't you worry now, my pretty, we'll see that Jethro's got well again, won't us?'

Bron felt her heart lighten, and she smiled back at him.

CHAPTER THIRTY-SIX

The horseman let his mount walk slowly up the steep hill on top of which stood the church of Beoley village. On the crest of the hill, he reined in the animal and sat motionless in the saddle, gazing across the valley of the River Arrow to where on the hills above the river lay the buildings of Redditch town. From this distance, the town looked pretty and peaceful, and even the smoke curling from the tall stacks of the many needle mills only added to the intimacy of the scene.

The rider was of medium height, his youthful face deeply suntanned, but thin and worn. He wore the dark green uniform with the slung pelisse and cylindrical hussar busby and black accoutrements of an officer of the Rifles; and across the back of one thin hand, running up to lose itself under the sleeve of the coat, he bore the livid scar of a sabre slash. He gazed intently across the valley with its sun-flecked river and he smiled in contentment.

Mark Purcell had come home.

'Annie? Annie, Where are you?'

Anne Bartleet was sitting at her open bedroom window enjoying the summer day when her sister came bursting into the room.

'Why did you not answer me?' Abigail demanded.

Anne sighed and gave her attention to the younger girl.

'How do I look?' Abigail pirouetted across the room.

Dressed in a flowing lavender gown, a dainty bonnet upon her shining hair and twirling a feathery parasol, she was so beautiful that for a moment Anne found herself fiercely resenting the passage of years which would inevitably erode that beauty. She swallowed the lump that had risen in her throat and replied, 'You look quite pretty today.'

'Only quite pretty?' Abigail assumed an expression of mock dismay.

'Very well then,' Anne laughed. 'You look lovely.'

'That's better,' her sister giggled. 'I only hope that Harry feels the same way.'

'You may be sure that he thinks you to be the most divine creature that was ever created,' Anne said fondly. 'When is he coming for you?'

'At any moment now,' Abigail answered. 'Anne? What do you think of Harry? Tell me, truthfully.'

Anne took the girl's gloved hand in her own. 'I think that Harry Washford is a very fine man, and a true gentleman,' she said gravely. 'And I think that any girl who had him for a husband could count herself very, very fortunate.'

'Do you mean that? ... Truly?' Abigail begged.

Anne nodded. 'Truly!' she affirmed.

Abigail smiled radiantly. 'Oh, I am so happy Anne, and I will tell you a secret, but you must not speak of it to anyone. Will you promise?'

'I promise.'

'Well, Harry Washford wants to marry me ... I can tell.'

Abigail's face mirrored her surprise at her sister's reaction to the news. Anne threw back her head and laughed long and loudly.

'Why are you laughing?' Abigail was mystified.

Anne could only shake her head helplessly.

'Oh my dear!' she finally managed to say. 'That secret must be the most widely known fact in the whole county. Everyone knows that Harry is dying of love for you, and wishes to marry you. He asks father at least ten times a week for your hand; and father keeps telling him that although he finds him eminently satisfactory as a prospective son-in-law, yet Harry must ask you himself, since father is not a Mussul-man and does not believe in the custom of arranged matches.'

Abigail dissolved in happy laughter. 'If he is too timid to ask me to marry him, then I shall propose to him ... this very day!'

Anne was shocked. 'Oh no, Abi! That would not be lady-like.'

The younger girl removed her glove and snapped her

fingers above her head.

'That is what I care for being ladylike,' she said scornfully, and they giggled together until Abigail chanced to look out of the window. She gave a faint cry of surprise.

'What is it? What is the matter?' Anne asked anxiously.

Abigail pointed. 'It is he!'

'Who?' Anne went to look also. 'Oh, my dear God!' She closed her eyes and swayed.

Abigail leant from the window and bawled in a most un-ladylike manner, 'Mark Purcell, you great booby! If you do not come up here this instant and kiss my sister hard enough to prevent her fainting, which she is doing now, then I will break my parasol across your head.'

It was to be a double event, they all decided. Anne and Abigail Bartleet would wed Mark Purcell and Harry Wash-ford at the church of St Stephen, just as soon as the banns could be called. Among the older, more staid inhabitants of the district, eyebrows were raised and whispered asides exchanged. Charles Bartleet himself was censured for allowing his daughters to behave in such a headstrong fashion; and it was most unseemly, the staid ones whispered, for young women to show such haste to enter the marriage bed.

Charles Bartleet hid a smile, and said in reply to his critics, 'I have long since conceded defeat in the battle to make my daughters conduct themselves in a ladylike manner.'

CHAPTER THIRTY-SEVEN

Doctor Murdoch completed his examination of Jethro, and called for Jos and Bron to come into the turf leanto that Jos had built for Bron and Jethro to live in.

'Ye'll be happy to hear that I think that I can cure his paralysis,' he told them both.

'And his loss of sense, sir? What of that?' Bron asked him.

The stout, red-faced Scotsman looked at her with wise eyes.

'If I said that I was an expert on the workings of the human brain, then I would be a liar, my wee lassie ... But I think that as a result of the wound at the base of the skull, a pressure of fluids has been caused, affecting certain areas of the brain. I hope that when I operate and drain the fluids, then the pressure will be relieved and he will regain his intelligence.'

'But you'm not sure, sir?' Jos questioned.

The Doctor pursed his lips judiciously. 'No!' he admitted. 'I'm not certain. Only hopeful.'

'When will you operate?' Bron wanted to know.

'Immediately,' the doctor answered. 'But ye'd best find a couple of strong men to hold him still. The operation's a wee bit difficult to do, in fact I've only ever done it once before, and that was on a monkey that my sailor nephew brought home from Africa.' He patted Bron's cheek and his eyes twinkled. 'Don't you worry, young woman. There's a hell of a lot of similarity between yon monkey and the human body.'

He winked at them both. 'I'd no' be at all surprised to find out that, contrary to what our religious brethren would have us believe, the noble monkey is our cousin and ancestor, not that fellow Adam. In fact, when I read about the tricks some of our monarchy and government get up to, then I'm damned sure of it.'

223

He waved his arms.

'Away wi' ye, get the table scrubbed clean in yon shanty, and fetch the men to help.'

When all was prepared, Jethro was carried into the shanty and laid face downwards on the freshly cleaned eating table. Two friends of Jos's had come to help, and when they had secured Jethro, the doctor removed his coat and rolled up his sleeves.

'I've give him a wee something to make him drowsy,' he told his helpers. 'But he'll still feel me cutting, so take great care that he does nae move his head or neck. If my hand were to slip, he could well be paralysed for life.'

They took their positions and the doctor cut with his scalpel. As the soft skin parted, a gout of black blood and yellow pus welled from the gaping wound, and a foul smell filled the onlookers' nostrils. For a moment Bron felt sick with apprehension, then the skill of the surgeon absorbed her and all worry dropped away. The trancelike hush ended when Doctor Murdoch tied the last stitch to hold the edges of the wound together and straightened his back with a groan.

'Guid God Almichty! This damned Sassenach damp will cripple me yet ... That'll do fine now. This young man should be walking around as good as new in a few weeks.'

Bron thanked him with tears in her eyes. The doctor waved her thanks and praise away.

'Don't thank me, young woman,' he pointed at Jos. 'Give your thanks to that one there who is paying me very well for my trouble, and can rely on my discretion in this matter, I might add. The pity is that I don't know if it will have any effect on Stanton's intellect. You may now have a full-grown, active man to care for who has an empty, useless mind; and if that is the case, then I have no idea as to what the remedy would be. I have done all I can. We must hope. If ye're religious ye can always try prayer ... Though personally, I have little faith in that exercise.'

After Murdoch had left the camp and Jethro was sleeping soundly in the leanto, Jos Boswell led Bron a distance away from the camp.

'I want to talk wi' you, Bronny,' he said, when they halted in a spinney of young larches. 'It's bin weeks now sin' you come to the camp. Now when I found out about your feelin'

224

for Jethro, I didn't press you to be my woman, but you 'eard what the Doctor said, Jethro's mind might be gone for good, then 'e'll be a loony for the rest on 'is life. Now you'll not be able to care for 'im on your own ... ull you?'

'It's not certain he'll be a loony, and even if he was I'd still take care of him,' she answered bravely.

'It wun't be possible, and you knows it wun't,' he told her brutally. 'You'd do better to jump the broomstick wi' me, Bronny. Then the two on us ull care for 'im ... Come on, now,' he coaxed. 'What does you say? I knows that you reckons you loves 'im, but remember, girl. The Jethro you loved could'a gone, and all that's left then is a loony, who's no more use than a blind puppy.'

'But suppose his mind does come back? What then?' she protested.

He stared at her in great sadness and when he spoke his voice was gentle.

'Be honest wi' yourself, Bronny. Does you really think that Jethro Stanton ud ever marry you? If by any chance he ever did, it ud only be out o' pity, and you wouldn't want that.'

Her face was tragic for she knew in her heart that what Jos said was the truth. She made one last despairing effort.

'Perhaps, deep down, he does love me!'

Jos took her gently by her shoulders and with one hand he tilted her chin so that their eyes met.

'Bronny, my love, if that be right, why is it he's never once called for you all the time he's bin badly?' His soft loving tones hardened a little. 'I'se 'eard him night arter night, acallin' out in 'is sleep for a girl named Abigail, whoever that might be. His "darling Abi".'

For a long minute she stared at him with hopeless eyes, and he waited patiently. Then, her face expressionless, she asked, 'Did you mean what you said, Jos? About helping me care for Jethro for ever, if he's not cured?'

He nodded solemnly. 'I swear it, girl! Only be my woman. I'll be good to you, Bron, becos I loves you. With all my soul and body, I loves you.'

She made her decision. 'Very well then ... I'll be your woman.'

'When?' he questioned.

'Whenever you want.'

'Right, my pretty!' He grinned happily. 'We'll jump the broomstick next payday.'

In the early hours of the following morning, Jethro woke. He groaned softly and stirred. In an instant Bron had left her sleepless bed and was beside him.

'Lie quiet, Jethro! I'll bring light.' She fumbled in the darkness for a stub of candle and went to light it at the glowing ashes of the shanty cooking fire. When she returned, she saw in the wavering glow Jethro, lying propped on his back on a bed of sacking, feeling with one weak, uncertain hand the curious contraption that the doctor had fashioned from laths of wood and leather straps to immobilize his patient's head and neck.

'Bronny?' His voice was puzzled and half-fearful. 'Bronny? What's happened to me?' Suffering twisted his features. 'My father's been killed, murdered! And so has Batten ... Where am I? What ...'

'Don't speak, honey!' she begged, and going to him she placed her finger across his lips. 'Don't say nothing for a while.'

Fighting to hold back tears of joyous relief at his recovery, she began to tell him of what had occurred, and why and where he was. It was almost an hour later when she finished, and the stub of candle had long since melted to nothingness.

'There is so much that I have to do,' Jethro said, when she fell silent. 'I must bring my father's murderers to justice, and I must repay your kindness to me.' The sadness and strain in his voice was overlaid by a note of determination. 'I shall do both those things, but first I must grow strong and well once more.' His voice softened. 'For apart from those things, I cannot go back to my Abi as a helpless cripple.'

Bron's tears fell freely now, but this time they were of grief.

'I've lost you, Jethro,' she thought. 'God forgive me for wishing it, but I would that you were helpless and mindless again, for then you were mine and mine only.'

CHAPTER THIRTY-EIGHT

Harry Washford had shares in the Canal Company and followed the progress of the Tardibegge Tunnel with great interest. Today being Saturday, he had arranged to make a carriage party with his bride-to-be, her sister and Mark Purcell. They made a fine show as they set off, the girls in flowered gowns and wide floppy-brimmed hats, and the men dressed like a pair of London dandies in the height of fashion. Under Abigail's urgings, Harry's normally sombre clothing was gradually being discarded. Today he wore fine ruffled linen, and a brightly coloured waistcoat and cravat under a plum-shaded coat, and white breeches tucked into soft high boots.

The party reached the workings in the early afternoon and were met by Charles Anderson and Mortimer. Over in the camp they could see the navvies lounging about, surrounded by swarms of hucksters and market-women selling all manner of produce. Even as they watched, a cheer went up from the waiting navvies at the sight of a wagon loaded with barrels and crates of bottles lurching into the camp. Charles Anderson laughed at the puzzled faces of his guests and explained.

'It's payday for the men. They're going on one of their sprees, isn't that so, Mr Mortimer?'

The big contractor nodded. 'They goes on the randy every time they gets their money ... And there's no work to be got from them until all the rhino's spent. It'll be worse this time,' he added. 'There's going to be some stick-jumping later, that's always good for a damned riot ... Pardon the expression, ma'am.'

'What in the world is stick-jumping, Mr Mortimer?' Abigail asked.

'Well, ma'am, it's the navigator's way of getting married. They calls it "Jumping the broomstick". They takes their woman and they jumps over a broomstick three times, then they are counted as man and wife.'

'Oh, how quaint!' Abigail said delightedly. 'Would we be able to see the ceremony, Mr Mortimer?'

The big man was hesitant. 'Well, ma'am, I don't rightly know if it would be a proper thing. They'm a terrible rough bunch, ma'am, and the language and rows are something vile when they're on the randy. Not to mention the sights you might see.'

Abigail seemed disappointed. 'Mr Anderson?' she appealed. 'Cannot you persuade Mr Mortimer to let us see the ceremony? I am sure that both I and my sister would be able to disregard the language.'

The engineer glanced at Harry Washford, trying to gauge the wishes of this important shareholder. Harry smiled dotingly at Abigail and added his plea to hers.

'Be a good chap, Anderson, let us see the ceremony. I've heard that the navigators, for all their rough ways, are most welcoming and hospitable to visitors.'

Anderson shrugged helplessly. 'We are at the mercy of your decision, Mr Mortimer.'

Mortimer shook his head, then said doubtfully, 'Very well, ladies and gentlemen, I'll see what I can do. But it will be some time yet before they start to jump. They've got a thirst to quench before anything else.'

'Excellent!' Charles Anderson smiled. 'That will give us ample time to view the workings and enjoy a little picnic meal that I've arranged.'

Gaily the party went towards the tunnel entrance, leaving the big contractor looking after them ambiguously.

'Yes,' he muttered. 'I'm sure that you fine gentry will enjoy seeing the labouring beasts having a merry-making. Maybe it'll even open your eyes to the fact that they'm human beings.'

'Away, Geordie man! Let's hear thy music.'

The eating had finished and now the navvies tumbled everything out of the long shanty except for benches lining the walls and the trestles supporting the barrels of ale and cider.

228

In one corner they improvised a small platform from planks raised a couple of feet above the floor on bricks. On this platform the three fiddlers, led by Northumberland George, tuned up their instruments. A pair of young girls stood with them, one with a tambourine, the other with a tabor.

The tiny hump-backed fiddler, his face glowing bright red with the effects of the gin and rum he had been pouring down his throat, ignored the shouts for music until he felt ready to play. Then he tapped his foot twice on the platform and called, 'Away, lads ... Give um the "Rowan Tree".'

The tambourine and tabor jangled and rattled out the rhythm, the fiddles swung in to join them and the dancing began.

Navvies in their party rig of velveteen breeches and waistcoat, coloured shirts, bright red or purple kerchiefs around their thick brown necks, with white stockings ending incongruously in heavy clogs, stamped and turned and jumped high in the Northumberland reels, the Irish jigs, Lancashire clog dances, Highland flings and Cotswold Morris steps. Their women in richly coloured shawls, ribbons tied in flowing hair, white petticoats frothing under raised skirts, swayed and dipped and matched the intricate footwork of their menfolk.

'Browns Reel', 'Father O'Flynn', 'The Hag with the Money', 'Highland Whisky', 'The Dairy Maid', the fiddles soared high, swooped low and soared again, while the tambourine tinkled and the tabor rattled. The ale and cider, the gin and rum flowed, shirtsleeves were rolled up displaying mighty arms and bodices were loosened across full, heaving breasts. Outside in the dust, the children pranced in solemn imitation of their elders.

At times, individual dancers and pairs would hold the floor alone, performing miracles of tapping, stamping, high-stepping, high-kicking footwork, and the applause would thunder, drowning momentarily the strains of the 'Irish Washerwoman', 'False Knight on the Road', 'Jack's Choice', 'Bryan O'Lynn', 'The Masons Apron' and the 'Rakes of Mallow'. Sweat ran down bodies, darkening shirts and dresses and voices grew hoarse through shouting slurred with drinking, and husky with loving. At intervals, noted singers would render their offerings. The lively:

> '*It's of a London Cockerney, I now will relate*
> *Who went into the countery to find himself a mate,*'

The sentimental

> '*Lay still, my bonny shepherd, and don't you rise up,*
> *It's a fine dewy morning and my love it's wet.*'

And the popular roaring, ranting choruses of

> '*Still I sing, bonny boys, bonny mad boys,*
> *Bedlam boys are bonny ...*
> *For they all go there and they live on the air*
> *And they want no drink or money.*'

'You sing, Bronny, I knows you got a lovely voice. I've heard you singing.' Jos kissed her on the cheek and pushed her on to the platform. He jumped up beside her and held up his arms. 'Now listen, cullys, give my woman here a chance to sing, will you.'

The din lessened a trifle and Bron, half-dazed by drink and the excitement of the happiest time she had known for many, many years, opened her mouth to sing. As she did so, two drunken Scots began to moan a lugubrious lament. A dozen pairs of hands lifted the drunks bodily and hurled them through the door of the shanty.

'Goo on now, Bronny!'

'Gi's your song, lass.'

She thought for a moment of Jethro lying in the turf leanto, and she wept inside for her love of him. When she sang, she sang for Jethro, but she smiled at Jos, dark handsome Jos, standing so proudly beside his woman.

Her pure voice filled the room and quietened even the most heedless and uncaring, managing to touch for an instant the buried softer feelings of the most hardened and callous.

> '*As I walked out one morning in the springtime of the year*
> *I overheard a sailorboy lying beside his lady fair.*
> *They sang a song together, made the valley for to ring*
> *While the birds of the spring in the meadows gay*
> *Proclaimed that love is green...*'

'What a beautiful song!' Abigail exclaimed as the sound of Bron's singing reached the party nearing the shanty. 'Shh!

230

Let us stand and listen,' she said, and they halted until the last haunting notes of the melody died away.

The hushed shanty erupted in a storm of cheering and clapping. Then the wild wailing of the fiddles started up again and the wooden floors thundered with the dancers' clogs.

Before entering the shanty, the visitors stood admiring the colourful scene. A good-looking young navvy, the flash kiss-curl called the Newgate knocker plastered down on his forehead, was performing a jig with his long-haired woman, and their heavy clogs skipped across the floor. They ended their solo and other couples joined in. Shepherded by Mortimer, the visitors entered the shanty and stood to one side. The navvies ignored them, except for a few nudges and winks and whispered admiring comments about the girls' beauty. A woman brought mugs of ale and offered food to the visitors. Anne sipped the ale and remarked, 'How well they dance.'

Mortimer bent and said, 'Strange is it not, ma'am, that even the lowest can show appreciation of music and enjoy themselves without bestiality.'

Anne regarded him searchingly, then said quietly, 'Mr Mortimer, I think you misunderstand our motives for wanting to see the celebrations. We do not believe ourselves to be in some menagerie for strange wild animals. On the contrary, our family has always stood as good friends to, and respecters of, those who have been unfortunate enough to possess less of the good things of this world than ourselves.' She gave a quick smile. 'I apologize if that statement sounds as pompous to you as it does to me.'

The big man instantly softened towards her. 'I beg your pardon, ma'am, for the manner in which I spoke; and I mean that most sincerely.'

Abigail watched the dancers with bright eyes.

'I think it is wonderful!' she told Anderson. 'They have so much colour and vitality, and look at the different characters to be seen here! Why they make us seem insipid, don't they?'

Harry Washford nodded ruefully. 'I must agree with you, my love.'

But Mark Purcell laughed. 'It does my heart good to see it. With all the poverty and hardship in our country at present, it is good to find that all joy of life has not disappeared, or been crushed from the poor.'

'Oh lord! Not another Radical joining our family?' Abigail teased him. 'Poor father is being submerged in a sea of them.' She turned to Harry. 'Are you enjoying it, Harry?'

'Yes, sweetheart,' he answered, adoring her with his eyes. 'It's like one of Pieter Breughel's paintings of peasant dancers.'

'Isn't it really so,' she agreed happily.

The jig ended, and while the dancers wiped their sweating faces and gulped at huge jugs of ale, Bron sang again. This time it was a song she had learned in the coalpits. Her pure voice effortlessly poured out in sad lament.

> 'Rap her tae bank, me canny lads
> Wind her away, keep turning.
> The backshift men are gannin' hyem
> They'll be back here in the morning.'

As the tale of tragic happenings unfolded, Abigail whispered to Mortimer, 'What is it she sings?'

'It's a colliers' song ma'am,' he told her. 'It comes from the north, but I've heard them sing it over in the Black Country.'

'How does she know of it?'

'Why, ma'am, she was a pit wench.'

'A pit wench?' Abigail was plainly surprised. 'But she appears such a sweet-faced, fragile creature, and she is crippled, is she not?'

'Yes, ma'am,' Mortimer explained. 'It was a rock fall that caught her. But she's a whole lot tougher than she looks. She's jumping the broomstick with that young man standing by her.' He indicated Jos Boswell.

Abigail looked hard at the swarthy young man.

'I could swear that I know his face,' she murmured.

'I doubt it ma'am,' Mortimer grinned. 'He's of tinker stock.'

Impulsively, Abigail asked, 'Might I meet the young woman? I would love to speak with her and learn something of her life in the pits.'

Mortimer left her side. When the fiddlers struck up a reel, he returned bringing with him Bron Elliot. He presented her to the visitors and she blushed shyly and curtsied.

'Now then, Bronny,' Mortimer said bluffly. 'This lady is Miss Abigail Bartleet and she wants to hear something of you.'

At the mention of the name, Bron paled and stepped back with shock.

'Are you all right?' Abigail asked.

Bron's mind raced. 'I'd like a breath of air, ma'am. I feel a bit faint all of a sudden.'

'I'll come with you,' Abigail said. 'And then you can tell me about yourself ... I'll not be long,' she told the others, and followed the crippled girl outside.

It was now approaching dusk and the lamps were being lit in the tents and shanties. While Abigail asked question after question, Bron answered automatically and studied this beautiful young creature. She knew without doubt that this must be the girl Jethro loved, the one that he had called for and raved about in his delirium. Finally, unable to restrain herself any longer, she blurted out, 'Please, ma'am, Jethro Stanton is here at the camp!'

Abigail halted in mid-speech, fear and shock mingling in her face.

'What did you say?' she gasped out.

Bron felt strength surge through her. 'Come with me.'

She took Abigail's soft white hand and led her to the leanto.

'Wait a moment.' Bron lit the lantern that hung from the turf wall and beckoned the other. 'In here, come now!'

Warily, Abigail entered the leanto. Jethro was asleep, still wearing the wood and leather brace.

'Don't be alarmed, ma'am,' Bron said. 'He was hurt bad, but he's all right now and ull soon be able to leave that thing off.' She bent and woke the sleeping man. 'Jethro? Miss Abigail has come to see you.'

His eyes opened and he stared in blank disbelief.

'Jethro?' Bron was near to tears. 'It's Miss Abigail has come.'

She caught Abigail's arm and forced her down until their three faces were illuminated by the lantern. In Jethro's eyes the disbelief was swept away by incredulous joy.

He blinked hard, once, twice, then smiled and said, 'Abi, you've come ... Abi, love!'

The girl's expression was momentarily confused, then it hardened and from behind the mask of her beauty, the petulant, spoilt, capricious child burst through.

'Why did you come back? There is nothing I can do for you, Jethro, and there's nothing to be said between us. I no longer love you and in a week's time I am to marry Harry Washford.'

Without another word she rose to her feet and was gone from the leanto. Tears spilled from Bron's eyes when she saw the shocked pain in Jethro's face.

'Did I dream that?' he asked, pitifully. 'Did I?'

'No, Jethro, you didn't dream it. It would have been better if you hadn't got your memory back than to see this happen,' she sobbed.

Almost an hour passed before Jethro spoke again.

He said, 'I remember when my father was murdered, I heard the voice of the man who did it. Now that Abigail is lost to me I've only one goal left in my life . . . to kill John Mence.'

In spite of all Bron's entreaties, he would say nothing more and eventually she despaired of him and returned to the festivities. Abigail and the visitors had gone and Jos was too drunk and merry to question her about her absence; and when she saw his happiness, she knew that she could do nothing to destroy it by telling him what had happened. If she told him he would insist that their union be postponed and he was too good a man to be tormented in this way. Besides, she had made a bargain with him, and she would fulfil her part of it.

'It's time!' a woman screeched; and quickly the people in the shanty who could still stand upright formed two lines facing each other down the length of the room. Three broomsticks were produced and held thigh-high at intervals spanning the gauntlet. The promised couples paired off and the fiddlers played yet another jig, while the crowd stamped, clapped, cheered and exhorted. Pair by pair the couples ran hand in hand through the gauntlet, leaping together over the broomsticks.

Bron looked with shame at her crippled legs. 'I'll not be able to jump, Jos!' she choked out.

He laughed at her, his white teeth gleaming in the flaring light of the lamps. 'There's no need for you to jump, my pretty,' he shouted joyfully. 'I'll do it for both of us.'

He snatched her up in his muscled arms and ran the gauntlet, jumping as lightly as a mountain goat over the broomsticks.

The navvies cheered his gesture wildly as he took Bron in his arms when he had finished the run and kissed her with passion.

'You'm really my woman now,' he breathed into her ear.

She closed her eyes, and in her heart she called for Jethro Stanton.

CHAPTER THIRTY-NINE

The weeks passed and the summer was drawing to an end. Jethro had long since discarded the headbrace, and each day as he grew stronger he would walk for ever-increasing distances through the woods and fields surrounding Tardebigge, but always avoiding Redditch and its environs. Once he met a party of riders cantering along a bridle path and suddenly found himself face to face with Abigail. Not by a tremor of her beautiful features or even a flicker of her black eyes did she acknowledge him. Staring at him as if he were a total stranger, she galloped past, and, as the tiny tufts of earth and grass thrown up by her horse's hooves struck his body, Jethro forced himself to return her stare impassively. It was only in the hours of darkness that he surrendered to his bitter grief and, in the privacy of his crude leanto, wept for his lost love.

For Harry Washford, Jethro felt no animosity. He knew too well the fascination that Abigail, now Harry's wife, could exercise upon any man; and deep within himself he began to wonder whether any man would ever hold that lovely, self-centred creature.

Denied his love, Jethro surrendered to the opposite emotion ... hate. Hate for John Mence. Night after night, Jethro lay sleepless on his hard pallet and promised himself, 'Some day, Mence, you will find yourself looking into my eyes and at that moment you will be facing your death.'

Early one fine morning, as the autumn winds blew boisterously across the countryside, stripping the dead and dying leaves from the trees and hedgerows, and scattering them across the shorn fields, Bron brought Jethro his breakfast of onion porridge. She found him awake and busily wrapping strips of sacking around his boots and calves.

'What are you up to, Jethro?' she asked.

He smiled at her and went on tugging at the sacking.

'I'm starting back to work,' he told her.

'But you're not fit to,' she protested. 'Why, you've not got enough strength back to toil.'

'Perhaps not,' Jethro answered. 'And if I go on like this, I'll never get it back. I must start to use my muscles again, before they waste away ... No!' he cut her short. 'There's nothing to be said. I've already decided. I'm going to speak with Mortimer this morning, Jos says he'll support me.'

Her gentle face flushed and she snapped, 'I'll give Jos a piece of my mind for this.'

Jethro shook his head. 'No, you must never do that,' he said quietly. 'He's too good a man to be badgered.'

Bron's flash of temper subsided as quickly as it had risen, and softly she replied, 'Aye, Jethro ... He is too good a man indeed.'

Jos had been true to his promise and had helped Bron to care for Jethro, and treated her always as a precious possession, constantly giving her tokens of tenderness as a mark of the love he felt for her. Bron had not grown to love him in return, in spite of her own desire to do so. Her heart was still held by the man who had rescued her from her purgatory, but she felt great tenderness for Jos and came sweet to his bed at nights, never showing by word or action that she still loved Jethro Stanton and could not conquer her burning jealousy towards Abigail Washford. She had tried one day to talk with Jethro about his ex-sweetheart, but he had refused to answer, merely saying, 'That part of my life is dead, Bron. Let us leave it buried in its grave.'

Jethro scraped the last savoury remnants of the onion porridge from the wooden bowl with his horn spoon and handed both utensils back to the girl.

'My thanks, Bronny.'

She looked fondly at him. 'You'll be needing more than this tonight, I'm thinking.'

'If I've energy enough left to chew,' he smiled, and left her.

He made his way through the bustling encampment, where at this hour of the morning the women were sweeping shanties and bothies, the swarms of children were screaming and shouting at play, and the packs of dogs were already snarling and tussling for old bones and stinking refuse. At the tunnel workings, Jos was standing by the entrance with the contractor, Mortimer. The big man regarded Jethro shrewdly. 'Have you done any tunnelling work before, young fellow?' he asked.

'No, sir. I was a carter,' Jethro told him.

'I've carters to spare.' The contractor's voice was harsh. 'And by the looks o' you, I don't think you'll be able to keep up wi' the navvies yet ... When Jos here told me he had a friend who wanted work, I thought you was a tunneller, or a navigator.'

'Look 'ere, marster ...' Jos began, but the contractor silenced him with a wave of his hand while continuing to look hard at Jethro. He went on, 'You've done no tunnelling, you're not strong enough for the navigating gangs, and I've sufficient carters ... What the Hell do I need you for?' Mortimer turned away.

'Hear me out, Mr Mortimer,' said Jethro, no trace of begging or humbleness in his tone. 'Never mind my strength, I'm asking no favours because I may still be a trifle weak. I'll do my share.'

The contractor shook his head. 'Look, young fellow, it takes a year's solid slogging to make a navigator. It takes that length o' time just to toughen his work muscles and stiffen his back so that he can keep up wi' his mates, and that's even when he comes in full vigour to work. When you come on to these works you was a helpless cripple ... oh yes!' He nodded at the expression of surprise on the men's faces. 'I know what goes on in the camp there, and when anybody new comes ... If I put you in a gang, your butties 'ud be at your throat and kick you from them if you couldn't keep up the pace.'

He went to turn away once more, but Jethro clamped one hand on his arm and held him.

'Is there a job on these works that no one will stick for more than a few days? ... Is there toil that's so ill-paid that no one wants it? Then give me that toil, Mr Mortimer; and I'll do it, and what's more I'll do it well.'

Jethro's determination was such that, in spite of himself, Mortimer was impressed. Unexpectedly, his hard face grinned. 'Take this young bugger to the puddling gang,' he ordered Jos. 'Tell Yorky Mitchell from me, to gie him the start.'

'Thank you, Mr Mortimer,' Jethro said.

The contractor laughed. 'I doubt you'll thank me for very long, young fellow. Still, you deserves a chance, I reckon. I likes the spunk you shows.'

Back in the camp, Bron was busy cleaning the turf-walled, wood-floored and roofed hut that Jos and his friends had built for his bride. The large single room was whitewashed and contained a rough-fashioned table and chairs and a plank bed, while in the corner was Bron's pride and joy, a brick fireplace with baking and roasting chambers ingeniously placed to draw controlled heat from the fire. To the side of the fireplace was a large wooden box in which she kept her brightly burnished utensils. Since the marriage, Bron had gathered rags and worked them into colourful bed-coverlets and tablecloths and even curtains to hang across the door and the two small glazed windows. Daily she gathered herbs and wild flowers in their seasons and arranged them in jars and old bottles around her home, lightening and sweetening its shadowed corners. She put aside her broom of twigs and drew water from the rain butt outside the door. Placing the container on the table she started to gut and clean a rabbit that Jos had snared the previous evening. A sudden commotion outside made her run to the door once more.

Across from her hut was the long shanty where she had first met Jos on her arrival at the camp. The old woman who had befriended her, Durham Jill, was now lying outside the shanty wailing and screeching in pain and fury. Straddling her half-naked body another woman, younger and heavier, was tearing at Durham Jill's sack rags of clothing. Attracted by the noise, more women and the inevitable swarm of dogs and children came hurrying to see what was happening.

'You besom bitch! You dirty, thievin' besom bitch!' the younger woman grunted, then in her turn screamed in agony as Durham Jill's filthy fingers gouged into her eyes. She rolled back her head and tried to drag the old woman's fingers from her face. As she did so, Durham Jill reared violently and toppled her over. Before the younger woman could recover her balance, the old crone scuttled on hands and knees to where Bron was standing outside her hut and grasped the girl's long skirts.

'Help me, hinny!' she begged. 'Dinna let that cow get me agen!'

Without pausing to consider, Bron lifted the old woman to her feet and pushed her through the doorway of the hut. The younger woman, Meg Mitchell, wife of the puddlers' ganger man, Yorky Mitchell, was by now on her feet. She wiped tears from her gouged eyes, swearing vilely in deep gruff tones. Bron guarded her door and waited for whatever might happen. Meg Mitchell was fat and large, a slatternly, meaty-armed virago who ate, drank and swore like a man and could trade blow for blow with most men. She topped Bron by some inches and her bulk made Bron's pit-toughened body look frail by comparison. Mitchell finished wiping her eyes, then stared hard at the girl.

'Wheer's that old hell-bitch? 'As you got 'er in your shant?'

'Yes, I have.' Bron faced her bravely. 'Why were you fighting with her?'

'Wot's that to you, gowky legs?' the woman spat out.

Bron's hands, still clasping the half-gutted rabbit, began to tremble. For an instant of time she was back in her mind in the coal pits, a fragile gently nurtured young girl facing a vicious breed of bully, the like of which she had never encountered before in her whole life. That instant passed in a flash, Bron had learnt well how to fight and hold her own in the rough and tumble of coal mining and she felt no fear of this woman in front of her.

'It's whatever I choose to make it,' she said coldly. 'And I'll thank you not to becall me, my legs are what a fall of rock made them ... What made you resemble a fat sow?'

Meg Mitchell's face whitened at the insult and she cursed loudly. 'I'm agoing to break your bloody back for that, gowky legs; and then I'm agoing to tear that thievin' old bastard's 'ead from her shoulders.'

'Ye're a bleedin' liar, Meg Mitchell!' Durham Jill's indignant face appeared round the edge of the doorway. 'I didna pinch nothin' frae you. Ye're a bleedin' liar!'

Those standing watching began to urge the old woman on. Meg Mitchell was disliked and feared by most of them.

'That's right, Jill! Gie the fat cow 'er character!'

'Ahr, you tell 'er wheer her gets orf!'

'Iffen I was fowerty year younger, I'd tear your bleedin'

'ead orf arlright!' the old woman screeched defiantly.

'Gerrout o' my way, gowky legs,' Meg Mitchell threatened.

Bron stood her ground. 'What is it she's done?' she asked.

The other woman ran the back of her hand across her mouth and spat on the ground. 'Her's stole a bokkle o' best gin from me,' she shouted. 'And I means to take it out on 'er stinkin' 'ide!'

'Ye're a filthy liar!' Durham Jill screeched. 'May God strike me dead iffen I did. May he strike me stone cold dead! You bleedin' liar!'

Meg Mitchell cursed deep in her throat and came forward in a rush, arms outstretched to catch and tear. Bron acted instinctively, she ducked under the reaching hands and whirled the gut-hanging rabbit up between them. The coils of blood-slimed intestines smacked into Meg Mitchell's open mouth and the woman halted in her tracks, her eyes bulging in horrified amazement.

Durham Jill seized her chance. Snatching up a piece of rock, used by Bron as a doorstop, she darted from the shelter of the doorway and struck Meg Mitchell with all her strength on the side of the head. The woman's eyes rolled up and she buckled to her hands and knees. Old Jill lifted the rock again, but before she could strike, Bron tore it from her hands.

'Leave it Jill!' Bron ordered sharply. 'There'll be no more nonsense from this one.'

The old crone grinned toothlessly.

'Arl right, hinny.' She took Bron's arm and hurried her into the hut.

Still on hands and knees, her greasy hair hanging down, Meg Mitchell swung her great fat from side to side.

'Me bleedin' head's broken,' she wept. 'And 'er stoled my gin! 'Er stoled it!'

The crowd wavered and broke up, going in search of other pursuits now that they sensed the excitement had ended and that Meg Mitchell had no more fight in her.

Inside the hut, old Durham Jill laughed gleefully and stroked Bron's arms and shoulders with her filthy, broken-nailed hands.

'Arl right, me pretty hinny! Ye're arl right! I could see that frae the first day that ye come to the camp ... Here!' She fumbled in her rags and pulled out a nearly full bottle of gin.

'Take a drap o' the swate cratur, hinny.'

Bron's expression was one of deep suspicion.

'Now tell me the truth, Jill?' she questioned sternly. 'Is this Meg Mitchell's bottle?'

The old crone cackled her delight, holding her sides in merriment while tears of utter joy streamed down her withered cheeks.

'Tell me,' Bron snapped. 'Is this Meg's bottle?'

Durham Jill choked and gagged for breath, the spittle spraying from her toothless collapsed mouth. At last she managed to gasp, 'Nae, hinny! Nae it's not Meg's ... It's her man's ... Yorky's!'

She pealed off in a paroxysm of laughter and Bron's angry reaction at being used in such a way by the old woman faded. She could not help but chuckle herself.

Jill calmed herself and again offered the bottle. Bron took a sip. The old woman observed her with faded, cunning eyes.

'Ye're happy here, aren't you?' she said.

Bron thought for a moment and then realized with a shock of surprise that in fact she was happy. At least, happier than she had been in many years.

'Ahr!' The old crone grinned at her. 'I can tell that ye are, hinny. Ye've found a good man and a home here at the war-kins. Ye're a navigating woman now, hinny; and ye'll be a navigating woman till the day that ye die ... Old Durham Jill knaws these things. Ye can mark my wards, I knaws, because I've sin it all before on the canals ... I knaws.'

CHAPTER FORTY

THUNK. THUNK. THUNK. THUNK. THUNK. The heavy wooden chopping shovel cut into the red clay in steady relentless rhythm. Jethro's muscles ached and his hands blistered, the blisters swelled and burst, blood and fluid mingled with sweat and pain, scalded the insides of his palms and fingers. For seemingly endless hours he and the other eight men of the puddling gang wielded the wooden shovels and fought with the clay, struggling to break down its toughness and render it soft, pliable and submissive.

They worked on the floor of the canal, with the sun beating on their bowed heads and shoulders. The lumps of clay were hurled from open carts standing above them on the raised banks, the red dust flying out on impact to cake thick across mouths, eyes, nostrils and sweat-soaked skin. Water was pumped from above to fall in a continuous trickle over the piled clay and the puddler's task was to beat and chop the mixture until the clay became a worked smooth layer a foot deep over the rock spoil which was the primary lining of the walls and a barrier through which no moisture could escape. Underfoot, the red clay sucked voraciously at the men's boots and legs, clogging on leather and cloth until men's feet were huge balls of muck and to lift a leg from one footing to another was a joint-wrenching, muscle-straining battle between the man and the earth.

The ganger in charge, Yorky Mitchell, was broad-shouldered and barrel-chested, a brutal product of the Yorkshire Dales and as hard and bleak in his outlook as his own winter moors. Now, late in the afternoon, he stood on the bank and scowled down at the men toiling beneath him. One man paused and straightened his back, rubbing the aching muscles.

'Gerron wi' it, tha bloody Jessie!' Yorky Mitchell growled. 'Iffen tha stops agen, tha'll goo from the works wi' me boot up thy arse.'

'Now then, gaffer. Rome warn't built in a day, you know,' the man quipped, and his mates grinned tiredly.

The ganger's face didn't alter. 'Nay lad, I know it warn't . . . But then, I warn't the ganger on that job. Now bend thy back and move tha bloody shovel.' Grumbling to himself the man resumed his work.

Jethro toiled in a daze of pain. His hands felt as if they were being seared by red-hot bars and his head throbbed agonizingly without respite. He had long since lost all sense of feeling in his shoulders and back, and lifted and drove the wooden shovel in a state of numbness. The ganger watched the newcomer closely. On each man's performance his own wages depended, and he drove men until they dropped so that each two or three weeks he could pocket enough golden guineas to slake his gargantuan appetite for meat, drink and women. He had lost all desire for the fat, flaccid body of Meg, his wife, but the young girls he lusted after were costly, and he could only earn sufficient money to buy their firm flesh by breaking men's bodies with excessive labour. In fairness to him, he too had puddled the clay for long years under other hard-driving ganger men and was only carrying out his job in the way he had been conditioned to. He stared at Jethro and felt satisfied with his new man.

'Tha's soft in the body as yet, lad,' he thought. 'But tha's got the bottom to stick it out until tha hardens to it. Tha'll do well enough for me.'

At last the day's toil ended and the ganger shouted the men from the channel. Jethro dragged his feet from the clay and made his way haltingly back to the camp. He still slept alone in the ramshackle leanto at the rear of the big shanty and when he reached it, Jethro fought against the overwhelming desire to sink on to his hard pallet and rest. Instead, he forced his bone-weary body to fetch a bucket of water from one of the rain butts and, stripping off his clay-stiff clothing, he soaped and washed his head, legs and torso. The harsh lye soap bit savagely at his raw hands but tiredness numbed his senses so that he hardly noticed the pain.

Bron served Jos with his rabbit stew, then took a bowlful

to Jethro. When she entered the leanto, Jethro lay upon his bed, snoring loudly. She placed the savoury, steaming bowl on the ground and tried to rouse him. He lay as if he were dead and she was forced to leave him asleep. As she turned away his hand fell loosely open at his side. Bron drew in her breath, wincing at the bloody rawness she saw. Later, when Jos went to smoke and talk with friends in another hut, Bron took home-made herbal ointments and dressed Jethro's hands. Even then he did not wake.

The next day, and the next, Jethro's body felt as if it would break in its tortured stiffness and it took the full force of his will to drive it on and to make his wounded hands keep their grasp on the shovel. But slowly at first, and then increasingly quickly, his muscles strengthened and his hands grew hard and calloused, until in only weeks he could outlast any other of the puddlers.

He remained withdrawn and silent, rebuffing all overtures of friendship and having social intercourse only with Bron and Jos, and even this he kept to a minimum. When his shift was finished, he would take his food and eat alone, then either go for long solitary walks, or sleep, not drinking or joining in any of the games of cards, dice, knur and spell, quoits, badger-baiting, otter-hunting, hare-coursing, fist-fighting and wrestling that his workmates spent their few hours of leisure pursuing.

When he had fully regained his strength, Jethro began to talk occasionally with a young carter who came from Redditch, and in that way kept in touch with events in the town. He learned that Jacob Stone and his men had gone to the North Country to continue hunting for Luddites; and that John Mence was in London, passing his days in feverish debauchery. Jethro mastered another useful and important skill in those long days of waiting. He learned patience ...

At last, one bright cold morning in late October, the young carter brought Jethro the news that John Mence had returned from London. Jethro paid the man well for his information.

'And mind!' he warned. 'Not a word about my asking for him, or that I'm in the district.'

'Doon't you fret about that, Jethro,' the carter, a cousin of the Fishers', assured him. 'I'd gie anythin' to see that evil bugger taught a lesson. He give a babby to a wench I was fond on when her was a servant at his house. Only a slip of a kid, her was ... And now her's gone to the bad altogether ... I'll gie thee a tip, Jethro,' the man went on. 'Theer's to be a bull-baiting in the Star and Garter meadow at Crabbs Cross next Sunday. Mence is sartin' sure to be theer. I'se 'eard tell as how 'e's brought a dog from Lunnon that corst him two hundred and fifty guineas. He claims it's a champion "Pinner".'

Jethro grimaced in satisfaction. 'I'll be there,' he promised.

CHAPTER FORTY-ONE

Sunday afternoon was unseasonably warm and after the midday drinking session, crowds of needle pointers, some of them with their dogs, headed for the village of Crabbs Cross which lay a couple of miles from Redditch. The meadow in which the bull-baiting was to take place had a wooden post a foot thick hammered deep into the ground in the centre of the field and an iron ring was clamped to the post. By the time Graham the butcher brought his prime bull to the post, the meadow was filled with rowdy needle men and their women. All were busily swigging from jugs carried out from the Star and Garter, and disputing vociferously about the merits of past and present bulls and bulldogs.

Jethro had walked from the tunnel workings early that morning and now sat quietly alone in a high corner of the field and watched for the appearance of John Mence.

Each owner who wished to let his dog bait the bull paid Graham the butcher five shillings a turn. After the event, if the butcher decided to kill the bull he would find a ready market for the beef which people considered was made tastier and more tender by the ordeal the animal had undergone.

A stocky tough-looking man was watching the securing of the bull to the post. He was known as the Berrod, and was in charge of the baiting. A rope about twenty-five yards long was brought on to the field and then tied about the animal's horns and knotted on to the iron ring on the post. The Berrod then shouted for order. Jethro recognized the man, George Wells, an ex-cavalryman who had brought his old sabre with him for the occasion.

'Now then, you buggers!' he shouted. 'Who wants the first run at this fine beast?'

A bunch of young needle pointers rushed forward, dragging with them a fine specimen of a bulldog, tall on its legs, barrel-chested and with a short thick muzzle.

'Here, Berrod!'

'What's the name of your animal?' Wells asked.

'Slasher,' one man replied.

The Berrod swung his sabre over his head. 'Slasher makes the first run,' he shouted.

Bets were hurriedly laid and taken on the dog's showing and the pointer released it.

'Goo on, Slasher,' he urged.

The bull stood motionless by the post, bemused by the noise and hubbub surrounding it. The dog slunk forward, ears back against its head, eyes intent on its prey. Suddenly the bull scented danger and began to paw the ground, lowering its wicked sharpened horns. The crowd waited, tense and expectant. The dog, its lean flanks quivering with excitement, leapt at the bull. Almost contemptuously the beast flicked its mighty head and sent the dog spinning into the air.

'Catch it! Catch it!' screamed the crowd, and a pointer ran under the dog spreading his white apron. The dog bounced into the apron and landed unhurt. Trembling and yelping hysterically, it ran back at the bull which charged to meet it. The impact sent the dog rolling over and over, squealing in terror with the bull's horns punching against its body. On they scrabbled, divots of earth and grass flying until the end of the tether was reached and the bull jerked abruptly to a halt. The dog lay limp and bleeding until the young owner came to retrieve it amidst the jeers of the crowd.

The afternoon wore on and dog after dog was pitted against the bull, and dog after dog was sent hurtling, ripped and bleeding, crushed, battered and broken. One animal received great plaudits for its bravery as with its entrails dangling it dragged itself time and time again to the attack. Money changed hands in large amounts and still the bull had not been pinned. To pin meant to get a grip on some part of the bull, normally the muzzle, cheeks, eyepiece or even tongue, and for the dog to hold the grip so firmly that the bull would fall to the ground in its efforts to free itself from torment.

'That bloody bull bin baited before,' one irate owner

shouted, cursing over the broken dead body of his favourite dog.

'B-B-B-B-B-B?' a wag in the crowd shouted.

The Berrod waved his sabre threateningly under the man's chin. 'So what if it has?' he scowled. 'What if it is a game bull?'

The man took a long, long look at the battle-pocked blade and shut his mouth.

Jethro took no pleasure in the baiting, he had eyes only for John Mence, who had appeared in the meadow with some drunken cronies and leading a vicious snarling dog.

'Is there anyone else wants a run?' the Berrod shouted. 'If not I'll freshen the bull and then we'll have all the dogs together . . . the Smut.'

A stream of small boys ran to him carrying buckets of water and Wells sluiced the liquid over the animal, washing away the lathered sweat and the blood from the bites covering its legs and flanks. When he had finished, a man stepped forward cradling a dog in his arms. The dog was smaller than the ones that had gone before and when the man placed it on the ground, it was seen to be peculiarly twisted and lumpy-boned.

'It's Jem Wright and his dog Kit.' The news flew through the spectators and they craned their heads, eager to see the most famous bulldog in the country. It had had nearly every bone in its body broken and had been badly gored on countless occasions, yet it was reputed that the dog had pinned every bull it had ever been pitted against. Its master matched the dog, a leather-skinned, lean, tough whip of a man whose ferocity in a brawl was notorious even among the notoriously savagely brawling needle pointers.

'That's a game bull you got there, Berrod,' Jem Wright said. 'But I've got ten guineas that says my Kit here will pin the bugger.' He stared around the crowd. 'Any takers?' he challenged.

'I've got a better wager than that,' John Mence swaggered arrogantly up to them, leading his large glossy-coated, strong-bodied brute. 'I'll match my dog against yours, Wright, at ten guineas a turn.'

Jem Wright, poker-faced, sized up Mence's dog.

'You'm on, Captain,' he said, after a second or two; and

amid excited comments from the crowd, the bets were made and the details agreed.

Jethro was moving through the crowd very slowly, taking great care to avoid drawing any attention to himself. In the right-hand pocket of his loose-fitting coat he held the haft of an open knife. 'When you've looked into my eyes, Mence, and you know who I am, then that's the moment you're going to die,' he thought, and stalked his quarry like a hunting savage. He had no fear of the consequences of his action; he sought only the blood of his father's murderer.

Jem Wright loosed his chain and the famous Kit went into movement. Belly to the ground, ears laid back, fangs bared in a snarl, the dog snaked forward. The bull trotted to meet it, its head came down and it charged. Kit leapt to one side, avoiding the thrusting horn, and twisted in a blur of speed to clamp the bull's cheek between its jaws. The bull bellowed and tossed its huge head frantically, trying to shake the dog loose. Kit hung on growling and the bull tripped itself to fall with a bone-jarring smash on its side. Jem whistled and the dog released its hold and, tail wagging, scurried cringing back to its master. The whole episode had taken place in seconds.

Jem Wright patted his dog and grinned at Mence.

'Well, Captain?' he asked, insolently. 'Does you still think you'se got a better dog?'

Mence laughed blusteringly. 'That took twenty-three seconds, Wright. I'm willing to bet you another ten guineas that my dog Bouncer does it in less.'

Wright spat on the ground. 'You'm on, Captain.'

Mence loosed his dog. 'Sink him, Bouncer!' he shouted.

The handsome animal surged forward and dodged the bull's thrust, but, try as it could, was not able to get a grip. When the three minutes, allowed in the terms of the wager, were up, the Berrod beat the dog away with the flat of his sabre, and Mence, cursing his luck, paid the twenty guineas with bad grace.

'Same terms, Captain?' Wright questioned mockingly.

Mence scowled at him. 'We'll double them.'

'That's fine by me.' Wright grinned and as he released Kit he snatched up a long stiff bamboo pole that a bystander had fetched him. The dog went forward as before, but this time the bull was wiser. He lunged, the dog leapt and twisted and the bull caught it under the ribcage with the wide of his horn and tossed it high into the air. Jem Wright darted under the line of fall and, as the furry misshapen body cartwheeled down, he slipped the bamboo pole up under it so that Kit slid harmlessly down the smooth rod to the ground. The dog immediately snaked back to the attack and caught the bull by the muzzle, bringing it crashing to the ground once more. The spectators' roars of approval drowned out even the agonized bellowing of the bull.

The Berrod jabbed it to its feet with the point of his sabre and the tortured animal stood, flanks heaving, with lathered sweat and blood streaming down its muddied sides and long thick strands of mucus dangling from its mouth and nostrils.

Mence let go his dog and shouted it on.

Jethro was now almost directly behind him. He measured the distance with his eyes.

'Four yards,' he estimated. 'Four yards, Mence, that's the span of your life.' He slipped the knife from his pocket and readied himself to spring.

Bouncer was dodging the bull's short rushes, and then he leapt in and gripped the ripped cheek. The bull bellowed and tossed its head, the dog's fangs tore loose the hanging shred of cheek and it went somersaulting high over the bull's head. It reached the apex of its flight and dropped back towards the earth. The bull heaved upwards and impaled the shrieking dog on one horn. The crowd's blood-howl shattered the air.

'Mence! John Mence!' Jethro bellowed, and bounded forward. But he struck at emptiness.

Mence, in a paroxysm of rage, had snatched the sabre from the Berrod's hand and rushed at the bull, flailing at it with the curved blade. His first wild blow decapitated the shrieking dog, his second bounced off the bull's horn and slashed through the tether rope. The maddened bull smashed Mence to the ground and punched into his soft body with its vicious sharpened horns. Screaming in pain and terror, Mence tried to scramble out of the bull's reach but with the tether cut there was no escape, and again the horns thrust and punctured his body, battering him against the ground, crushing, ripping and destroying.

Jethro and the Berrod tried to beat the bull from the

smashed, bloodied body, but it was only when more men from among the scattering spectators joined them that they succeeded. By then it was too late ... Mence was dead.

Jethro stared down at the broken body of his father's murderer and could only feel that the man had met with the death he deserved.

He turned on his heel and walked slowly from the meadow.

CHAPTER FORTY-TWO

'Don't go, Jethro!' Bron's eyes were sad and pleading. 'Stop here with Jos and me. We're your friends.'

They stood outside Jethro's shelter and he hefted the small sack containing his few belongings across his shoulder. He smiled at her and when he spoke his voice was affectionate.

'I have to go Bronny, I'll come back at times and see you. I shan't be far away.'

'But where are you going? What are you going to do?' she pleaded.

'I'm going back to Redditch town,' he told her.

'Oh no! You'll only be going back to trouble if you go back to Redditch, I know you will.' Bron bit her lips to stop the grief in her heart spilling from them.

He touched her cheek and said quietly, 'I'm my father's son, Bron. He was a man who, when trouble came, met it face to face, and turned the other cheek to no one. He would expect me to do no less.'

'And where will you live, pray, and what will you do for work?' She showed a flash of temper.

'I think I'll maybe become a needle pointer and live with Doll Greenaway.' He smiled, then sobered and went on, 'Listen, girl, the worst abuses of this world we live in are not to be found here on the canal workings. They're back there in the mills at Redditch, and the factories and mines and sweat shops of a hundred other towns. My father was murdered by men who want to keep this life unchanged for ever. I'll not shame his memory by failing to stand with those who want to fight to change it.'

'But it's not your fight, Jethro,' Bron said tearfully. 'You can stay here and be at peace. You're well regarded by Mortimer, and Jos says that you'll soon be made ganger.'

253

'Try and understand me, Bron.' He was very gentle with her. 'I've no wish to be at peace, I'm sure that my father isn't at peace, wherever he may be. How can it be possible to rest peaceful, while this fight remains to be fought.'

'Your father is dead!' she burst out desperately. 'Let the dead bury the dead! You cannot bring him back to life by fighting the masters and the gentry.'

He shook his head.

'I know only too well that I can't bring him back, Bron. But this is a war, not a skirmish that ends with the death of one man, or even a thousand men. I am not returning to Redditch to avenge my father's death, no matter that I loved him dearly. I tried to kill his murderer but failed, a poor tortured beast killed the man for me. I'm going to Redditch because I am a man in my own right, a free-born Englishman, and this is my country. It belongs to me just as much as it belongs to the masters and the gentry. I want to sweep aside the old ways and replace them with a more just way of life. There are many thousands who feel as I do. Perhaps when we have achieved our aims, then I will be content to live at peace,' he grinned wryly, 'even become a ganger on the canal ... But, until I begin to fight against those who oppress us, then I will never know what it is to be able to laugh with joy again.' He patted her cheek. 'Is that such a poor ambition? To want to laugh with joy once more?'

He smiled at her as if in farewell, and unable to control the longing she felt for him, she reached out, flinging her arms about him, and searching hungrily for his mouth. He moved his head, and her eager lips found only the light stubble of his chin and jaw.

'I'll be back, Bron,' he said quietly, 'when I am able to do that.'

She watched his tall figure trudging away from her until he disappeared around the curve of the hill. She blew a kiss fancifully.

'I'll be waiting, Jethro—till the Day of Judgement,' she murmured; and went weeping to the shanty where Jos, her man, was shouting for his dinner.